Little Gracie

H. Ronald Freeman

AmErica House
Baltimore

First printing

ISBN: 1-58851-258-4
PUBLISHED BY AMERICA HOUSE BOOK PUBLISHERS
www.publishamerica.com
Baltimore

Printed in the United States of America

Author's Note

Most of the events in the story of *Little Gracie* are fiction. The story is about a child who lived in Savannah briefly during the late 19th century. Grace Watson is buried in Bonaventure Cemetery in Savannah.

Little is known about Gracie or her family other than they came from Charleston and her father was part owner of the prestigious Pulaski Hotel in Savannah. After her death, her father assumed management of the new and grand DeSoto Hotel in the city. A few years later, he left Savannah and apparently remained in the north until his death.

This story is based on that family and the real events of the day in Savannah and Charleston. Many of the characters and places in the story were real. Most of the events happened but in truth, they happened to others and were only combined here for storytelling purposes.

Little Gracie's statue is practically a shrine in the cemetery in Savannah. Her grave is visited annually by thousands of tourists and other visitors to the city. It is very real. She was real. Hopefully this story will do nothing to disparage her memory or that of her parents.

H. Ronald Freeman

To Gracie

*May she always represent
the innocence and purity
of children everywhere*

Chapter 1

Gettysburg, Pennsylvania
July 2, 1862
General Longstreet's Army

"Sammy? Are you scared?" asked Russell, not really looking at him. Sammy knew what was running through his younger brother's mind. They had been marching for several days and had already been exposed to the sights and sounds of two days of intense fighting.

They lay on the ground with others in their unit under a small clump of trees. Night was falling and the hot dustiness of the day was being replaced by a heavy dampness of evening dew. Sammy knew his brother would place great stock in his answer and knew he must answer with care.

"No," he said, not looking back, "Just eager I guess."

"Yeah, me too. It's hard to tell what's going on and when we'll see action, if at all."

"I've heard some of the troops say that we have the Yanks on the run and tomorrow we'll probably run them out of Pennsylvania. If so, then that'll leave Washington open for the taking." That'll put old Abe on his guard.

"That's all above me," said Russell. "I would just like to see some action. You know, just to have something to talk about when we go back home. Sammy?"

"Yeah?"

"Do you wish we'd stayed at home, like Pa asked?"

Sammy knew again that Russell would place great importance on his answer. It was difficult for him to totally divorce himself from what was happening around him and still get in synch with the doubts that were stalking his brother.

"I think he realized he couldn't keep us there. Every generation has its war. This one is ours. Pa knew that. He knew us going was the right thing. Eventually, he knew we would answer the call. We couldn't stay home. It was our time."

"Yeah, but I still miss Mom and Pa and the farm. Have you written them lately?" asked Russell.

"No, not for a while but I probably will after we finish up here. You?"

"No, but probably will tonight."

"That would be good. Be sure you do."

The next afternoon, their division, led by General George Pickett of Virginia, made a historic charge over more than a mile of open field in a futile assault on an entrenched Union position. Never had such an army marched on the enemy en masse.

"Stay close to me Russell, we'll be okay." They only had to look in each direction down the long gray Confederate line to feel confident with their strength in numbers. They were like the waves in the ocean approaching the shore. It was impossible for such a body of armed men to be defeated.

"Do you think they'll break when we get closer, Sammy?"

"Got to. Colonel Alexander's softened them up with all that artillery. Besides, they wouldn't send us up till they were ready. Pay attention now. Stay alert."

They were rapidly approaching a fence, about 100 yards from the Union wall. Southern boys were having to place their rifles on the other side as they took the time to scale the wooden poles. Enemy cannon were beginning to open up on the advancing troops, firing both shot and chain. The troops held their ranks. Huge hunks of their lines were being decimated by the constant fusillade of Yankee cannon. True to their training, the Southern lines held rank.

Suddenly, without warning, Russell cried out as a cannon ball exploded only a few yards to his left. Sammy saw him fall and ran to where he was sprawled on his stomach.

"Russell! Russell?" Sammy turned him over.

The shrapnel from the exploding metal had torn a gaping furrow across his chest. He could only watch as he saw the life draining from his brother's face. Russell tried to speak, but was unable. His eyes flickered and his last attempt to talk was only a bloody bubble. Sammy held his brother and watched as life eroded and death prevailed. Then Russell was gone.

"No!" cried Sammy, feeling responsible for his brother and unable to grasp the horror of the moment. The gravity of the event closed in and with it the emptiness of all the slogans and enticements of the recruiting posters.

"Move on, move on, Perry," screamed the sergeant, prodding Sammy with his rifle.

"He's my brother, dammit," screamed Sammy.

"Keep moving so they can't get their sights on you, son, now move."

Sammy realized the truth in the sergeant's prodding and reluctantly started forward again. No sooner had Sammy begun than the bugle call was sounded to fall back. He looked around the field, and for the first time realized the extent of the mass carnage of the dead and dying. Everywhere were the sounds of men screaming for help. Some with missing limbs from cannon shot and others just were lying in lifeless heaps.

Sammy started, slowly, dragging back with the others, but determined to come back for his brother.

It was the cruelest moment of war. That time when one realized the cost of glory. Men writhing in pain with limbs missing from canister shot and faces maimed, never to recapture their innocence. These were the thousands who numbered in the undead. Unable to go out in glory and cursed to remain on the earth as unproductive cripples, swept aside and ignored by North and South alike.

Later that evening, Sammy went in search of his brother. He knew the futility in calling his name. Retracing the earlier charge of the day, he went forward. He was not alone. The field was filled with hundreds. Most were calling the names of fallen comrades. Others, like himself, only staggered forward with determination, knowing they were too late to save but only hoping to identify and preserve. Sammy plodded onward to the point where he was certain Russell was struck. Cautiously, but reverently, he turned multiple bodies. None were Russell and after several hours, he realized the futility of his mission. Apparently, Russell's body had already been loaded on one of the many burial wagons actively collecting the dead.

The next day at dawn, Lee's defeated army began its slow retreat back to Virginia. Sammy wrote the letter he dreaded to his parents.

July 4, 1862

Dear Mom and Pa,

It is with heavy heart that I must tell you of the loss of your son, and my brother, Russell. He was kilt while we were attacking the Yankee army on the last day at Gettysburg. I was with him when he died. Russell will be buried on the battlefield with many others from both sides. He was very brave and I can't begin to tell you how sick I am of war and how I feel responsible for talking Russell into this. I'm not sure who won the battle.

I wish to God that I had never let him leave the farm with me. Please forgive me, oh God forgive me. Russell was fine and I know I had him kilt. I am okay. I must stay and see this thing through. Pa, you were right. I love you both.

Your son,

Sammy

Sammy did stay. He continued on to serve in Longstreet's army and went on to fight in the Wilderness campaign, Cold Harbor and finally--Petersburg. It was there, when he was weary of war, and a hardened veteran 21 years of age, that he suffered the bayonet of a young Union soldier. Due to other wounds, he was unable to defend himself. The war was near its end but Sammy wouldn't be counted among those weary veterans returning home. His commander sent the sad letter back to his family.

For the Perry boys, the war was over. Their glory had been found in the carnage of Gettysburg and the muddy trenches of Petersburg.

Chapter 2

Bonaventure Cemetery is said to be one of the most beautiful places in the world. Although I haven't seen the world, I would agree. You see, I stay here and have for some time. My name is Grace Watson, Little Gracie to most people. I came to Bonaventure when I was six years old and have called it home ever since.

Originally, Bonaventure was a Georgia rice plantation near Savannah. It was the place where the French camped during the Siege of Savannah in the Revolutionary War. Eventually it became a cemetery in 1847, a fitting use if you ask me. Large Oaks draped with Spanish moss give it an aura during the day and a stillness at dusk, when the gates close, that really must be experienced. Come springtime, the entire area is in full bloom from the thousands of azaleas here.

Bonaventure has become very popular, with all the interest in the Bird Girl statue. Since I sit near one of the main avenues to her location on the river, much of the traffic also stops by to see me.

Usually they make remarks to the effect of "what a loss," or "to die so young, she had yet begun to live." I find these comments interesting, but I often wonder what they would say if they knew the whole story of how I came into being, and how I prematurely came to reside in Bonaventure.

In my early days here, many said I had the same wistful look on my face that haunted my mother before she died, just staring away, brushing her hair, preoccupied with her last thoughts.

I know, you're thinking, "what are you doing inhabiting a cemetery?" Notice I didn't say living in. Some people are sensitive about those things.

It's hard to say. I don't have all the answers. Many believe that at death, you suddenly possess all worldly knowledge, knowing everything amassed to date and everything to be discovered later. Based on my experience, and that of others in my situation with whom I've become acquainted, it's not true. The secrets of the universe haven't been revealed, at least not yet. But that's not important.

People tend to be frozen in their own circumstances and period in history. Occasionally, time gets out of focus, when past inhabitants of locations can appear in the same place, but at the present time.

It's happened to me several times. We don't know why, but we know we're the intruders. Our time in that spot has past and we now share the space with others. Maybe it's happened to you? If so, don't be frightened, it's only a warp in time. Things aren't always perfect. It's a lot like having strange dreams and then wondering what it's all about.

When I came to Bonaventure, my papa was part owner of Savannah's Pulaski Hotel on Johnson Square. It was the showplace in town, with 75 rooms, and Papa was almost as proud of it as he was of me, and of Mother.

Notice my clothes. I'm dressed the way we did in the late 1800's. In fact, it's my Easter outfit, the one I never got to wear. Don't you like my high-buttoned shoes? My dress is a tight basque with long sleeves over a high-necked blouse of sheer nainsook. My clothes and expression are copied from a portrait I posed for right before Easter. Papa took me. I was wearing my hair long to my waist with bangs across my forehead. I'm sitting very still with a smile and looking out at the trees before me.

I'm made of marble, not granite. Papa thought it would be better. To project my purity as he termed it with a white radiance of eternity. My right arm is resting on the stump of a tree. That was Mr. Walz, the sculptor's touch, denoting a young life cut down before its time.

I'll visit you again later to tell you goodbye. For now though, let's look at how it all happened.

Chapter 3

"Do you believe that most commerce will swing to the North and Savannah will continue to slump?" asked the builder, sitting in front of Rob's desk.

"No, that won't happen," answered Rob. "Savannah has a commercial base through the port. We will always be important as a port city." Savannah will continue to prosper because of where it is and what it is.

Rob's comments were based on fact. Savannah in 1888 was a bustling cosmopolitan town of about 30,000 souls. It was struggling to rebuild after the Civil War and the radical changes brought by the war to its economy. Before the war, the city had personified the cotton boom and the massive amount of wealth it brought to those involved in its production.

At war's end, with the liberation of the slaves, it was impossible to make the large plantations competitive. No longer did they have the access to cheap labor they relied on previously. Many of the old river rice plantations that used the rise and fall of the river to flood the fields were now being converted to industrial uses.

Rob felt totally transparent. He was now 45 years old and had been a part of the Savannah scene for the greater portion of his life.

He had been born in Atlanta but moved to Savannah at an early age. Now, his prime objective in business was to develop real estate in Savannah on his own, rather than financing it through the bank for others. If that goal could be attained, he saw himself as being part of the "monied class."

"You mustn't ever count Savannah out," he continued. "She is on the threshold of a new industrial age. Unlike Charleston, Savannah is looking forward and not resting on past laurels of development."

Rob was comfortable in what he knew of Savannah and its economy. He was employed by the Southern Bank and was good at his job. His primary function was to finance the burgeoning boom in real estate. Part of his charge was to be sure that Southern Bank received its share while not placing their funds at undue risk.

"Rob, that's your last appointment of the day," said his secretary.

"Thank you, Frances."

Rob drew his watch from his vest and checked the time -- 4:45. He silently read the inscription on the facing case as he did each time, and he looked at his hands.

His left still carried the scar of a musket ball that shattered several bones. It was a souvenir he received from the battle the day before the Southern surrender at Appomattox Courthouse. Rob had fought with the Savannah Volunteer Guards under General John Gordon of Atlanta. His left leg also carried a reminder from Cold Harbor when it was skewered by a Yankee bayonet.

Rob Truitt looked on the war as no more than a footnote in his personal history. He had been a believer in his cause and had served to the best of his ability. Looking back, he understood the economics of both sides had doomed the South to defeat. It was okay. It was behind him. The lost cause was one he couldn't embrace on a personal basis. It was history.

The North had more men to commit, more resources to employ, and more time to mark. The South had scrambled for victories with a strategy of employing a small finite army against a large expendable force. Looking back, it was easy to acknowledge what those other than the firebrands knew before the war; belief in a cause wasn't enough.

Rob was proud of what he'd accomplished since the war, but knew his life was not complete. Although he was a vice president of the bank and well thought of by the Board and senior management, something was missing.

He liked to think of his life in categories: his job, his friends, his social life, his community life, and so forth. He had been with the bank his entire working career and should have been pleased with his advancement.

Rob wanted to go on his own. He was surrounded by wealth and he knew that, if he could only get in the right situation, he could be successful, as well.

Frances had worked as his personal secretary for only a few months. She had been married seven years and had one child. It was only the previous year she had moved to Savannah with her daughter

14

and husband, Wales, from Charleston. Gracie, her daughter, was now six and Frances was 29.

Frances enjoyed working with Rob. He made her feel a part of what was happening in the life of the bank and always took time to explain why things were done as they were.

Rob and Frances were closer than most people knew but they attempted to keep their relationship on a professional plane. She was aware of his personal ambitions, to leave the bank and strike out on his own.

"Mrs. Watson, will you bring me the Marshall file?"

"Yes, Mr. Truitt, of course."

Each was careful to observe the protocol of business in the presence of customers.

The mahogany-paneled walls of the bank were beginning to grow dim in the Autumn afternoon shadows. Rob could hear the clatter of the telegraph key down the hall and the chatter of some of the younger staff in the bank. Frances suddenly rushed into his office in a panic.

"Rob!"

"What? What is it?"

"Something is happening on the street."

Rob leaped from his chair and sprang for the door to the hall. He tore down the stairs to the lobby and into the street.

The scene there was one he encountered repeatedly during his war years. A man in a carriage was wielding a bullwhip to a frightened horse. He repeatedly laid into the animal to force him forward. A crowd had gathered.

Rob mounted the step to the carriage, seizing the whip and wrenching it from the man's hand. The man's attention jerked to Rob's direction.

"How do you expect the animal to heed a command from someone who is more afraid of the situation than he is?"

The man cowered, and those who thought they knew Rob absorbed the situation, gaining a new respect for the man they had only known through business dealings. Rob tossed the whip to the ground and went to the front of the carriage to calm the horse. Frances was standing

15

close by. As Rob met her gaze, she turned abruptly and went back to the bank.

He was unaware, but Rob had marked himself as one to be watched and avoided in tense situations. As he walked back to his office, the crowd was murmuring, "Who was that?"

"I believe he's a vice president works for the Southern Bank," one said.

As he reached his second floor office, Frances was there ahead of him. She was pacing and waiting for him.

"Why did you do such a foolish thing? Someone would have come along and brought order to the situation."

"That's just the point," Rob said. "Most people are waiting for others to rectify the problem when the problem is lending itself to a simple solution. The only alternative is that someone needs to act."

Many times during the war, Rob had seen identical settings. Whatever the crisis, it only took initiative in a timely manner to set it straight.

"Please don't do anything so foolish again," she said. She was visibly shaken. Rob knew he needed to carefully frame his response so as to assuage her fears but, at the same time, to defend what he thought had been the proper action.

"Frances, we don't live in a vacuum. Things happen. When they do, you respond. You don't think about it. And besides, it was not dangerous." Rob began his customary pacing while not looking at her as he was speaking.

"What you don't realize," she said, " is that we are back again in a civilized environment, not your war days. You are not rewarded for risking your life, and, frankly, you have become too important to me to see you in danger."

"If -- ."

"What?" she asked.

Rob remembered back to earlier days when you had better act or you and the lives of those depending on you would be in sudden jeopardy.

"Nothing." He took a deep breath. "I appreciate your concern. Next time I'll think before I act."

To Rob, it seemed like an eternity ago that his family had moved to Savannah from Atlanta. Actually, the year was 1850, and Rob was only eight years old.

His dad had taken a job with the newly formed Central of Georgia Railroad as an engineer on the mainline from Savannah to Macon. His older brother, Edward, also found a job, since he was 14 at the time.

Rob hated to leave his friends in Atlanta, but soon after arriving in Savannah, was easily able to assimilate himself into the mainstream of school and activities in the seaport town.

Savannah proved fascinating for Rob, from the salty fragrance of the waterfront, where ships were being laden, to the taverns and general press of the people as they went about their daily lives.

By 1858, talk of war was in the air. Rob and most of his friends could discuss little else. The local firebrands, advocating secession from the Union gave speeches day and night in Johnson Square.

The arguments and reasons were all beyond Rob and his young pals. All they knew was that a line in the sand had been drawn. The North was telling the South what to do, and the people of the South were eager to show they would not be pushed.

They didn't know what lay ahead, and like most Southerners, they thought that if war came, it would be over in a matter of weeks. After all, everyone knew the men in the South were much better soldiers than men from the North. They could shoot straighter, live on the land, and had more training in military tactics.

Rob joined the Oglethorpe Light Infantry, one of the many militia groups that had formed in Savannah. It was definitely the "in" thing for an able-bodied young man to belong to a military unit. Colonel Francis Bartow, a young attorney in Savannah and a leading voice in the secession movement, commanded the regiment.

Bartow was an eloquent orator, a Cicero of his age. Because of this, and his advancement of the Southern argument, he was elected as a delegate to the secession conference in Montgomery, Alabama. At the conference, Bartow was again rewarded for his convincing oratory and was appointed Chairman of the Committee on Military Affairs.

One of the early tasks of the committee was to select a standard uniform for the soldiers who would serve the Southern cause. Since he was already enamored with the striking gray worn by the Savannah's Oglethorpe Light Infantry, he naturally suggested that the Confederate forces adopt it. It was approved.

Back in Savannah, the secession fires seemed to burn day and night. Once South Carolina seceded from the Union, Governor Brown of Georgia took haste to secure the entrance to the Savannah River from the sea.

He ordered several Savannah militia units to sail immediately downriver to Fort Pulaski, guarding the river's entrance, and wrest the fort from Union control. This was accomplished without bloodshed -- the first hostile action of the war. The taking of Fort Pulaski was accomplished even before Fort Sumter in Charleston harbor was fired upon.

The Oglethorpe Light Infantry was one of the youngest units to take the field. Colonel Bartow, at 35, was commanding a youthful regiment, most in their late teens and early twenties.

They cut a fine figure in their dress grays but were soon bored of repeated drilling on the parade ground in Forsyth Park. They were eager to take the field, and Bartow was eager to lead them. Governor Brown thought otherwise.

In a scathing letter to Bartow, he forbade any of the Georgia units to leave the state. He wanted all to remain within the boundaries of Georgia to protect against invasion from the North. This, however, was not in Bartow's plan; he craved action for his unit. How else could he prove himself. He knew he had to be in the fray before the war abruptly ended.

Bartow offered the services of his unit directly to President Jefferson Davis, whom he knew from the convention in Montgomery. Davis graciously accepted. Shortly thereafter, the Oglethorpe Light Infantry was marching north to Virginia to join other Southern forces in what would be the first battle of the Civil War. They converged near a town called Manassas and a creek known as Bull Run.

Governor Brown, in another fiery letter, ordered Bartow back to Georgia immediately, or face dire consequences. Bartow penned an equally caustic reply to the Governor. He said "You sir, again make your common mistake of supposing you are the State of Georgia. It's a mistake in which I do not participate. With due respect, I have the honor to be your nonobedient servant."

The Georgia unit didn't have to wait long for the opportunity to prove their worth under fire. At dawn of the second day of battle, they were asked to move to support General Beauregard in an area taking heavy Union fire. The Georgia troops were positioned at the extreme end of the line and Bartow had been given the admonition to not let the Union troops flank them. They must hold.

He repeatedly rode down his lines exalting his men to stand firm and make Georgia proud. Rob was just a young kid, his thoughts more on survival than glory. He was excited but cool and had the ability to sense a good position to lay down fire at the enemy without unduly exposing himself.

Colonel Bartow, more the lawyer than the warrior, was not as calculating or fortunate. As he rode past his lines in the thick of battle, he suffered a shot directly to his chest, and abruptly fell from his horse.

The boys close by quickly gathered around their commander with the helpless feeling of those who knew the uselessness of administering aid. Bartow too, knew the wound was mortal and told his men, "They have killed me, boys, but don't give up the field."

That was the beginning of four long years for Rob. He was able to see the conflict with a much older perspective. Survival, that was the key. Don't let "bound for glory" commanders place you in a position that could get you killed. Know your fight, know your odds, and know how to survive. Cowardice never entered into it, only survival.

From Bull Run, he would go on to fight at Chancellorsville, Fredericksburg, and Gettysburg. There he was captured and spent over a year in a prison camp in Maryland before escaping to rejoin General Lee's army outside Cold Harbor. Rob was able to find the Savannah Volunteer Guards fighting under General John Gordon of Georgia.

It was with this unit in April 1865, that the last Confederate assault of the war was made near a town called Appomattox Courthouse in Virginia. Reality had finally caught up with the South. All the superficial bravado and states' rights arguments combined with a lack of goods and manpower, ran head-on with reality and the cause was lost forever.

It was time to reassess. Rob and thousands of his comrades turned toward home. It was time to rest, time to rebuild, and for many, a time for lifelong resentment.

Chapter 4

"Rob, we've got to do something."

He glanced at Frances and knew immediately she had the same thing on her mind as he did. It was early Monday morning and the office was just opening. She wore her auburn hair tied up in a bun as was the fashion of the day and more manageable than when worn under her hat.

"Well, it seems we have some private time. Why don't you come into my office?" Once they were seated Rob said, "Tell me if what's on your mind is the same thing that's been on mine all weekend?"

Frances nodded, reading his thoughts. "I'm tired of living like this. Even with our situation aside, I still feel as though I have been a captive in my own home for the last seven years."

"Tell me what you want to do?" asked Rob.

"I'm going home to tell Wales I want a divorce. I feel my father's debt to him has been repaid."

"Your father never owed that kind of debt. Are you sure you want to do something?"

"I keep thinking about it. It scares me but I just can't continue to do nothing." She came over and squeezed his hand, looking at his face with concern.

"I love you," she said.

"I love you too."

* * *

Rob lived within a good walk from the bank in a townhouse on Gordon Row. As he walked through Johnson Square, he felt a sense of comfort with the city. Although it was changing, it still offered the same sereneness he remembered as a boy.

It was March and there was a still a bite to the air. Over the street noise of the carriages and drivers, he could hear the calls of the workers on the river only a short block away.

After about fifteen minutes, he reached his house. As he ascended the stairs to the parlor floor and entered the foyer, he wondered what it would be like to come home to a wife and family. He would announce he was home for the day and his wife would be bustling in the kitchen preparing the evening meal. She would ask how his day had been.

It had not turned out that way. Rob always believed that after the war, when he settled into a job or career, he would meet someone, the right person. Actually, he had. It was just that the circumstances at the time were not right. She had an obligation to carry out, and he tried to understand. Many times since, he doubted the wisdom of that decision. It seemed so long ago.

* * *

McIntosh was a small farming community in central Florida. As the railroads began to develop the state, many moved inland from the coast to cultivate the rich delta topsoil. Sam Perry, Frances' father, was one of them. Frances was born in McIntosh, and it had been home to her since. By many, it was considered to be little more than a whistle stop in the farming belt. It was about twenty miles below Gainesville and fifteen above Ocala.

In 1881, Frances was twenty-two years old and very much involved in the social life of her town. There were church picnics, tennis matches in the local park, bicycling, swimming; her focus was on her friends and social life. McIntosh was her world and she had little reason to question its adequacy. After the crops had been harvested for the summer and fall was approaching, she decided to visit her cousin Fanny in Savannah.

Fanny was the daughter of her mother's sister and was only a year older than Frances. After Frances arrived, they scarcely allowed themselves an idle moment. Both were caught up in a whirlwind of parties, theater, and daily shopping excursions about the town.

One afternoon, as they were idly window shopping along Barnard Street, a seaman burst forth from a tavern onto the walk and bumped roughly into Frances.

"Watch where you're going," said Fanny. "You almost knocked her down."

The man regained his composure and started toward Fanny.

"Maybe you lassies ain't accustomed to the presence of a real man," he slurred. "Why don't I buy you a drink and we'll forget it happened?"

"I don't think so," said Frances. "I think we'll just be getting on our way."

"You think you're too good to drink with Sean O'Leary, do you?"

A crowd was beginning to gather.

"Please excuse us," said Frances. She stooped to pick up her parcel. O'Leary seized her roughly by the arm.

"I'll show you," he said.

Suddenly, from out of the crowd, someone rushed in and slammed O'Leary against the tavern wall.

The breath went out of the seaman. The man quickly grabbed his feet and pulled them forward, jerking him off balance and sending him sprawling against the wall in a sitting position. Like a snake striking, the man clutched O'Leary by the throat and spoke directly into his face.

"Go back in the tavern and leave these ladies alone. I won't tell you again."

O'Leary rose unsteadily to his feet and said dejectedly as he headed back in the door, "Another time, mate."

"You people go about your business," the man said to the onlookers. He turned to Frances and Fanny. "I'm sorry. These things happen in a seaport town more than others, but they shouldn't. I'm Rob Truitt." He looked at Frances. "I hope you're okay."

Frances just gaped at him. He was the most handsome man she had ever seen. He was lean and over six feet tall, with the movements of a dancer. His hands were slender without being delicate. His hair was brown and full and worn in a brushed-back style that emphasized the high cheekbones of his face. A penetrating gaze from his brown eyes seemed to peer into her soul.

"Miss?" he said.

Frances recovered. "I'm sorry, yes, I'm fine. Thank you so much for coming to our aid."

"I guess we should have crossed the street and not walked in front of the tavern," said Fanny. "Frances is from out of town and new to this type of thing. Next time we'll both know."

"Can I escort you home?" Rob asked.

"Oh, we're okay," said Fanny.

"I insist," said Rob as he reached to take their parcels. "Where are you from?" he asked Frances.

"From a small town in central Florida, really just a farming community."

"She's up here visiting me for a week," said Fanny. "She and I are cousins. Her mother and mine are sisters. I'm Fanny Ellis, and she is Frances Perry."

"I'm pleased to meet you," said Rob.

"What do you do here in Savannah, Mr. Truitt?" asked Frances.

"I work at a local bank, the Southern Bank & Trust Company."

They continued walking south on Barnard until they reached South Broad Street--in earlier days, the southern boundary of the city. Fanny lived in a brick townhouse on the south side of the street.

"This is it," said Fanny as they approached the door. Rob handed the packages to the ladies.

"I've enjoyed meeting you both. May I call again?" asked Rob. As he said the words, he looked directly at Frances. To Fanny this was no surprise, since Frances always seemed to turn heads when they were out together.

"Perhaps," said Fanny.

"It was a pleasure to meet you Mr. Truitt," said Frances as she looked briefly into his face and then demurely to the ground. Rob only hesitated for a moment.

"Ladies, have a pleasant evening," he said as he departed.

Fanny and Frances climbed the steps to the parlor floor and entered the hallway. As the door closed, Fanny looked at Frances, smiled an impish smile and scrunched her shoulders.

"I think you have made a conquest," she said.

"Oh really, he was more interested in you than me."

"If you think that, cousin, you are either being overly polite or you did not see where his eyes were focused as we walked to the house."

"Do you really think?" said Frances.

"Just wait."

Men and emotions were not a new thing for Frances. During her school years she had had several affairs of the heart. But this was different; this was grown up and real. Still, she could not believe he could be interested in her, a simple farm girl.

* * *

Rob was not sure what he felt, but his step was lighter as he made his way back to his apartment. Here he was, a mature man of 37 and, yet, he felt like a young boy.

"Damn," he said aloud. "What a girl."

The streets were active as he made his way home but he scarcely noticed the traffic. Earlier in the day, he did notice two attractive ladies walking idly down the street, more intent on talking and laughing than where they were heading. One in particular caught his eye. She was the taller of the two. There was something about the way she carried herself, with a poise and grace that exuded confidence. He knew he could not dare approach them. Then, as if fate intended, the roughneck burst on the scene. Maybe I should go back and thank him, thought Rob.

It was one of those situations where everyone is sympathetic but, at the same time, intimidated. Rob knew it was whiskey courage with the seaman and, once confronted, he would not be difficult to subdue. He had witnessed it many times before.

Now, as he reflected on the events, his single- minded purpose was to see Frances again. She would only be in town a short period longer and he had to make a definitive move.

"Nothing ventured, nothing gained," he mumbled. "Fortune goes to the brave."

He decided to stop by Grant Dawson's apartment. He just didn't want to be alone at the moment and he needed someone to use as a sounding board.

He and Grant had served in the war together with the Oglethorpe Light Infantry and other Georgia units. Grant was an impetuous but sensitive rogue who could at times be a good listener.

He walked toward Grant's apartment, not a great distance from his own, and rang the bell. There was no response. He rang again. Finally, through the door, he thought he heard the sound of movement.

"Just a moment," came Grant's muffled voice.

Rob heard someone approach the inner side of the door.

"Who is it?"

"It's Rob. Are you alone?"

"Well, not at the moment, but I can be freed up in short order. Why don't I meet you at Houlihan's in twenty minutes."

Rob smiled to himself. "I'll be waiting."

Houlihan's was one of many tavern eateries in town. It was located on Bay Street, only a few blocks from Grant's apartment. Houlihan's was where they met occasionally for drinks during the week. The cocktail hour would be boisterous and noisy and, yet, they would be able to talk.

Houlihan's catered to the professional class in town and was already busy as Rob entered. He recognized several familiar faces and nodded in greeting. The bartender recognized him and motioned him over. "What can I get for you, Rob?"

"Just a draft, Vic. Grant is meeting me here in a few minutes."

The bartender drew a cold mug of beer and placed it before him. As Rob took a sip, he turned to survey the crowd, mentally recording how the faces remained the same. He thought if someone were to paint a mural of the afternoon drinking crowd and compare it with the actual scene five years later, there would be little change. The patrons were truly loyal to their watering hole. It occurred to Rob that he would probably be one of the ones in the mural.

He moved away from the bar and over to the side of the room where a small shelf lined the wall. After only a few minutes Grant ducked in the front door with a smile on his face. He walked with feline quickness to where Rob stood.

"Good to see you, old man," said Grant. "Sorry I was wrapped up at the house."

"Who this time?" asked Rob. "Wait, I don't even want to know."

Grant motioned to the waitress and pointed to Rob's stein of beer. She acknowledged his order and went toward the bar.

Grant, like Rob, was a regular in Houlihan's and knew most of the other patrons. He detested being interrupted while expressing a thought and would usually raise his voice and continue as before.

"So what's on your mind today, old friend?" asked Grant.

Grant and Rob had served together in several Savannah-based units during the war and had the easiness between them that most close friends possessed. They could be honest with each other without fear of trampling on one another's feelings. Usually there was light-hearted banter between them, and those who didn't know would think they were adversaries rather than the closest of friends.

Grant was close in physical makeup to Rob, tall and wiry. His hair was more of a sandy blond and his complexion was freckled without being ruddy.

Rob knew Grant would never let a friend down. They had saved each other in tight situations in combat and Rob knew from those experiences that Grant could always be counted on when he needed him. No one had more courage, and he was the one Rob would immediately select to accompany him in a delicate situation.

The waitress delivered Grant's beer.

"Thanks Dorrie," Grant said and turned his attention to Rob. "Okay, let's have it."

"I've just met a girl."

"What's new about that?" You're always meeting women. You're about as bad as me."

"This one is special. It's hard to describe."

"The one, huh?"

"I don't know about that, but I do know I want to see her again and I want you to help me figure a way to do it."

"Why don't you just ask her?"

"She's only in town for a week and staying with her cousin. I just bumped into them on the street and was able to escort them home."

"Simple." Grant raised his voice a decibel and continued with deliberate phrasing. "You just go back to the house, inquire about her well being, and ask if she will accompany you on a stroll through town. You're making too much of this. It isn't like you."

"I guess I'm afraid of rejection from this one. It would make a difference."

"You won't be rejected -- go for what you want. Then I can meet her."

"I'm not sure she's ready for that."

Chapter 5

Rob woke the next morning thinking of little else other than what he would wear, what time he should call, and where they should go if she accepted.

He dressed in his best suit and decided about 10:30 in the morning would be proper -- not too early and not approaching lunchtime. Mentally, he continued rehearsing his opening lines. Not too casual and not too eager.

The distance from his apartment on Marshall Row to Fanny's house was only a few blocks, and he strolled along immersed in his thoughts. His hands were cold and wet. He rubbed them against his trouser leg. That seemed to warm them as well as dry them off.

As he came to the house, he paused at the base of the steps and took a deep breath. Then, quickly, he ascended to the porch and rang the bell. He could hear footsteps in the hall. An attractive woman he judged to be in her late forties opened the door.

"Yes?" she said.

"Good morning, ma'am. I'm Rob Truitt. Yesterday I escorted Miss Fanny and Miss Frances home and I wanted to inquire as to their well being."

"I see." He could feel her scrutiny. "I'm Fanny's mother, Clara Ellis. Won't you come in and I'll let them know you're here."

Rob entered the house with some trepidation as Mrs. Ellis led him into the living room and offered him a seat. He selected a side chair next to the fireplace facing a large camel back sofa.

As she left, he observed his surroundings. The house was as impressive on the inside as it was uniform with other townhouses in the row outside. There was a large chandelier suspended from a dome inset in a twelve-foot ceiling. The walls were papered in a damask flock design above a white wainscoting

"Impressive," he said to himself.

The floors were of random plank pine and strategically covered with oriental rugs of varying sizes. The mantel was sculpted in white marble with a gilt-edged oval mirror above and brass sconces on each side. On the walls were an eclectic array of old masters and pen-and-ink drawings. His confidence was rapidly eroding.

Suddenly, there was a rustling noise on the stairs in the hall and Fanny entered the room. She was wearing a simple everyday dress with her hair pulled back in a bun. Rob rose.

"Hello, Mr. Truitt. It's good to see you again."

"I hope I haven't caught you at a bad time. I wanted to check on your well being after yesterday."

"Not at all. It's kind of you to call. Frances will be down in a moment."

Fanny could tell by Rob's expression there was a slight look of apprehension that Frances had not come down with her.

"I trust today will be a better day for you ladies than yesterday?"

"Well, actually, yesterday wasn't bad until the incident."

Frances entered the room. She was dressed in green with her hair pulled back with a barrette but not in a bun. To Rob, she looked radiant.

"Hello, Miss Perry. How good it is to see you again. I hope I'm not intruding on your morning."

"Nonsense," said Frances. "Fanny and I were just discussing what we might do to fill the day."

"Could I make a suggestion?"

"Which is?"

"I was hoping I might be able to escort you on a stroll about the city. Maybe we could stop and have lunch."

"What do you think?" said Fanny as she looked at Frances.

Frances felt herself flush. "That would be lovely."

* * *

The day was overcast with a gray sky. It was fine for walking. Rob suggested they head in the direction of Colonial Park Cemetery, which was actually a small municipal park. It was the final resting-place for many of the founders of the colony and was usually filled with sightseers.

They walked down South Broad with Rob on the curb next to Fanny and Frances on her other side. He was hoping conversation would flow and not be awkward.

As they passed Independent Presbyterian Church, Fanny pointed out that was where she and her family attended.

"Fanny, how long have you lived in Savannah?" Rob asked.

"All my life, except a few years off at boarding school."

"And Frances, how long have you lived in Florida?"

"All my life, too. My father is from Atlanta and my mother from Woodbury, not too far from there. He moved to Jacksonville where my mother was working and not too long after that, they married. Then he bought the farm in McIntosh and the family has been there ever since. It's where we live now. What about you?"

"Oh my history is not so interesting. My family moved to Savannah when I was young. I've been here all along, except for the time I spent in the war."

As they approached the park they could see the entrance to the cemetery, set in a corner. Street traffic was bustling since most of the people in the surrounding area came to the city on the weekend.

"My two brothers were in the war," said Frances. Russell was killed at Gettysburg and Sammy at Cold Harbor, near the end of the war. I was too young at the time to really know them."

"I'm sorry," said Rob. "I was at Cold Harbor, too."

"It was a hard time for everyone," said Fanny. "I've heard stories from my mother about how Savannah was blockaded by the Yankees and the city literally starved. The only supply boats that could get in or out were the blockade runners."

They entered the park, and now Frances was walking next to Rob since Fanny had adroitly moved to the outside.

"It's not very well maintained," observed Frances.

"True, it's really slipped from when it was as the city's primary burial ground," agreed Fanny.

"At one time it was a proud place but the Yankees took care of that in the month they occupied the town," said Rob. "Compared to what it was, it's in a sorry state."

31

"What happened?" asked Frances. Fanny waited for Rob to answer.

"Some of General Sherman's troops camped here during their occupation in December 1864. They ransacked the graveyard in search of valuables. It seems they heard local residents had stashed their gold and silver in the burial vaults to hide it from the Union army. Although the rumors were not true, the troops desecrated the vaults and graves in search of treasure. The city has yet to restore the park."

"Maybe one day," said Fanny.

"I've an idea," said Rob. "Why don't we go to the White Horse for lunch. If Frances hasn't been there, she may find it interesting."

"I think that's a great idea," said Fanny. "Frances will love it."

* * *

The White Horse was an easy walk from Colonial Cemetery, only a few blocks. The building had operated as a restaurant and inn with rooms upstairs as long as most residents could remember. The inn was built with brick masonry on the ground floor with a frame clapboard exterior on the second. They entered under the canopy that extended to the street.

"Oh, it smells so good in here," said Fanny.

Frances was taking in the beamed ceilings, the brick flooring, and the two fireplaces in the large single room that served as the restaurant. Both boasted a glowing fire.

"I love the ambiance," said Frances.

"I think you'll like the food, too," Rob laughed.

The maitre d' seated them at a table next to the wall where they had a good view of the entire room. The ceiling was low and the exposed heart pine joists were visible the entire length of the room. Each table had its own small candle in a hurricane glass.

Out of nowhere appeared the waitress to take their orders and left a basket of freshly baked bread. Rob asked if they would like a glass of wine before the meal. Both ladies deferred.

Fanny and Frances decided on a quiche that was one of the luncheon specials and Rob diplomatically ordered the same thing.

When the food was brought, they ate, laughed and talked as if they had known each other for a good while.

"Rob, how did you happen to be on Barnard Street yesterday when you came to our aid," asked Fanny.

"Actually, I was just leaving the city market building and was doing a little window shopping myself. If I'd known in advance you two would be there, I would have made it a point to be there and make it look like happenstance."

Fanny laughed, "Maybe it was all preordained."

"Maybe so," said Frances, in a more serious tone.

He was easy to talk to and the conversation flowed. He asked them to call him Rob, and they became Frances and Fanny in turn.

After lunch, they walked the short distance to Bull Street. Bull was the primary promenade in the city for strollers, and Wright Square was filled with people and children playing.

"What a beautiful church," Frances commented. "What denomination is it?"

"It's Lutheran," said Rob. The Lutheran Church of the Ascension, It's one of the most beautiful churches in the city."

"My church in Florida is so small it would fit inside."

The threesome walked back toward South Broad and Rob pointed out different sights along the way. He knew Fanny was well acquainted with the city, so his comments were usually directed to the different shops and street scenes. He was careful not to say anything injurious about anyone in fear that she might know them.

Eventually, they approached Fanny's house. All three were aware that the time was rapidly approaching where Rob needed to ask if he could call again, assuming he was interested. They also knew a choice must be made. Rob pondered on how he would ever see Frances alone. The three ascended the steps and reached the porch.

"Rob, this was delightful," said Fanny.

"Yes," said Frances. "Thank you so much for an interesting day and being so attentive."

"It was my pleasure. Thank you both for being such good company. Why don't I rent a carriage tomorrow and take you both for a ride outside the city."

"Well," said Fanny looking down, "I can't, even though I would love to." She looked back at Rob. "I must go with Mother on something she has scheduled, but I'm sure Frances would enjoy seeing some things outside the city."

"Well, I don't know," said Frances blushing. "Would it be proper?"

"Of course, you silly farm girl," said her cousin with a laugh.

"It would be fun if you could," said Rob, not believing his good fortune in getting Frances alone.

"Okay. Could you call after church and lunch, around two?"

"That's perfect. I'll make the arrangements and see you tomorrow."

The choice had been made.

* * *

Fanny and Frances entered the house and Frances turned to Fanny. "You don't have anything to do tomorrow afternoon -- what are you doing?" She could hardly suppress her smile.

Fanny laughed. "At this point, three's a crowd," she said holding three fingers aloft. "I see how he looks at you when you look away and he thinks no one sees."

"Oh god, I'll be nervous as a cat," said Frances wringing her hands. "What'll we talk about? Do you think he likes me, really? You and he seemed to do most of the talking."

"I think he's funny, and witty, and oh so handsome, but I don't have that same feeling for him that you do."

"What do you mean?" asked Frances, walking into the parlor.

"Frances, it's written all over your face."

"Do you think he could tell?"

"No, silly, but I've been around my cousin long enough to know when she sees something she wants."

"I'm a nervous wreck. What will I wear?"

"Don't worry, we're the same size and I've got some country clothes that will do fine. Now, let's do some strategizing."

Chapter 6

Rob left the house playing back almost everything that had been said and where they had walked. Where had the time gone? The threesome had been together for almost five hours and yet he could not believe it passed so swiftly.

His mind was buzzing as he replayed the conversation in his head. What he said. How she reacted. What she said. And oh, Fanny said some funny things, too.

"I wonder if she likes me," he said to no one.

He went back to his apartment by way of the Marshall House Stables to reserve a carriage for Sunday. I must make an impression, he thought.

Rob entered his apartment and began getting ready for the evening. He was attending a party, but his mind was focused only on the next day.

His apartment was furnished with a masculine flavor but was tastefully done. It was on the ground floor of a row house and consisted of only three rooms. These were in the same configuration as the house upstairs. There was a side hallway from front to back that connected living room or parlor in the front, the bedroom, and a kitchen in the rear. A small bath lay between the bedroom and kitchen. His windows were cracked slightly and there was a cool autumn breeze blowing across the rooms.

Rob's mind was on Frances and what they would do to spend Sunday afternoon together. He found himself unconsciously pacing the length of his apartment and back again. Everything needed to be perfect.

* * *

It was early Sunday morning and Frances awoke, both dreading and at the same time being wonderfully nervous about the day. She dressed and went downstairs to a full breakfast of scrambled eggs, grits, and toast. She liked hers with marmalade, the same as Fanny's dad, her Uncle Charles. Fanny was already at the table. It was set with a white linen cloth and sterling serving pieces. The food was on the sideboard next to the table. Frances began helping her plate.

"What are you doing today, Cousin Frances?" Fanny chided.

"As if you didn't know. You even set it up."

"I was beginning to wonder if we would have to prod him a little to plant a seed in his mind. Fortunately, we didn't."

"You mean '*you*' didn't."

"Whatever," said Fanny. "Sometimes it doesn't hurt to make things happen. Even destiny needs a little push at times."

"What will I wear?" asked Frances.

"I told you, I have clothes for you. I promise you'll look just ravishing."

"What if we find we can't talk to each other. What if it starts to drag?"

"It won't, silly. Now stop worrying and relax. You're going to have a marvelous time. Then you can tell me all about it."

The girls went back upstairs and dressed for church. They lived only a few blocks from Independent Presbyterian, where Fanny's family had attended for generations.

The church had the highest spire in the city, adorned with a copper roof that had weathered to a burnished green. The massive church covered almost an entire block on the corner of Bull and South Broad.

The minister preached from a mahogany pulpit raised high above the congregation. The acoustics were such that it seemed as if the voice of God himself was speaking. Fanny leaned over and whispered Frances' ear during the sermon, "Two o'clock is drawing near."

Frances jabbed her in the ribs with her elbow. After properly mingling and visiting with other members after the service, as was the custom, they walked slowly back to the house. Lunch was light and afterwards, the girls thanked Fanny's mother and rushed upstairs giggling.

"We need to fix you up in something interesting," said Fanny.

"Interesting?"

"Right. Let's pull your hair back in a French twist and dress you in a color to accent its auburn cast. Maybe the green suede jacket as an accent over this rust-colored dress --- yes, I think so. Try these on."

Fanny pulled Frances' hair back and clipped it into a roll. Frances changed into Fanny's clothes and looked at herself in the full-length oval mirror. She smiled, pleased with the transformation.
"You wear them like they were made for you," said Fanny.
"Are you sure?"
"Trust me. If they looked that good on me, I'd go in your place."
"Would you stop." Frances smiled.
"It's almost time; let's wait up here so you can make an entrance down the stairs. Besides, I'm supposed to be going somewhere with mother. Fanny winked.

* * *

Rob woke about eight on Sunday morning. He lay in bed for a spell, focusing on the day. He knew he had some time to kill before he would call for Frances and decided he would shave and bathe at a leisurely pace and generally get himself to a point where he would be as inoffensive as possible.

He drew several pails of water and placed them on the kitchen range to heat. The embers were still faintly glowing from the night before and he added a few coals and stoked the fire to take advantage of them.

When the water in the pails was beginning to warm, he poured a small amount into a wash basin and carried it to the bathroom to shave. Slowly, he stropped the razor to insure its keenness and made a mental note to be extra careful. To cut the small mole on his upper lip would make it bleed for hours, like he was hemorrhaging.

Rob mused, I wonder if they know how much we go through to get ready for them.

After he cleaned up, he threw some old clothes on and went out to get a newspaper. That would give him some time to mull over the events of the day with his coffee, and he brought it back to his place to enjoy with his coffee. Still having ample time, he stopped by the livery again to confirm his reservation. He had been specific about a shay with a gentle horse. No sense asking for trouble, he thought.

Everything was confirmed and ready, and all he had to do now was wait. At 1:30 Rob walked again to the Luke Carson's stables at the Marshall House. He thought the best plan of action would be to drive out toward Bonaventure Cemetery on the Wilmington River. Maybe an hour out, an hour back, and an hour or two in between.

As he entered the livery, he was struck by the sounds but especially the smells of the stable. There was a mixture of sweating horseflesh combined with that of oiled leather. It was a man's world and one Rob was comfortable in. His rig was ready and he still had the luxury of time on his side.

All horses were somewhat different, and he knew it would be smart to drive the carriage about town a few minutes to get the feel of the horse before calling for Frances. As he suspected, the horse and shay had been out many times, and there was no problem.

At five minutes to two, he drew the horse up in front of Fanny's house. He tied the reins off on the seat and attached the retaining anchor to the loop on the horse's bit. Taking a deep breath, he started up the stairs to the door.

His knock was answered by Fanny, who was jabbering to Rob about how nice the day was and how she knew they would have a good time and so on. Rob heard little of it.

As he looked to the head of the stairs, he saw Frances and he could not deny his feelings. She was lovely.

"Hello," he said. "Are you ready to see a little more of what lies around Savannah?"

"Absolutely." Frances smiled. "It will be an adventure."

* * *

Rob helped her up and into the carriage, unhooked the anchor and seated himself beside her. The reins felt like old friends in his hands and he expertly drove the horse eastward on South Broad.

They were heading toward the Sea Island Road that extended out about eight miles out to Bonaventure. The horse had an easy gait and he figured it would take them about an hour to get there.

"I'm glad you could come today," said Rob. I kept thinking I would get a note saying you couldn't make it."

"I admit to being a little nervous about it, but I have trust in you. Is it misplaced?"

Rob looked her in the eye and said with a serious smile, "Never."

"Do you have many lady friends?"

"I have friends that are ladies, but I wouldn't say that I have many, if any, lady friends. How about you? Are you the heartbreaker in McIntosh?"

"Hardly," she laughed. My father has scared off almost every boy in Marion County with his stern looks."

The wind felt good on their faces and the horse seemed to be enjoying the work. Rob relaxed and shifted in the seat. The tenseness had melted.

"How much longer will you be in town?" he asked.

"About three more days. I received a letter from Mother saying some things had happened at home that she needed to discuss with me. I hope everything's okay. I wish I could stay longer." She glanced sideways at him.

They had reached the winding Bonaventure Road, the direct approach into the cemetery.

"It seems strange to those outside the city," said Rob. "But on Sundays in Savannah, it's always been quite the fashion to visit the cemeteries."

"I'm sure it's refreshing to get out of the city for a while," said Frances. "Maybe a change of pace."

"It's probably as much a park as a cemetery," said Rob. "Kind of like Colonial Park in town. It was laid out with wide avenues for carriages and places for strolling and picnicking on the weekends."

"Is it old?" asked Frances.

"As a place, yes. Bonaventure was a plantation that was home to one of the early governors of the state. It's only been in use for public burial since right before the war. "Rob slowed the horse to a walk as they entered the grounds.

"It's beautiful," said Frances. "The oaks are simply overwhelming."

39

"Yes, many say it's one of the most beautiful spots in the country. You should see it in the spring when the azaleas are in full bloom."

Rob guided them to the right of a single vault near the entrance that said simply "Gaston Tomb" at the top of the door.

"Why is that sitting apart from the others?" asked Frances.

"It's an interesting story. It was actually moved from Colonial Cemetery. You know, where we were walking yesterday with Fanny. When that park slipped into a poor state of maintenance, the city decided it would be a good idea to move it to Bonaventure for better keeping.

"Was he a military hero or a local politician?"

"Neither. Gaston Street in the city is named for Mr. Gaston. He was president of the Planters Bank before the war and a confirmed bachelor. It's said that no one ever visited Savannah who was not welcome at Mr. Gaston's house and table. He became the legendary host of Savannah."

"But why the vault?" asked Frances.

"Gaston died suddenly in New York City while on a business trip. His friends thought it would be a noble gesture to erect a tomb called the 'Stranger's Tomb.' The idea was that in addition to Mr. Gaston being there, anyone who died unexpectedly in Savannah could reside with him until their remains could be transferred to their hometown. They thought since he was the ultimate host in life, he could continue being as hospitable in death."

"Is there anyone in there with him now?"

"I don't know, but it's nice to think so."

"What a story. Almost romantic."

Rob slowed again and motioned to the horse to stop.

"This is where the old plantation house was located. It burned many years ago and was never rebuilt. It must've faced out across the marshes to the river."

"I have the strangest feeling here," said Frances. "It's almost like a ghost is stalking my shadow. I want to go but yet something is pulling me back. Have you ever been somewhere new but yet feel as though you know it?"

"I know. Every time I come to Bonaventure, it's as if the place is calling me. With all the fighting and hardship we went through in the war, I never experienced the same pervading feeling."

"Tell me about the war."

Rob sighed. Four years of misery and butchery came back to him in an instant. "I'd like to. Maybe when we have more time," he said it with a steely closure.

"I didn't mean to hit on a sensitive topic. I'm sorry."

"It's okay. And it's not sensitive. It's just long and I'm not sure I can do it justice."

Rob nudged the horse ahead and drove on down the short distance to the bluff on the river. Pulling off the road, he tied off the reins, anchored the horse, and went around to help Frances out.

"I thought we could walk a bit," he said.

He reached up to help her down. As she stepped down, she unintentionally lost her balance and lurched against him.

"Careful," he said, supporting her.

"Sorry," she said, looking directly in his eyes.

"No problem," said Rob.

They walked a short distance from the carriage along the river. She took his arm for balance. The autumn sun was getting lower in the sky and the day could not have been more beautiful.

"Frances?"

"Yes?"

"Can I see you again? Before you have to go back?"

Frances didn't hesitate. "You'd better, Rob Truitt."

When they returned to the carriage and headed back toward town, there was an easiness between them. Frances lay her hand on his for just a moment.

What am I doing, she thought. It's so bold but so right.

Both floated home in the carriage.

LITTLE GRACIE

Chapter 7

No sooner had Frances entered the house than Fanny was all over her.

"Well?" said Fanny.

"Well. It was nice. He was charming and we had a great time. We rode out to Bonaventure. What a beautiful place."

"I know that, cousin. And what a beautiful man. What did you talk about? Tell me! Tell me!"

"Oh, you know. Just getting-to-know-you talk. What kind of work he does and where he's from. His family and so forth."

"Did he touch you?"

"No, but we did hold hands for a minute."

"I knew it -- he's interested. Did he ask you out again?"

"I told him I only had three more days in Savannah and he asked if I could have dinner with him tomorrow."

"Ah ha. You've captivated him. He's hooked."

"Well I don't know about that, but it certainly was easy being with him. I think he enjoyed it, too."

"Let's go get you changed so I can hear every detail. I want to know everything that was said the entire time. How exciting."

* * *

Rob drove the shay back to the livery and settled up with Luke Carson. He was pleased with the small investment in the rig and was already making plans for dinner the following evening.

What would be a good place? he thought. Somewhere not too formal but not too casual. A place where she will know I think she's special.

He decided on The Pink House, originally a private residence and only a block from the bank where he worked. He stopped by and made a reservation for 7:00 the following evening. He made certain the maitre d' would hold the table in the corner by expressing his gratitude in advance. Rob placed a gratuity in his waiting hand.

"Thank you, Mr. Truitt. We're so happy you will be joining us tomorrow evening."

"Thank *you*, Marcel."

Rob walked back to his house with a spring in his step. He felt as if he had done all that he could for now. It was time to start working on the direction he wanted the conversation with Frances to take.

He felt it to be a verbal chess match and he tried emphatically to think of her reactions and responses to his lines. He would say *this*, and she would respond with *that*. He played it over repeatedly in his mind.

Damn, this is hard, he thought.

Darkness fell early in the autumn months and there was a crisp feeling to the night air.

"Interesting how the town takes on an entirely different ambiance after dark," he mused. Rob knew time was growing short. In a few days Frances would be gone. When and if she would return was unknown. Would she want to? Somehow he had to accelerate the relationship. How? If only there was more time, he thought.

Tomorrow was a business day. Normally, he would think ahead on Sundays to mentally anticipate the coming week. He thought of pending items left on Friday that would need to be addressed.

Oh hell, he thought, tomorrow will take care of itself.

* * *

Rob was right. Monday was an extremely heavy day, but he was in the best of moods.

"You seem to be unusually chipper this morning Mr. Truitt," his secretary said, "did you have a pleasant weekend?"

"Yes, Mrs. Arnold, it couldn't have been better."

"Good. You have a full day of appointments and there is a meeting of the loan committee at 10:30 with all members expected to be in attendance."

"We're ready for it."

With all he was involved in, there was still the glow in the back of his mind -- Frances.

44

Perhaps he should give her a parting gift as a remembrance. Then again, perhaps that would be too forward. Hard to say. Better hold off. Don't want her to think I'm trying to buy her affection like some damn carpet bagging Yankee.

The day passed swiftly. He had only taken a short respite for lunch down the street at Louie's. He wanted to eat something filling so that he would not be consumed with an eager appetite in the evening.

Back at the office he was immersed in reviewing construction drawings and, before he realized it, the bell in the city exchange was chiming the hour, signaling the shopkeepers of closing time at 5:00. He straightened his desk and headed for the door.

"Goodnight Mrs. Arnold," he said in passing.

She looked up, surprised to see him leaving so punctually.

"Goodbye, Mr. Truitt. Have a good evening."

Rob literally streaked down the flight of stairs to the street. It was important that he get home for a change into fresh clothes and allow time to freshen up.

Frances would be expecting him to call at 6:30 and he wanted to be comfortable with his appearance.

At 6:15 he left his house to walk the few blocks to the stand and retain a taxi to pick up Frances. He wore a gray suit with a dark vest and a freshly starched white shirt. He wondered what she would wear this evening.

As they stopped at her house, Rob instructed the driver to wait, then proceeded to the door. After his knock, it was opened a few moments later by Frances herself.

She was stunning, dressed in a full-length burgundy dress with pleated bottom, lace yoke, and a matching bowler hat. He felt his heart jump. He smiled and said "Don't you look lovely tonight. Are you ready for some dinner?"

"I've been looking forward to it."

He assisted her down the stairs and into the waiting carriage.

"The Pink House," he told the driver.

"Yes sir."

As the carriage started off to the restaurant, Rob settled back into the seat with Frances. She exuded cleanliness and the subtle fragrance of perfume, in stark contrast to the well-worn leather of the carriage.

"Did you have a busy day?" asked Frances.

"Yes, Mondays are always active, but today was especially busy. We have our weekly loan committee and there were several meetings with clients. The day seemed to slip by before I knew it. How about you?"

"Fanny and I went marketing for Aunt Clara, and that took up most of the morning. Then, after lunch, we visited a friend of hers who paints landscapes using watercolors. She has her own studio, down on Factors' Walk overlooking the river."

"It sounds as if you had a full day, too."

"It was fun. Where are we going tonight?"

"It's called the Pink House. A wealthy planter built it in the late 1700's as a private residence. Later it was used as a bank, the one where Mr. Gaston was president. Now it's been converted into a restaurant. I hope you'll like it. The food is good and it has a nice atmosphere."

The carriage drew up in front of the restaurant and Rob paid the driver. He helped Frances out and she tucked her arm in his for support. As they entered, Marcel spotted them and hurried over immediately.

"Mr. Truitt, how nice to see you this evening. And how lovely your lady is. I have a wonderful table for you in the corner."

Marcel took two menus from his stand at the door and led them to their table. He held the chair for Frances and assisted her into her seat. Rob stretched his hand out to thank him and Marcel pocketed the bills with a fluid and practiced motion. After Rob was seated, Marcel gave each of them a menu and lit the small candle in the hurricane globe on the table.

"Your waiter will be with you in only a moment," he said and returned to his station by the entrance.

"Rob, it's beautiful; so old and with a special character. Thank you for bringing me here."

"I thought you would like it. I think you will like the food, too. They specialize in seafood dishes, but the steaks are always cooked to perfection, as well."

The waiter came and asked if they would like a cocktail before dinner. Frances agreed to a glass of Chardonnay and Rob ordered another for himself.

"It's nice to be with you tonight," he said.

"I've looked forward to it all day."

"I was hoping in addition to having a good dinner we would have a chance to talk some more."

The waiter brought their wines and proceeded to name the special dishes of the day that didn't appear on the menu. Also, Rob thought to himself, they never mention the prices.

"Would you like more time?" the waiter asked.

"Yes, can you give us another minute?" said Rob.

As the waiter left, Rob mentioned to Frances that the flounder stuffed with crabmeat was a specialty of the house she might enjoy if she didn't get much seafood in central Florida. She agreed.

"And I'll join you," he said.

Rob motioned to the waiter and when he returned, placed the orders.

As the waiter left, Rob turned to Frances and said, "You really look lovely tonight."

She smiled coyly. "Well thank you, kind sir. You cut a rather dashing figure yourself."

"I must tell you again that it distresses me you will be leaving in a few days. Do you have any idea when you'll be able to come back?"

"It's hard to say. I received a letter from mother saying I was needed back home, but she was vague as to what is going on. I hope everyone is well."

"I do, too."

"If there is a crisis, I must go back to be there. Do you understand?"

"Of course. If I give you my address, do you think you could write me? Also, I would like to write to you. Would that be possible?"

"Oh Rob, I would be disappointed if I didn't hear from you."

"I know we've only known each other for a few days, but you have grown to mean a lot to me in that short period of time."

In a bold move, he reached across the table and covered her hand with his.

"Let's make a toast," he said.

She smiled. "You start it."

Raising his glass and looking at her, he said. "Whatever you may do, in thought, word, and deed, either intentionally or naturally, and wherever you may go, it matters. Surely you were conceived and packaged just for me."

"Oh Rob, what a nice thing to say but that's not a toast. I can't drink to myself."

"Well, I can." He smiled and took a sip of his wine.

"Here's one," said Frances. She raised her glass. "To new friends from distant places, may the distance grow small while the friendship grows large."

They touched glasses and sipped their wine.

"That's a beautiful thought," said Rob.

About that time the waiter came with their meal. It was presented on Wedgwood china and accompanied by a large basket of freshly baked bread. He placed their plates in front of them and then graciously disappeared.

"I hope it's as good as it smells," said Frances.

"Let's find out." Rob picked up his fork.

The couple ate in silence while they tasted the flounder and side dishes. Their few comments were on the food and how it was prepared. As they finished, Frances said, "That was delicious."

The waiter came to clear their plates and to entice them with the desserts offered by the house. Rob talked Frances into a mudbottom pie that was rich in chocolate and a specialty by many restaurants in the Savannah area.

"You have something, too," she said.

"No I couldn't."

"Then you'll have to share mine." To the waiter she said, "Please bring two forks with the pie."

They ordered coffee to have with the dessert.

"I would like to see you again before you have to leave. Is that possible?" asked Rob.

"Yes. I would be very upset if I thought I couldn't spend as much time with you as I can before I leave. What can we do?"

"We can take walks, we can have dinner, and perhaps you and Fanny could meet me for lunch. I would like you to meet my friend Grant, whom I think you will find entertaining. I just want to see you and spend time together.

Frances placed her hand on his and looked at him.

"And I want to spend as much time with you as you will let me. Maybe you could come visit me one weekend in Florida."

"I'd like that."

They lingered and talked for a long while over dessert and coffee about trivial things that people falling in love gravitate to. None of the answers meant anything to anyone except the one asking, who in each case was falling strongly in love and out of control.

"It's getting late; I better get you home," said Rob. He called for the check and settled the bill with the waiter. In escorting Frances to the door, he noticed as several heads turned silently in their direction. Rob smiled to himself as he read the envy on the faces of the men.

* * *

He led Frances to the first taxi waiting in the street. The two settled back in the seat for the ride home.

"This was such a lovely evening," said Frances. "I'm sorry it has to end."

"Hopefully we'll have others."

"Yes," she said, looking at him directly with a slight parting of the lips.

Rob felt himself being drawn to her. She still held his gaze. He eased his arm behind her and drew her slowly to him. Her mouth was warm, sweet, and softly yielded. He stroked her face gently with the back of his hand as they kissed. She sighed as they parted and rested her head against his chest.

"How could you know I love to have my face rubbed? My dad always did that when I was small and he put me to bed."

"He must be very fond of you."

"Rob, things are going so quickly, but I feel our time is running even faster. It's like sand in the hourglass. Someone once said, 'picture the future and act now.' Is that what we're doing?"

"No. We're probably being more honest with each other than people would otherwise be if they knew they had more time. When we were in the war, Grant always had the philosophy of imagining every day being your last but still believing you'll live forever."

"Yes, don't waste a moment."

"Maybe we should follow your advice." Rob kissed Frances again. This time, a little more intensely.

Other than a few street noises, the only sounds were from the horse's hooves and the occasional mutterings of the driver to the horse as they clip-clopped through the dimly lit streets of town.

"Do you like my face?" she asked.

"Of course, it's beautiful. What kind of question is that?"

"I think my nose has a slight hump in it. I wish it didn't. I've heard that there are new techniques where doctors can totally reshape your face. I believe it's called plastic surgery. I've read that criminals use it to change their identity. If I had the money, I might change my nose."

"If you did, you would get a severe argument from me. Leave it alone."

"Okay. For now." She laughed. Do you think your friend Grant will like me?"

"Absolutely. And you will like him, but I warn you, he's different."

"In what way?"

"Grant's an attorney by trade, but his avocation and love is his writing. He's written several pieces of crime fiction that have been published in men's detective magazines."

"So he writes whodunits?"

"Yes, but his genre is more in the area of action mystery. It seems to be more palatable to a male audience."

"Sounds interesting."

"Do you think maybe you and Fanny could meet us for lunch tomorrow? If so, I'll muster up Grant and we could meet you at the Hunter's Place at a quarter of twelve. Fanny knows where it is. If we go a little early, we could dodge the noon rush and get a good table."

"Let's plan on it, Frances said. "Unless you hear from me otherwise in the morning, we'll see you for lunch."

The carriage stopped in front of Fanny's house and Rob kissed her goodnight. This time again sweetly. Her fragrance and the headiness of the moment was totally captivating him.

He escorted her to the door and bade her goodnight by the shadows and flickering of the gas lamps at the door. A chill was settling in to the evening and before long, the first frost of the season would arrive after the unusually hot summer.

Rob let the driver drop him at his apartment. The small hallway was dark and he lit the gas sconce near the archway to the parlor. That should be enough light to get to the bedroom, he thought. All he wanted to do was to get his clothes ready for the next day. He would call it an early evening.

In the morning he would stop by Grant's and ask him about lunch. He knew even if there was a conflict on his friend's schedule, he would break it to accommodate him. Grant would much rather be with two attractive ladies than any possible business luncheon.

Chapter 8

Before the clock on the night table could chime its half-past-six wake-up call, Rob reached over and killed the alarm. He had been awake for several hours. It seemed the harder he tried to get back to sleep, the more futile it became. Thoughts of Frances crept into his mind until he could no longer stave the flow.

He dwelled on things like what they did the night before and, of course, what they said. Where was all this heading, and where did he want it to? Those were the thoughts he had swirling but he was not ready to focus on them with a direct attack. In a few days she would be leaving and he didn't want to confront that fact. He didn't want to acknowledge how emotionally involved he had become in only a few days.

What is different? he thought. Why this girl? I've had many other girls that were as pretty; and intelligent; and witty. Why this one?

The web that entangles all that are smitten was entrapping him. They then turn to analysis to sort out their predicament. Scared to death to commit, but even more frightened of the thought of not seeing that person again. Usually another meeting only whets the appetite for another -- and another. It becomes an addiction. The other person hasn't filled a need as much as become one.

"Oh what the hell."

He made his bed and put his room in order. Even though he had few guests, male or otherwise, he didn't want his landlady to think him a disheveled person, should she have the need to enter his quarters while he was away. Usually, he knew the place would be just as he left it when he returned -- silent and empty.

Rob's apartment was only about six blocks from Grant's and he enjoyed the crisp morning air as he walked over. Grant was surprised to see him so early, but said to count on him for lunch. He didn't remember on his calendar from Monday if he had a prior engagement, but said not to worry. They would meet at the restaurant at 11:35, then secure a table.

Rob went straight to the office. Like Grant, he was not sure what awaited him for the day. There were several row house apartment dwellings that were being developed in the city and he knew he would be meeting with architects, builders, and developers in the course of arranging and getting all documentation into place for review by the committee.

At 11:30, Rob left the bank so he could arrive at the restaurant and secure a table. As he entered, he didn't see Grant. He let the waiter show him to a table and told him there would be four in the party for lunch. Luckily there was a booth open and he chose that, knowing it would work better for the ladies.

* * *

The Hunter's Place was a popular lunchtime spot on Whitaker Street in the business district of the town. The food was good, the service relatively fast, and there were always the familiar faces of those who worked in the downtown community. Rob caught the aroma of today's lunch being prepared in the kitchen along with the stale smell of beer from the adjoining lounge.

He sat facing the front door so he could see the others as they arrived. A few minutes after he was seated, he saw Grant come in and visually sweep the room. He motioned him over to the booth.

"You got us a good table, old man. How's it going?"

"Typical Tuesday, everything in full swing. Everyone in town seems to be building something. I hope we didn't interfere with anything important you had going."

"What do you care?" said Grant, laughing. "You would have insisted, anyway. But no, there was nothing pressing going on. What time do you think the girls will show up? I believe I've met Fanny before, but only casually. She seems to be a fox."

"I'm sure you'll find out."

About that time the girls entered the door along with others in the lunchtime crowd. The restaurant was beginning to fill up. Rob went to meet them while Grant kept the table.

"Hello, you're right on time. We've got a booth over near the rear. Come on back, Grant just got here himself."

Rob led them back to the booth and Grant stood to meet them.

"Miss Fanny Ellis and Miss Frances Perry, this is Grant Dawson."
"It's a pleasure," said Grant. "I believe Fanny and I have met some
time before, although I don't recall where, do you?"
"I'm not sure, either," said Fanny.
Grant turned his attention to Frances. "And are you the lady who's
been monopolizing Rob's time and attention span?" Frances reddened
slightly. "He's been very kind to show me around the city."
The ladies sat next to the wall with Grant next to Fanny and Rob
next to Frances. As the restaurant continued to fill, many of the
patrons nodded in acknowledgment to Rob and Grant. The waiter
came for drink orders and they ordered cider and tea, except for Grant,
who opted for a draft beer.
Grant was rolling into his entertaining self, which usually
consisted of telling stories that were embarrassing to Rob. He was
always relating some escapade they'd been involved in that Rob wished
he would hold until another time.
Grant was actually born in New York City and came to Savannah
when he was only a year old. His father had been a jeweler who died
when Grant was very young. Actually, he had no memory of his father
at all. It always galled Grant that he was not a native Savannahian, but
he knew the rule was one of birth.
The proof of that was the story of a Greek merchant in town who
had been living in Savannah with his family since he was two years
old. He was 94 when he died. His obituary cited him as a native of
Athens, Greece.
Rob always needled Grant that it was the Yankee coming out in
him that made him act as he did when meeting women.
"What do you mean?" Grant had once asked.
Rob explained his observation of the Southern approach to getting
acquainted with women compared to the Yankee method. Northern
men usually tooted their own horns. They would tell the girl about
how cultured their family was, their bloodline, how much money they
made, or how smart, brave, or strong they were. On the other hand,
Southern men said little about themselves until they knew someone
very well. No talk of money, family, or what they excelled in.

Everyone seemed to be in good spirits and Rob felt Frances acknowledge his presence with a slight pressure against his leg. He returned the gesture.

The waitress brought their orders and everyone set in to make a production of the food before them. As they ate, Rob and Grant continued their good-natured banter with each other.

"Do you see that painting on the far wall," asked Fanny, "I wonder who the artist is? There's an English artist who does bucolic scenes much like that one." Rob offered to walk over with her to examine it.

When the two left, Grant looked at Frances. "You have a thing for him too, don't you?"

"It's moving along quicker than either of us thought or planned, I'm sure. Unfortunately, I only have two more days in town before I must return home to Florida."

"What then?"

"It hasn't been said. Hopefully, Rob will be able to come down and meet my folks. I'd like to show him around my small town."

Grant took a deep breath and let it out slowly. "Rob Truitt is one of the most honorable but violent men I've ever known in my life. I feel fortunate to call him my friend. I wouldn't want him as an enemy."

"What do you mean?"

"When he sides with a person, he's loyal -- to the end. Be sure you want that, Frances. Don't lead him on."

"I never would, but I don't fully understand. Do you think Rob would hurt me?" She thought back to the day of their initial meeting and how quickly he had come to her aid. Also the look of fear on the seaman's face as Rob subdued him.

"Let me tell you a story to illustrate," said Grant. It was toward the end of the war. We were in Petersburg with General Gordon under Lee. Rob and I had been asked to take a small patrol and reconnoiter the enemy position. At that point in the war, both sides had been dug in for months.

"Rob and I, along with four others, eased out right after dark and moved in a slow and cautious path toward the Union lines. Everything seemed to be going fine, and one of the unseasoned men became less cautious. He began casually talking to himself and others and making entirely too much noise while moving through the underbrush."

"That seems very foolish," said Frances.

"It was. Unknown to us, there was a Union patrol close by. That was not unusual. It was common for both sides to send out patrols at night as listening posts to learn whatever they could about enemy position and movement. The next thing we heard was 'halt, don't move.'"

"Oh no. What did you do?"

"Slowly we rose from our squatting positions. 'Drop your weapons and raise your hands,' the voice said. We stood up and followed his directions. The group emerged from their cover in the woods. There were seven of them, including a sergeant in front who was doing the talking. He herded us into a close bunch and had one of his men gather our weapons.

'You men are now our prisoners; sit on the ground in a circle with your backs to each other.' The young private with our patrol who was responsible for us being detected was scared to the point of shaking. A corporal on the Union patrol detected this and began to jibe at him, calling him names and telling him what they would do to him. Rob was sitting next to the private and told the corporal to leave him alone."

"I'm sure that only made it worse."

"It did. The corporal then turned on Rob, demanding to know what he thought he would do. When he leaned down close to Rob's face, he was suddenly jerked from his feet with his rifle falling toward us. The whole thing was so quick no one could really comprehend what was happening. While we were all wondering, Rob grabbed the rifle and shot the corporal in the chest. Point blank."

"Rob did?"

"Without hesitation. Then, since he had the element of surprise, he shouted to the rest of us to charge. The next few moments were absolute bedlam. There were shouts of alarm, rifles being fired, screams and curses. When the smoke cleared, there were two Union men dead and one wounded, with one of ours dead and two wounded. But at this point the tables were turned and they were our prisoners."

"Unbelievable." said Frances.

"That's not all. We could have marched them back to our lines and probably tortured them the way they had planned for us, but Rob said no. There was nothing to be gained from it. He's always had the uncanny ability to see both sides of a question regardless of how it will profit him. He firmly told the leader of the Union patrol, the sergeant, to take his dead and wounded back to his lines and we would do the same."

"There's so much I don't know about Rob," said Frances.

"Well, the point of it is that he's a man that will act in a split second but will be aware of the motivations and consequences on both sides. Quick to action and quick to heal -- that's your man. Never underestimate him."

Fanny and Rob walked back to the table and were laughing about some of the regulars in the bar. "Same old crowd," Rob said. "Nowhere to go and nothing to do. Drink your lunch and drink your dinner. They will be here again after work as soon as the city bell rings."

The foursome continued on at the table for another half- hour with Grant telling funny stories about clients and cases and, fortunately for Rob, leaving him out of most of them.

As the group broke up, Rob and Grant offered to walk the ladies to a taxi stand for the ride home.

"No thanks," said Fanny. "We plan to do some shopping and we can walk back in that direction."

"I'll see you tonight? Frances asked Rob. "You know you're expected for coffee and pastry."

"I'll be there.

* * *

The two remaining days sped by, and suddenly it was time for Frances to board the train back to Florida. It was scheduled to leave the station on Liberty Street at four in the afternoon. Rob agreed with Frances he would be there to see her off.

The station loomed as the sun dropped lower and the chill of afternoon settled on the city. It had been a center of activity since its opening. Along with the terminal on the other side of town, it served as a lifeline for travelers in and out of Savannah.

The lobby inside boasted a white floor made up of small octagonal tiles and a rotunda dome listing the cities of destination and tracks for the trains that were always coming and going. The waiting benches were constructed of oak, and there was a shoeshine stand in a prominent location near the snack bar in the lobby. The trains backed in, and a solid cube of concrete at its terminal point buttressed each track. To date, no train had entered the station at an excessive speed and tested the fail-safe mechanism.

Fanny, along with her mother and father, had also accompanied Frances to the station to send her off. As her train was called, they all proceeded through the turnstile and onto the platform next to her train. She was assisted with her bags and trunk by a porter with what appeared to be a huge wagon. Since she had planned to stay for a few weeks, she had brought most of her clothes. In addition, she had a small bag with personal items.

"I hope everything will be okay," her aunt Clara was saying. "Now we want you to come back as soon as you can. I feel like your vacation was interrupted."

"I will, Aunt Clara. Thank you."

Everyone said his or her goodbyes but Rob. Out of courtesy, the others deferred to him while he took Frances' handbag and boarded the train with her to assist in finding a seat. The car was not crowded and she was able to sit next to the window. She was on the same side where Fanny and the others were waiting. He placed her bag on the seat beside her.

"Be careful and please write," said Rob. "Come back to me as soon as you can."

"I will, and you write to me, too. You have my address."

"Don't worry, you'll hear from me." Rob drew her close and gave her a tender parting kiss. "I love you, Frances," he said softly. "I think you know that."

"I love you, too. It's been such a quick few days. I wouldn't trade anything for them, though."

"All aboard," cried the conductor.

Rob left the car and joined the others. Frances waved to them from her window seat. What am I going back to, she wondered. What will I find?

Chapter 9

With a jerk, the train slowly started forward. It brought memories back to Frances of the many times she made the trip to Savannah and back with her parents and sisters. The familiar stale odors of the coach and the double- breasted uniforms of the conductor and porter brought the past trips into focus.

Taking the train was romantic. The way it glided through the small towns and swamps between Savannah and McIntosh made her think that she was isolated from the world. It was out there, outside the window, while she was inside as a disinterested observer. Nothing could touch her, nothing could harm her. The clickity-clack of the wheels on the rails was like a soothing balm. It was a good time to reflect on the past few days and her blossoming relationship with Rob. The ride to McIntosh would take about six hours, putting her home about 10 o'clock in the evening. The trip would give her time to think. She knew her father would meet her.

The whirlwind affair had been exciting, heady, and very flattering to the ego of a farm girl from a small town. She found Rob to be witty, yet sincere. He was interesting and very attentive. She would like to think she had found her soul mate, but realized she had only seen a few facets of his personality. She always believed you never really knew someone until you saw them under adversity. Time will tell, she thought, and hopefully they would have much more time to be together.

By the time the train arrived in McIntosh, most of the passengers were sprawled in contorted positions on the bench seats, trying to find some comfort for sleeping. There were only two sleeper cars on the train and most travelers could not afford the added luxury. For those staying on to Miami, it would be a long night.

The conductor came through the train announcing to each car the coming stop. "McIntosh. McIntosh. McIntosh, Florida. Isn't this your stop, miss?" He glanced at the colored stub attached to the window shade. This was the railroad system of monitoring passengers and their destinations. When your ticket was collected and punched by the conductor, he placed a color-coded stub in your windowshade. Then he would know, at a glance, your destination. "Do you have any bags you need assistance with?" he asked.

"Thank you, no. I have only a handbag; the others were checked to the baggage car."

The train jerked slowly as it decreased speed and finally slammed to a screeching halt. Frances peered out the window but her father was not visible at the darkened station.

She rose and headed toward the end of the car with her bag.

"McIntosh. All out for McIntosh," the conductor repeated again as he proceeded through the train.

Frances stepped down from the car with the aid of the metal stool and a friendly assist from the porter. She saw her father coming toward her and she went to him.

"Oh Daddy, I've missed you." She embraced him and they kissed each other's cheeks.

"And we've missed you, too. The house never seems as filled with life with you gone."

"Is everything okay?"

"Everything's fine. We'll talk later. Let's collect your bags and get you home. Your mother waited up to see you but we know how tiring travel can be. We'll get you to bed so you can get some rest."

The train started out with it's familiar jerking. The wheels from the locomotive spun as it struggled for traction under its load. Slowly, slowly -- ever so slowly, until was victorious in the struggle and the cars gained speed and moved out into the night.

To Frances it seemed nothing could be so still or dark as a tiny depot in a small town when the reason for its existence has departed. Frances became aware of the cacophony of the night. Noises which she seldom heard while in Savannah. With her bags loaded on the wagon, they started out for home. It would be about a twenty-minute ride.

As much as Frances enjoyed the city with its activities and excitement, she couldn't imagine growing up anywhere else but here. It was small enough that everyone knew and was known by everyone. Rambling farmhouses dotted the countryside. Most were built during the years when rain was plentiful and crops were abundant.

Much of the community's income was from the numerous orange groves. The fruit ripened in winter and the primary fear of growers was a winter chill. Some years, unexpected cold waves could plunge the temperature below freezing for extended periods. This caused the fruit to burst internally and rendered it unsalable.

The defense against the freezes were the innumerable smudge pots set in the groves. They burned a crude oil that emitted a smelly black smoke. The pots were essential, though, in generating enough heat to stave off the freeze.

There were years when winter freezes and summer drought combined to make the citizens of McIntosh and surrounding areas wonder why they ever thought farming would be an ideal life. Frances wondered what the experience was this year.

They rolled slowly past Watson's Dry Goods. The store had been a part of the town scene for about ten years. Mr. Watson settled in McIntosh after the war and the local residents knew little about his background or family. Some even said he was from the North. Frances had worked at Watson's on several occasions and thought he was a nice person, although quiet.

It addition to the store, Watson owned a packinghouse near the railroad. These were found in most farming communities and were used to wrap and box the fruit and vegetables from each year's harvest.

Mr. Watson's latest acquisition was the small hotel across the street from his store. Many thought he only bought it because the former owner was forced to move and unable to find a ready buyer. It seemed Watson had bought it as an accommodation and good-will gesture. Apparently it was to his good fortune since he had been heard to say he enjoyed that operation more than any of his other businesses.

On the other side of the street was the little Presbyterian church where Frances had spent so many Sundays in school and church services. In a small community like McIntosh, most of the town's social life revolved around the activities sponsored by the church.

Frances thought back to her days in the youth choir, picnics in the park, covered dish suppers on the ground, and the many other activities missed by those in the larger cities.

Life is a trade-off, she thought. Just listen to me. I'm only 22 and I sound like a worldly cynic.

The horse knew the way home and needed very little direction from her father. Occasionally though, he would nudge him with the reins. Suddenly he said, "Frances, Bounder died while you were in Savannah." Bounder was the beagle Frances had raised from a puppy.

"What happened? Why didn't you write me?"

"It seems age just caught up with him. He went out hunting one night and in the morning, he didn't come back. Mr. Wood from down the road found him near his house the next day. It seemed it was just his time. We didn't write you about it since we didn't want to spoil your visit. We buried him out by the camphor tree you used to climb as a little girl."

"That's a good place; thank you. He would like it. He was a good friend." She wondered if this was the news that had called her home.

The wagon creaked to the front of the house and Frances stepped down with her small bag. Her father unloaded the trunks and other bags and carried them to the large porch that wrapped around the front of the house.

"Leave those bags for me. I just need to unhook Ginger and put her in the barn. After that, I'll be right up and bring in your bags."

The door opened and Frances' mother came out and put her arms around her. "Frances dear, we've missed you. I know you're tired. Can I fix you something to eat?"

"No Mom, thanks. I had a sandwich on the train. I think I'd just like some rest."

Like an old friend, the house seemed to welcome her. The rooms were spacious, with high ceilings and large windows for circulation on hot summer days. The wainscoting was paneled in a varnished mahogany that had darkened over the years. It was this paneled finish that Frances' father installed for her mother, years before when the house was built.

It was two stories with a large central hallway running between the drawing room and living room, and there was also a dining room at the end of the hall. A single staircase ran along the right wall of the hall to the five bedrooms upstairs. Frances slowly ascended the steps behind her mother who held an oil lamp to lead the way.

Frances lit a lamp in her room, told her mother goodnight, and quickly changed into her nightgown. Familiar surroundings and weariness worked their magic, and sleep came quickly.

* * *

The rooster began trumpeting at the crack of dawn, about six in the morning. With that, the house gradually began to stir and even those committed to sleep found it a problem to remain in bed much beyond eight.

Frances lay awake in bed to acclimate herself to the new but familiar surroundings. So many mornings she had risen from this bed to go down the road to school or to work at the store.

She could hear her mother and younger twin sisters stirring in the kitchen. Mary and Martha were eleven and wanted to be involved in everything. That was okay. She was fond of both and couldn't wait to see them. They could tell her about their recent adventures and fill her in on the local gossip.

The heavy iron bed creaked as she swung her feet over the side to the floor. She dressed for the day in a simple gingham dress suitable to help her mother in the kitchen and with household chores.

Frances went to the washstand and poured a small amount of water in the bowl. It felt good on her face as she dabbed with the washcloth. Straightening her hair while looking in the mirror, she felt she was ready to meet the day. Quietly she opened her door and stepped smartly down the stairs.

The smell of fresh coffee, bacon, and burned toast were coming from the kitchen. As Frances entered, the twins rushed her.

"Hey big sister, welcome home," said Mary.

"Yeah," said Martha, now we'll have someone else to help with the work around here." They both gave Frances a big hug.

"Good morning, dear," her mother chimed in. "Did you sleep well?"

"Like I was drugged. I guess I was more tired than I knew."

"We have juice, coffee, bacon, grits, scrambled eggs, and toast. I only have to scramble you some eggs when you're ready."

"Thank you, mother. For now I'll just have some coffee."

"You girls go clean your room," said her mother to the twins. She seemed somewhat nervous.

"Frances, will you tell us about Savannah later?" asked Mary.

"Of course; I'll do it after supper tonight." The twins scampered off.

Frances sat in one of the high backed, cane-bottom chairs at the large round table. It was draped with a red checkered cloth. Her mother poured coffee into a blue willow cup and placed it in front of Frances. She returned the pot to the wood-burning stove.

Frances took a sip and immediately was reminded how strong the coffee was that her parents enjoyed. She detected a hint of chicory in the blend.

"How are Clara and Charles and the children?" her mother asked. "I really wish we could see them more often. It just makes-- you wonder where the time goes. We're all so busy scurrying about with our lives, we scarcely look up to know what's going on with others. It's just not good, though. A person needs to keep up with his people."

"Everyone's fine, Mother. Like you, they're all so busy with their lives and earning a living that they aren't in close contact with far-off relatives, either. They said to give you and father their best. So did Fanny."

"And how is Fanny? I'm sure she's all grown up the same as you."

"Fanny's fine. She's beautiful and happy. She and I became very close during my stay. She's a real lifeline for me. Where's Father?"

"He went into town to do some banking and buy some feed for the cows. He should be back before long."

Frances was curious as to why she was called back to McIntosh early. She stirred her coffee. "How are things around here, mother?"

Her mother went back to the stove so that she would not have to look at Frances. She said in a halting voice, "Things are fine. You know."

Frances was silent. "Actually," said her mother, turning to face her, "things are less than fine. One reason your father went to town is so I would have this chance to speak with you alone."

She poured herself a cup of coffee and came to sit across from Frances, staring down at the table. Frances waited. This was unlike her mother.

"This has not been a good year for the farm," she said. "Following the hard freeze last winter that took most of the citrus, we've had drought and infestation with the cabbage and watermelon crops this summer."

"We've had bad times before," said Frances.

"But not to this extent. We really didn't have the funds to plant for the summer, but Mr. Watson agreed to advance the seed and fertilizer on credit as he has done in the past. As usual, he secures his loan with both the crop and the land."

"Well there should be more than enough value in the land to carry it. Certainly he knows that."

"Because of the bad year, some families have moved away. There is more land on the market than ever, and values are just not there anymore."

"What can we do?" Frances asked.

Her mother sighed and looked again at the table.

"Mr. Watson has offered to forgive the amount he has loaned if we will talk to you about -- a social matter."

"A social matter?"

Her mother took a deep breath. "He said he has always been fond of you. If a marriage could be arranged between the two of you, he would consider the debt a family matter which could be dissolved without consequence."

"Mother!"

Chapter 10

Frances felt her body numb as the realization of what her mother said began to sink in. She immediately thought of Rob and what they had been working toward. She was unable to identify with what her mother had asked. Finally she recovered. She pushed away from the table.

"No," she said, "absolutely not. How can you put me in such a position? It's not what I want, and I can't believe Wales Watson could even think such a thing. I must speak to him."

"We *have* spoken with him, both your father and I, at length. Your father has offered to work for him in the store, or otherwise, to retire the debt. Mr. Watson says he doesn't want that. He wants a wife; he wants you."

Frances rose from her chair and began to pace. "And what about what I want? I'm not a commodity that can be bartered for like a sack of seed." I'm a person with my own feelings and needs. My own dreams."

"Try to see it from our perspective," her mother began again.

Why now? Thought Frances. Why at all, but why now? Just when she was beginning to experience the good things about life and what it may hold for her. Suddenly the farm and house she had always felt to be her sanctuary became cold and threatening. She looked at the pump attached to the sink, the oil-burning lamps, the wood-burning range, and saw them all as trappings in a prison. She thought about her friends that grew up in McIntosh. Usually the boys remained to take over the family farm and the girls married and lived within a few miles of the community. She had no reason to believe she wouldn't follow suit, and it had never bothered her. But now it did; she was denied freedom of choice. Not this. How could they? No. What about Rob? What about any future they might possibly have?

"Your father has not been well," her mother went on. "As hard as he's worked--and then to have *this*. It's hard to believe it's happening to us. The farm is all we have; I just don't know what we'll do if we lose it."

Frances only stared silently.

"You don't have to give an immediate answer, just think about it. Now let me fix you some breakfast."

"I think not, Mother. I have no appetite. Besides, why can't he borrow the money? Uncle Charles in Savannah would be willing to help, I'm sure."

"I don't think so," said her mother. "Charles has always taken an elitist attitude when it comes to your father. He's always believed that farming was not a proper occupation for someone in his social strata. He and your father have had words in years past. Your father would never approach him."

Frances left the kitchen, strode to the front of the house and out the double doors to the large planked porch. It was a good five feet from the ground and covered with a metal roof supported by wooden columns, about 10 feet apart. She stood by the one closest to the door and encircled it with her arm, gazing straight ahead.

The house overlooked a cleared field extending about 200 yards and sloping down to the railroad. Beyond, about a mile farther, the mist was rising from Orange Lake. With a sigh, she turned and took a seat in one of the old rockers. She noticed the paint was peeling from the sides of the house.

* * *

Sam Perry had been a farmer for over 25 years. In 1855, he left his job in Jacksonville as an agent for the railway express to acquire land in Marion County and pursue the life of a farmer. He knew little of the methods of farming and agriculture but knew money was being made. Others were placing the rich delta land of the Florida interior under cultivation and doing well. Those he had spoken with assured him the work, although physically hard, was not difficult and success was almost assured. Sam, like many others of his generation, only wanted a chance to prove his worth and build something for himself. In doing so, he could also provide a good life and equity buildup for his family.

The first few years were exciting. Things went well for the farmers in the area, even the neophytes like Sam. The seed company had extended credit, fields had been cleared and crops planted. Labor was cheap, and in many instances was provided in exchange for the rent that was waived on a small cabin. Neighbors were helpful to each other, both in getting in the crops and sharing their tools and knowledge. The Perrys prospered.

On the national scale, conditions weren't quite as peaceful. Outside of Florida, war clouds were gathering for a clash with the North. While Sam and his neighbors were sympathetic with the South, it was hard for them to see how a war was necessary to preserve their tranquil lifestyle in central Florida.

His two sons, Sam Jr. or Sammy, and his younger brother Russell saw the buildup of tensions as exciting. They were eager to enlist for action and glory if it ever boiled into a war. It was the chance of their generation to march off to adventure and come home as war heroes. Wouldn't they have stories to tell?

Frances looked over to the barn and thought of how both Sammy and Russell had worked with her father in building the barn, the house and most other out buildings around it. Now it was all in jeopardy.

When war had broken out, all the boys in the area were eager to join up. They heard the talk of how it would be a short war. People in the South were saying it would only last a few months at best.

Some went immediately to Gainesville, or Ocala, to join one of the units being formed.

"Dad, they're raising a new unit in Gainesville that some of the local boys are joining. Russell and I would like to be with them. What do you think?"

"We've gone over this before Sammy. It's not our fight and you're both needed here. I can't allow you to go."

By 1862, a year into the conflict, they knew they must get into the fray or be passed by. The orange groves had been picked and spring planting was a few months off. This time it was Russell's turn to approach their father.

"Dad, if we promise to only go in for a six month enlistment and come back to in time to bring in the summer crops, would you agree?"

"Son, there's a lot more to this war than you think. People are getting killed. You and Sammy haven't thought this through. I can't permit it."

Perry insisted they stay on the farm where the family, which, by now, had grown to include a baby sister, needed them. The boys left anyway, without permission, knowing they were doing the right thing. They slipped out at night and both signed a short note written by Sammy.

Dear Mother & Father –

It's hard to know what to do. We don't want to disobey but at the same time we both feel the strong call of duty to defend our Southern territory. Other people we've talked to say it's the right thing to do and if we don't go, then after the war is over, we'll be ashamed. We don't want this to reflect on our family. Please understand and know we love you. We'll write often and plan to be back before summer.

Love,

Sammy & Russell

Sam Perry silently read the letter and passed it to his wife. She too, quickly read the missive.

"Oh no. God no, Sam, they're gone." Perry could only nod silently and hug his wife both for solace and comfort.

Knowing they only had a short time for glory, the boys elected not to join a local group but to travel up to Virginia and enlist where they would stand a better chance of seeing early action. They were able to attach themselves with a regiment from Georgia under the command of General James Longstreet.

They soon discovered that army life was nowhere near as glorious as they imagined. Camp life consisted of drilling in the morning and afternoon and nights that were filled with boredom and homesickness. The food was only tolerable and their uniforms weren't even complete. While it was true that their jackets were gray and each had a cap, they continued to wear their own trousers and shoes. Their rifles were smooth bore muskets that although adequate were not what they hoped for.

72

After a few months of restlessness, they received word they were marching north. General Lee, the supreme Confederate commander, had decided to take the war to the Yankees with a march into Pennsylvania. Now the Yankees would see what it was like to have enemy troops on their home soil. Finally, the army was on the move and the brothers would see action.

Frances thought, What a waste. The only remembrance she had of her brother Russell was the letter he had written the night of the second day at Gettysburg. It was later sent home by Sammy, along with his own.

July 2, 1862
Dear Mother and Father,

Sammy and I are gitting ready to go to the fight tomorrow. There has been heavy fighting for two days and they say we are winning. I don't know. We hear the sound of the guns and cannons but they have been far away.

I know you didn't want us to come up here and you were probably right. All I know now is we want to do our duty and support our friends who are counting on us. I am scared, but everyone says that's normal. I hope it will pass when the fighting starts. I love you both and wish I were home. I'm glad Sammy is here with me.

Your son,
Russell

Frances knew the rest of the story although it was one her mother and father seldom mentioned. Russell fell at Gettysburg and Sammy later, in the trenches at Petersburg. They never came home as planned. Her mother and father now had to endure a life without the sons that had been a primary joy of their existence. Her father never had a major problem with either. Now they had been unexpectedly ripped from him, never to return. He was not even be able to go to their graves and grieve. They were in some nameless pit in Pennsylvania and an unmarked grave in Virginia. Her father went on, but realized that one never recovered from the loss of a child.

Frances sat on the porch and continued to ponder on their lives on the farm and all the time, blood, and toil her father had stoked into it.

"Damn you, Wales Watson. How could you extort a man's life work and hold his daughter hostage?"

* * *

Frances heard a sound behind her as the screen door squeaked opened noisily on its springs. Her mother came to sit in the rocker next to hers. They were both silent for a moment. Frances waited.

"Mr. Watson knew you were coming back from Savannah last night. He asked if he could come over this afternoon to visit with you."

"Coming by to take a look at his goods, I guess -- size up the fatted calf."

Her mother looked down again and said with a measured voice, "Say what you will to me, I suppose I deserve it. But when you talk to your father, please be tactful. The man is just beside himself with all this. He feels like he has failed us all. With Sammy and Russell lost in the war and now this, he's just broken."

Frances thought about what her mother said and tried to place herself mentally in the position of her father. She loved him very much. Hurting him with harsh words would not be in her plans.

"Mother, you just don't realize what this will do to me. I'm trying to understand what's going on with you and father. I know what this place means to you and to him. But what about me and my life? What about what I mean to him? I have my own priorities and life to live. What about me?" Her mother reached over and patted her hand.

"I know, I know."

Her mother rose from the chair, leaving Frances sitting on the porch, and went back in the house. Frances was developing a terrible headache. What else can happen to me? she thought.

* * *

About three in the afternoon, Frances looked out her bedroom window and saw Wales Watson driving up to the house in his carriage. He was dressed in a dark business suit and carried a bouquet of flowers. He secured his horse and quickly ascended the front steps and quietly rapped on the door. Her mother responded and invited him into the drawing room.

"I'll tell Frances you're here. She will be down in a few minutes, Mr. Watson. Please make yourself comfortable."

"Thank you, Mrs. Perry," said Watson as he seated himself on a side chair where he could see the door to the hall.

Frances checked herself in the mirror. She thought she looked decent, but certainly not smashing. She didn't want to--only to be presentable and certainly not desirable.

Yesterday, I was happy and looking forward to exciting changes in my life, she thought. Today, I'm going through the motions. I'm in lockstep with a world I can't stop. Not unless I let Father down. His image quickly flashed through her mind. I can't do that. She took a deep breath and began descending the stairs to the drawing room. As she entered, Watson rose to greet her.

"Miss Frances, it's wonderful to see you again. You look lovely."

"Mr. Watson," she said cordially but evenly, "We need to talk."

"Frances--" Watson gestured with his hand and began to say something, and then he stopped. He seemed to be gathering his thoughts. He tried again.

--"Frances, I know this is unusual and seems cold, but I've thought a good while about this. I want you to know this is not sudden with me."

"If you were interested in me, why didn't you express yourself? Why didn't you call on me?"

Again he hesitated. "Frances, fear of rejection is a strong fear in most men. I'm sorry, I wish I had. But I have much to offer you. I am in a position to give you things you couldn't have otherwise. I am successful in business; we could have a comfortable life."

"I'm not surprised you're successful in business if you conduct all your affairs in the manner which you've treated my father," she said icily. "You've taken terrible advantage of him. Don't you realize you're playing with our lives? What gives you the right to play God with people? And what makes you think I could ever love you after the way you've handled this?"

"Frances, I'm not a bad man, just lonely. Perhaps I've handled all this poorly, but I was only trying to capitalize on a situation that seemed almost providential in the way it was presented to me."

"And what about the way it was presented to me? Does it seem providential to you from my standpoint? You've placed me in a terrible position."

"We could travel and go places. I'm able to buy you nice clothes and other things. We can build a beautiful house, just as you like. Also, your father can continue to farm and I'll never bother him again about credit from the store. I'll even help him."

"Right, as long as you hold the strings."

From the hall, the grandfather clock chimed the half hour. Afterwards, there was a strange stillness to the house.

Frances looked Watson directly in the eye. "This has all been too much for me for one day. I think I would do better if I had time to think on these things."

"By all means," said Watson.

"I'll give you my answer soon."

Watson nodded and said upon parting, "Very well. I'll await your decision."

Frances went upstairs to rest before dinner. She had just closed her eyes when there was a light tap on the door. It opened slightly and the hesitant voice her father said, "Frances?" She opened her eyes and turned toward the door.

Her father entered the room hesitantly and pulled a small straight chair near the side of the bed. The aroma of his sweat-stained shirt wafted up to her senses as he sat down. He wore the dark red suspenders that had almost become a daily uniform. He looked tired. She glanced at him and waited as he struggled to begin.

He deliberately scanned the room with his eyes. She waited. Haltingly, he started. "Sammy and Russell shared this room until they left for the war. I know I shouldn't, but sometimes I come here and it all comes back like yesterday. They were close with each other.

Everything Sammy did, Russell was eager to try. He idolized his big brother and Sammy loved him. When they didn't come back, I don't know what your mother would've done if you hadn't been here for her to focus on. It all seems like yesterday at times and at others, so long ago. Now it all comes to this. It never seems to end. I'm sorry."

Frances saw before her a man who was only a shadow of the father who had always projected strength and she had held in awe for so long.

"Father, I know the position you're in. I can't imagine why Mr. Watson feels he is justified in being such an opportunist on a personal basis. Anyway, let's not talk about this matter again. I need a few days to clear my mind and put my affairs and attitude in proper order. I want you to know I love you and I won't let you down."

She raised herself on the bed and took his hand. As she did so; she saw the tears begin to stream down his cheeks. Never before had she witnessed her father crying. She threw her arms around him. "Oh father, it will be okay. You'll see. Everything will be okay."

She realized the dread and despair that filled her father and knew that regardless of her fate, her love for him was such that he must be rescued. She would never forgive Wales Watson for what he was doing. True, the die may be cast, but she owed a certain loyalty to herself. She also knew she had unfinished business in Savannah.

LITTLE GRACIE

Chapter 11

The next days, Frances dwelled in the company of her family. She had the chance to spend a good deal of time with her mother and the twins. They wanted to know all about Savannah and especially about their cousin Fanny. Frances took long walks about the farm, just looking and reminiscing.

She thought constantly about what life would hold for her if she married Wales. It all came down to the realization that her personal dreams had been dashed. She was exchanging something positive and exciting for something resentful and mundane.

On the third day, she received a letter from Rob. It had the return address of Savannah and the thought of reading it made her burn. She went up to her room for privacy, sat in her rocker beside the bed, and slowly sliced open the top of the envelope. She unfolded the letter and read.

Dear Frances,

Although you've only been gone a few days, it seems like weeks. No sooner than the train pulled out of the station, that the entire town seemed empty. Life was so full with you here and so meaningless now with you gone.

I hope everything is going well for you at home. I know you had some concerns. I get the strange feeling that our time is passing like sand in the hourglass. It has only a finite number of grains and then will be no more. I hope I'm wrong. Please come back to me. I miss you terribly.

Love,
Rob

Frances read the letter again, savoring each word and the handwriting that formed them. She knew what she must do and how Rob would react to the news she would bring him. Their feelings for one another were only newly forming. Their relationship barely had time to blossom. If there were a love between them, it would certainly be redirected on his part. She couldn't bear the thought. It all hung over her like a heavy shroud.

Then, too, there was the matter with Wales. He was waiting for her answer. Politely for now, but soon he would become insistent. She knew what it had to be, although she also knew she would be in a position to dictate certain terms. If she elected to commit herself to a life of servitude in payment of a debt, she would enter the relationship with a loud voice.

She walked over to her small writing desk in the bedroom and took out stationery and a pen. Her reply back to Rob was carefully constructed.

Dear Rob,

I received your letter today and you must know how excited I was to hear from you. McIntosh and the farm seem so far removed from Savannah and you. I will stay here for probably a few more days and then come back to Savannah. I plan to write Fanny today and let her know a specific time to meet me.

Just as soon as I'm back in town, I'll get word to you. There are things we need to discuss and it will be better if we are there together. All love is tested at times; ours may be tested early. I hope it can endure. I miss you terribly.

Love,
Frances

Frances folded the letter and stuffed it into the envelope. She would give it to her father to carry to the post office to be mailed on the morning train. It would take two days before delivery in Savannah.

Next, she jotted a short letter to Fanny. She told her she needed to come back to Savannah and hopefully could stay with her again for about a week. She only alluded to things she needed to tell her and said she planned to be on the evening train at 8:30 this coming Friday. That letter was sealed and placed beside the other. Now, she thought, only one more note to write -- the easiest but the hardest. She again took a sheet a paper from the desk.

Dear Wales,

You asked for an answer and I will try to tell you how I feel about this entirely indecent "proposition". I use the word because that's all it is, even if it's in the formal sense.

When I was fortunate to secure a position in your store, I felt you were a person of high standards and even someone others could emulate as a role model. I even developed a fondness for you myself. Now, I know different and I feel a great resentment toward you.

This entire situation makes me feel like a commodity. It has stripped me of human dignity, and I feel it goes against all Christian teachings. I feel degraded, and I will never forgive you for what you are doing to my father. One day, you too may know the feeling of having your family ripped from you, leaving you alone and hollow.

I must return to Savannah to tie up some ends and will be back in about a week or more. Then, we can be married in the Presbyterian Church here in town. It won't be a large wedding, just family.

Respectfully,
Frances Perry

* * *

It was Friday afternoon. Frances waited impatiently with her father, as the northbound 2:10 train to Savannah appeared, slowly moving around the curve into McIntosh. It was made up of four coaches, a dining car, a mail and baggage car, and one sleeper. It was due into Savannah at 8:30 that evening. She looked forward to the ride and felt as if she was running to *someone* rather than away from *something*. In her mind, the distinction was important.

Her luggage consisted of only two suitcases and a small handbag. Her father would be able to stow the two larger bags in the rack above the seats in the day coach. As the train slowed for the depot, she looked in the windows and was relieved to see the coach was only about half full.

After her father placed her suitcases in the rack above the seat, he turned to her. "Frances, I don't know exactly why you need to go back to Savannah. But I want you to keep safe and know that your mother and I love you. Let us know when you'll be coming back so I can meet you. Send me a wire."

"I love you, too, Dad. And I'll be back, before long."

As she looked at her father, she knew he wasn't an old man in years but time had taken its toll. He was beaten. Two sons gone and now a daughter taken.

She thought about his life and the heartaches he had faced. Was that what life held for most? You start out with dreams and excitement and see them eroded over time as hardship and disappointment reduce your options, one by one? Were these things controllable or preordained? Are there those destined for prosperity and happiness while others are always downtrodden?"

Her father left the train and she heard the familiar call of the conductor, "All aboard." The train started with a lurch as she waved to her father. Another chapter had begun.

Fanny had agreed to meet her at the station and she hoped Rob had been informed of her arrival. How will I tell him? she wondered. Where would be the proper place? She wondered if she was being presumptuous in thinking it even mattered? After all, a single man as attractive as Rob would not lack for female companionship.

She tilted the incline of her seat back to where it would be more comfortable for the long ride ahead. The car was Spartan in its furnishings, almost devoid of creature comforts. There was little in the way of refreshments other than a water cooler at the front of the car. The seats each had a headrest cloth that was changed periodically for cleanliness but most looked as though the change had not been for some time. She removed hers. There was a noise at the end of the coach as the door opened between the cars.

"Get'm here, I got'm. Refreshing drinks, things to eat and other treats. Get'm here."

It was the sound of the news butch coming through and offering a variety of juices and other treats. She was always suspicious of their freshness and normally packed a sandwich for the long ride. However, she did buy a small bottle of juice to drink with her snack.

What will Fanny think of all this? Frances asked herself. She was such a take charge person that she would have had no hesitation in saying no if presented with the same situation. Let the chips fall where they may, everyone fend for himself. Maybe that was the proper course of action. Of course, Fanny never worried about anything monetary. Uncle Charles was a prominent and wealthy physician. Money never presented a problem, only selection.

About seven in the evening, the oil lamps in the coach were dimmed for the benefit of those who chose to nap. Frances enjoyed the moving panorama outside her window as the countryside slipped by and she and other passengers hurtled on into the night. The view was unchanging, especially when they crossed the St. Mary's River and entered Georgia -- flat land, palmetto scrub, and pine trees. Most of the land seemed low on both sides of the tracks, but she knew it was only because the mainline had to be high for proper drainage. She could see the water standing in shallow lagoons for miles beside the track.

Periodically, small boys and others at road crossings would wave to the passengers. No doubt wishing they could be on the powerful train as it slipped through the night.

As they neared Savannah, the porter came through.

"Savannah. Savannah, Georgia, the city by the sea," he announced. She smiled to herself thinking how each town called was followed by a comment of what it was known for. Savannah, the city by the sea. It had a ring to it. It certainly meant something to her. Hopefully it always would.

The porter helped her with her bags. "Now the train will have to back into the station, miss, so you'll still have about ten minutes before we stop."

"Thank you, John. It was a good trip." She handed him some change for assisting with her bags.

"Thank you, miss. Will you be needing a red cap to get your bags to the station?"

"No, someone is meeting me, thank you."

Slowly the train came to a halt. Then, with a lurch, it began its familiar backing into the terminal. Frances identified with several landmarks that could be seen in the dim light outside her window. At last, the columns supporting the station outbuildings came into view and she knew it would only be a few minutes more. Outside her window was another train on the adjoining track.

The passenger platform would be on the other side when the passengers unloaded. As the train came to a grumbling halt, she retrieved her handbag and joined the others who were disembarking through the end of the coach. She hoped Fanny would be there.

Fanny was nowhere in sight, and as Frances stared around the loading platform exasperated, a smiling Rob stepped from behind a column. Her heart leaped.

"Rob! Oh my god, I didn't expect you to be here."

"I hope that's not bad," he said. He leaned down to kiss her.

Her head spun. "No, I mean, I couldn't be more pleased." She looked at him. "I missed you."

"And I missed you. Come on. Let's get your bags and get you home. How was your stay in Florida?"

"Well, eventful. I'll tell you more when we have more time."

"What are you doing tomorrow? Can we have lunch and maybe spend the afternoon?"

"I'd like that."

Rob took her bags and walked with her to the taxi stand. He wondered how she would react to a gift. Would it be enough to show his feelings and convince her to come live in Savannah to maybe work and continue their courtship?

* * *

84

After Frances was safely inside the door of Fanny's house, Rob returned to the taxi. As Frances closed the door Fanny greeted her.

"So you're back?" was Fanny's inquisitive greeting.

Frances went to her cousin with a small smile and gave her a hello hug.

"Yes, and we need to talk. I need your support and guidance. Mostly, I just need someone to talk to."

"I'm listening."

"Could we go upstairs so I can unpack and we can maybe talk, a little more privately?"

"Good idea." Fanny picked up one of the bags and started upstairs to the bedroom. "Was it okay that Rob met you rather than me? When I told him you were coming back to town, he insisted."

"It was fine. He was such a surprise. After you've been with someone like Rob and think that maybe you have something going, you get away and then wonder how much if any of it was real. Maybe you just get caught up in the moment, you know?"

"And?"

"It's been fast but it's real. That's what I need to talk to you about. Everything has gotten so complicated."

"Maybe it just seems complicated. Let's see if we can sort it out," said Fanny.

Frances looked away, took a deep breath, and turned back to Fanny. "Wales Watson, who owns the store in McIntosh, threatens to ruin my father unless I marry him."

Fanny sat on the edge of the bed. "You've never even mentioned him other than to say you worked for him. Isn't he a good deal older than you?"

"Wales is fifty, but that's not the point. I feel nothing for him except resentment. I'm in love with Rob. Marrying Wales is something my parents have asked me to do."

"Why, what is the leverage he has on them?"

"Money, what else -- at least on my father. He's had a bad year with the farm, both with the oranges and his summer crops being ruined with the drought."

"How does that involve Watson?" asked Fanny.

"He's the one who extended the credit for the seed and fertilizer. For security, he holds a lien against the farm. His proposition to my parents is that if I marry him, he will cancel my father's debt. After all, as he says, there's no point in having one family member owe another. On the other hand, if I refuse, he will foreclose and my parents will be homeless and without the means of support. My dad's health is no longer good and he can't work for hire at manual labor. He's gone to the bank but they say it's not a creditworthy risk. At this point, I don't see where I have much choice."

"Frances, how awful. It's a terrible thing to imagine."

"I know, except this is real."

"He's wanting to marry you even though you don't love him?"

"I wrote Wales a note not mincing any words in how I felt about his taking advantage of the situation. Poor Father is an emotional wreck, and I can't blame him. He can barely look at me. Wales' first wife died of consumption a few years back and apparently he's looking for someone to share his travels and also keep up social appearances."

"An ornament, huh?"

"That's what it seems to me. He says we can travel and he can afford to buy fine clothes, a nice house, and other things to please me."

"And?"

"Those aren't the things I've dreamed of." She sighed. "They can't make me happy. What about what I want?"

"And *who* you want them with, right?"

"I've got to tell Rob and I don't know what to say. I was hoping *we* were going somewhere. What do you think he will say?"

Fanny stood and walked to the window. She pulled aside the curtain and looked down on the street. "My suspicions are that Rob was hoping you and he were going somewhere, too. I don't know how he will react; certainly it will be a test."

"I have this feeling that it's the first of many. I don't know why."

"Let's get you ready for bed. You've had a busy day and tomorrow will be, as well. Playing it over and over in your mind won't change things. What time is he calling for you?"

"Ten o'clock."

"It will be here soon enough. You get some rest; I'll see you in the morning."

"Fanny, what would you do with Rob in my situation?"

Fanny looked Frances directly in the eye. She seemed to read her secret thoughts. She answered with measured words.

"Probably the same thing that you came back to do. Now, you need some rest. Tomorrow is obviously a big day."

Chapter 12

The following morning when Rob awakened, the first thing on his mind was seeing Frances. He was happy, just knowing she was back in town. It reminded him of the old saying of what makes for a happy life: Interesting work to do, something to look forward to, and someone to love. At the moment, he had all three.

He formulated a tentative plan for the day. He wanted it to be romantic and perfect. Different parts of town came to mind and he decided the best thing to do would be to take Frances to Emmett Park overlooking the river. The view was outstanding and they could sit on one of the benches near the harbor light and talk. It would give him a chance to see what was bothering her. He would help her work through it. Afterwards, they could walk to a small out-of-the-way restaurant for lunch.

Precisely at ten, he arrived at her door. He had walked over from his apartment since it was only a few blocks between the two houses. Frances looked radiant and seemed to like the idea of walking to the park on the river.

Savannah was experiencing a true autumn day and there were many on the streets in sweaters, although it was still not cold enough for anything heavier. The row houses and shops along the way seemed to mesh with each other in a balanced symmetry.

Again, they walked through Wright Square in the heart of the city. Frances inquired as to what the construction was in the center of the park.

"That's where they are moving the remains of an old monument to Tomochichi, an early Indian friend to the colony."

"Where are they taking him?"

"Actually, nowhere. They're only moving him over to the edge of the square to make room for yet another monument."

"Oh?"

"Yes, the new one's for W.W. Gordon, one of the founders of the Central of Georgia Railway."

"It seems a shame to move one to make room for another. Is one more important than the other?"

"Well, it's politics. Tomochichi's remains have been there for 143 years and he was important to the colony. Without him, General Oglethorpe would have encountered much trouble with the Indians and the colony itself would have been in jeopardy."

"It seems then he should stay and they should build a larger monument to him."

"There are those in town that would like to erect a monument to Oglethorpe there with Tomochichi nearby. That would show the importance of the two figures and also their friendship."

"Seems like a good plan."

"Some have also argued the idea that the Bull Street squares should only carry monuments to military heroes. Obviously, Gordon, although a West Point graduate, was not in that role. There has been some talk about erecting a statue of Oglethorpe in Chippewa, the next square south."

"Money always wins out, doesn't it?"

Rob looked at her. "Why would you say that?"

"Just an observation," she said.

The couple continued on to the City Exchange building facing the river. There, they turned east toward the park. The warm salt fragrance from the river was in sharp contrast to the crisp autumn air.

* * *

"I usually come here to think," said Rob.

They were seated on a bench facing the river near the old harbor light. There were others in the park, but no one near enough to eavesdrop on their conversation.

"Have you been keeping busy since I've been gone?" asked Frances.

"I've tried; it always seems to help to have something to focus on."

"You know the reason for my coming back was you. You have been very much on my mind."

"And you mine." Rob turned toward Frances. "Want to tell me what happened in Florida?"

Frances' chin began to quiver. "Rob, there is no easy way to say this." He waited. Frances stood and began to pace.

"Last year was a disaster for farmers in McIntosh. The winter citrus crop was ruined by a severe freeze and this summer's vegetable crops were destroyed by drought."

"I've read they've had a bad year. It's a shame. To put forth all that hard work with nothing to show for it. But Frances, that's the life of a farmer," said Rob. "There are good years and bad years. It's all part of a cycle."

"I know, I know; we've been through it before so it's something you learn to live with. This time though it was different. My father used the general store in McIntosh to advance seed and fertilizer for the year on credit and now he can't pay them back.

"Aren't the others in the area in the same situation?"

"Yes, and many have had to sell their farms and move elsewhere. Actually, our case is somewhat different."

The owner of the store, Mr. Watson, holds a lien on the farm as collateral. He has threatened to foreclose unless--"

Rob watched her intently. "Unless what?"

"Unless I consent to marry him."

Rob sat silently for a moment as her words sank in. Frances again sat beside him. She was quiet.

He turned slowly toward her. "You've decided to do it, haven't you."

She refused to look at him. "I see no other option. I can't let my father down."

"Why doesn't he go to your mother's brother for help; your Uncle Charles, the doctor, here in Savannah."

"It's actually his wife Clara, who is my mother's sister. Apparently, there is some negative past history there. Besides, Father is much too proud to go to relatives to bail him out."

"And the banks?"

"They've turned him down."

Rob couldn't see it from her father's viewpoint at all. He didn't know Frances' father but he couldn't see a man letting his daughter be taken away from him and placing her in marital bondage. He held his tongue.

"When is this fait accompli' to take place?" Rob said with resignation, looking at the ground.

"Within the month."

"Within the month," he repeated. "It's a little late now, but I must confess I wanted so many things for us. I was not taking you for granted, but I had begun to plan things in my mind," he said.

"Rob, just because my situation has changed doesn't mean my feelings have. I still love you, I just don't know what else to do."

He nodded. "I love you, too," he said softly, as he stared into nothingness. "I'm just not ready for this dramatic turn. I never will be."

They sat in silence under the grey autumn sky for a few moments more, both happy with the company, but miserable with the situation.

"Where would you like to go for lunch?" he asked distractedly.

Frances turned and looked at him intently. "To your apartment."

Rob turned slowly to meet her gaze. There could be no doubt in his mind as to the intent of her statement, yet it was such a bold move that it was difficult for him to come to grips with all it implied.

"Let me be blunt," she said. "I'll only be in town for a few days and I don't know when we will see each other again. I want to spend as much of that time as is possible with you -- that is, if you feel the same way."

"Are you sure about this Frances?"

"Without a doubt."

"Do you feel like walking or would you rather ride?" asked Rob.

"Walking is fine," she said as they rose. She tucked her arm through his. The two walked slowly back on Houston Street toward Rob's apartment.

* * *

Rob slipped the key in the lock and gave it the familiar clockwise turn. Frances stood demurely by. As the door opened inward, she preceded him into the foyer. So many times, Rob thought, he returned to his quarters in the evening, only to be greeted with the same stillness he left earlier in the day. How different it was to have another fill the house. He reached back to secure the deadbolt on the inside of the door.

"Nice," she said, as she surveyed the room. "It's you."

She placed her purse on a small entry table and turned back expectantly to Rob. "Now, kiss me before I lose my nerve." She looked up at him.

Rob easily drew her to him and clasped her face tenderly in both hands. He kissed the tip of her nose, then her eyes, and finally her mouth. It was long, lingering, and hungry.

"Ummmmm," she said. "I missed that."

Lightly, he took her hand and led her to the bedroom. As she waited, he drew the curtains slightly so there would be a soft light from outside but closed enough to give them needed privacy. Rob removed his coat and walked back to her. She reached up and untied his bow tie. Again came the long look and another lingering, soulful kiss.

She turned her back to him. "If you will unpin my dress at the collar, I think I can get the rest. I believe it would be more comfortable for me if I undress and wait for you in bed."

"That's fine," he uttered in a rasping whisper.

Frances quickly shed her dress and undergarments and let her hair down. It draped almost to her waist and glowed with the sheen of long hours of brushing. She eased between the sheets on the side away from the door without the bedside table. She assumed the other would be his normal side. As he eased in beside her, she asked, "which side do you sleep on?"

"All over; I'm not sure I favor one."

They turned toward each other and she felt the press of his naked body.

"I know this is wrong," said Frances, "but I love you and I want you. I feel our future is being stolen. If we have no future awaiting us, I want the present."

"God, you're beautiful," said Rob as he caressed her neck and shoulders with the light touch of his fingers. He cupped her breasts with his hands and brushed them with his lips.

93

Rob felt his excitement increasing. He had been with many women before, but had never experienced the emotional depth that overcame him now. He wanted to be so good for her, so tender.

"Darling, you're gorgeous, too. You're dark from the sun and your muscles are firm under your skin." She rubbed his chest with her splayed fingers in loving fashion. His mouth greeted hers again and she parted her lips so their tongues could find intimacy. They played a touch and tag game, each marveling at being so intimate with the other.

Frances sensed his growing urgency and knew she, too, was in tandem with his stage of arousal. He moved over her in the dominant position and she shifted in accommodation. Rob grasped the pillow beneath her and jerked it to the floor, lowering her head gently down to the bed. He whispered to her, "Are you ready for me?"

"Yes darling, yes." She arched upward in expectation.

The two lovers locked eyes as he slowly descended into the vortex of sensual commitment.

"Rob, yes -- oh darling, yes." Frances had never known such happiness and emotional fulfillment. Why, oh why can't it be permanent, she thought. Don't care, don't care, my time, my man.

"Am I hurting you?" he asked gently.

"No, no, you're wonderful."

Rob looked down at the countenance on her face, studying the glow of her cheeks and the intensity in her eyes. Why can't I have her? he asked himself. Why, when after so long, I've finally found my soulmate, can't I have her?

They kissed again, this time frantically. The moment was closing quickly upon them. Frances clutched his face with her hands and looked at him.

"I want you to stay in me," she said, feeling her own urgency coming.

"Are you sure?"

"Without a doubt." Her breathing intensified and shortened.

Rob began to tense. "Oh god," he said and kissed her deeply and desperately.

And suddenly, they were one. Each frantically, joyously melting into and consuming the other. All the pent-up, held-back frustration of knowing they were without permanence for each other was released. But still, each was demanding and praying that the other realized the emotional bond and commitment being professed. She entwined her legs to hold him fast.

"Oh Rob, Rob," she sobbed circling her arms tightly around him. "I can't let you go."

"I know; I can't bear the thought."

They lay there for an extended period, refusing to disengage and saying nothing, just content with where they were and who they were with.

Finally, he stirred, rolling to her side and kissing her about the ear.

"We should have taken precautions," he said. "As much as I would love for you to have my child, I don't want to complicate things further for you."

Frances didn't hurry her answer. "Would you really? Want to have a child with me I mean?"

"Not only a child but a life. More than anything."

"I'm sure I'm okay; I'm very regular and in my safe period." Frances looked at the ceiling. "Rob, if we were married and had a boy I would name him after you. What is your middle name?"

"Lloyd. It's my grandmother's maiden name on my father's side. Robert Lloyd Truitt."

"Nice. It has a stately ring to it. And if we had a girl, I would like for her to carry my family name of Perry. I would let you choose her given name, though. What would you call her?"

Rob thought for a moment. "My mother died when I was relatively young. From all I've been told, she was a kind, happy person who loved her family and was very proud of her children. I would like her to know she is still loved and remembered. Her name was Grace. I would name the baby Grace and call her Gracie."

"Grace Perry Truitt," Frances said the name aloud for effect.

"I guess not," he said with resignation.

Frances was silent a moment. "Rob, the few days I can be with you I would like to be happy ones. I'm sorry for the news I've brought back. Believe me, I hate this situation more than I can express. But while we're together, please be happy with me. Spend time with me, make love to me, and know that I love you. Okay?"

He looked at her and smiled. "You've got it." He kissed her lightly on the end of her nose. "Would you like some lunch? Are you hungry?"

"Some, but I would like to see the rest of your apartment. Tell me about where you got your furniture and your pictures and if they are special. And then you can tell me about all the women you have over here all the time so I can hate every one of them."

They redressed, not being so modest this time about their bareness and took turns using the mirror to brush their hair. While she was brushing hers, he came behind her and encircled her waist with his hands and clasped them in front. She placed her hands over his and they looked at their image.

"I would like to have a picture of this," she said.

He kissed her lightly on the neck. "I have some deli ham and cheese and relatively fresh bread. We can make some sandwiches. I also have a bottle of California Chardonnay. What do you think?"

"I believe you have the makings of an indoor picnic. Sounds good to me."

The kitchen was on the rear of the town house and opened on a small garden. The garden was shared with Rob's landlords, the owners of the house. Actually, the few times he ventured out, he never saw them. The house had been built in 1855, shortly before the war, and consisted of three floors over a basement.

Since the water table in Savannah was high, few houses had actual basements, it was just the common name for the ground floor. Rob's building was a typical townhouse with the primary living area on the second, or parlor floor. This consisted of a living room in front, a dining room directly behind, and then a large kitchen on the rear of the house. The basement, or street floor, followed the same floor plan. In Rob's apartment, the kitchen opened directly into the small courtyard between the house and the carriage house on the lane.

The living area in the main house was designed for the parlor floor because Savannah was built on a sand hill and the grains were constantly airborne by the wind. This had the potential to create a continual housekeeping problem. Bedrooms were on the upper floors.

The townhouses were designed deep and narrow since most property owners were taxed on the frontage feet of the lot and not the total living area. It was a workable plan.

LITTLE GRACIE

Chapter 13

Frances planned to leave on the afternoon train Tuesday of the following week. Before then, Rob wanted to give her something meaningful. It was something he planned to do all along, but now it had a greater urgency and much more significance.

During his lunch hour on Monday, he stopped by Great Southern Jewelers on the corner of Bull and Broughton Streets. The store had a reputation for carrying some of the finest jewelry and unique pieces in the South. It was considered by many to be the southern Tiffany's. Rob was unsure as to exactly what he was shopping for but felt he would know it when he saw it.

He entered the store and walked cautiously up to the massive wood-framed glass cases. They were filled with watches, bracelets, earrings, necklaces, broaches, and other jeweled pieces. Since he was looking for ideas, he was filled with uncertainty.

"May I help you?" said an attractive lady of middle age as she approached him.

"Thank you, yes. I'm looking for a gift for a young lady and I'm searching for ideas."

"A very special young lady?"

"Yes."

"May I ask the range of value you're looking in?"

Rob thought. He hated to express his range in dollars. "Something certainly not cheap, but then again I couldn't afford a king's ransom. Something meaningful -- special."

She took several bracelets and rings from the case and presented them on the counter atop a small blue velvet pad. She discussed the merits and prices of each.

"I don't think so, I guess I'm looking for something unique that others would not have. Something exquisite." He looked at her for help.

"One of a kind?" she asked.

"Yes, exactly."

"Perhaps there is something. Excuse me." She turned and went to the rear of the store and asked Mr. Hamilton, the owner, if she could have access to the safe in the back room. He looked over to see whom she was waiting on and recognized Rob. Hamilton was on the board of the Merchants Bank, a competitor of Rob's Bank, but knew Rob in a friendly manner through business circles. As their eyes met, he nodded in acknowledgment.

A few moments later, the sales lady returned with a narrow jewelry box and placed it in front of Rob. It remained unopened while she spread another velvet cloth, this one in gray, about the size of a handkerchief, on the counter.

"This is something Mr. Hamilton obtained in an estate sale in New Orleans. We've only had it a short period and Mr. Hamilton has mixed feelings about even offering it for sale. Frankly, I've never seen anything quite like it."

She removed the top of the box with both hands and placed it aside. Then, she pulled a long gold chain with what appeared to be a large, black, smoky pearl suspended as a pendent. There were smaller natural pearls and diamond chips in a setting surrounding the dominant pearl.

"It's magnificent," said Rob.

"Yes, quite. This is known as the Tahitian Tiara," she said.

Rob stared. "It's the most beautiful piece of jewelry I've ever seen. It's perfect. I'm afraid to ask the price."

"I dare say, it's just out of the range you quoted – the upper end. It's not a king's ransom, but obviously it's one of a kind. Let me see what Mr. Hamilton will do."

She excused herself again and went across the room to confer with Mr. Hamilton. Rob noticed she took the necklace with her. As she talked with the owner, he noticed Hamilton took care not to look in his direction. What a pro, he mused. Nothing to make the customer uncomfortable.

The lady returned with a small slip of paper and placed it in front of Rob. He read the number and knew, although it was large, it was also extremely fair. For some reason Hamilton had made a concession. The lady looked inquiringly at Rob and raised an eyebrow.

Rob looked at the paper and then at the saleslady. "That's fine," he said. "I'll take it."

"Would you like it gift boxed and wrapped?"

"Yes, please."

Rob intended to see Frances that evening for dinner at his apartment. They had jointly planned what they would eat and both wanted to make it a private but formal occasion. It was important to him that he present it at exactly the right time. He wanted to include a brief note that would summarize his feelings and their relationship. He needed to work on it.

* * *

Frances was aware that her remaining time with Rob was growing short. She felt she had to leave him with something tangible, something leaving no doubt as to her feelings and commitment. She wanted it to be an item he would use daily and with each use, think of her.

Monday morning she visited Desboullions Jewelers on Bull Street, across from the Screven House hotel. Fanny had suggested she go there and see Mr. Adolph Sack. She knew he was very knowledgeable about men's accessories and had exquisite taste. The shop was small but complete; it gave one a feeling of permanence and security. Everywhere there were beautiful pieces.

"May I help you," asked the kind-faced man who was polishing a silver service.

"Yes, are you Mr. Sack?"

"He smiled. "That's me. What can I do for such a lovely young lady?"

"I would like to buy a gift for someone very special to me."

"A man?"

Frances smiled and reddened. "A man."

"Did you have anything particular in mind?"

"No, but I would like it to be something personal, something that could be inscribed."

"A ring, a tie pin, a money clip?"

"I don't think so. Maybe something more personal, more expensive."

The little man closed his hand and placed his fist to his chin. He closed his eyes. Frances waited in silence as he pondered. As he opened his eyes and pointed upward with his finger, it seemed he had reached his conclusion.

"Most men don't possess a good watch unless it's a family heirloom passed down by their father. And it's rare that the father would have one. The beauty of giving a fine watch is that it's something he will look at many times a day. You could do worse."

"I agree. Would you show me some?"

"Absolutely."

Mr. Sack directed Frances to the proper case and displayed several watches for her to see. He pointed out the merits of each style, those with a protective hunter's case versus those visible when extracted from the pocket. Assuming the watch was quality, she was more interested in the style and appearance of the face than other functionality.

She was especially taken with a gold Hampden watch in a porcelain dial with Arabic numbers and fleur-de-lis hands. It had a small inset second-hand dial at the bottom of the face.

"Is it prohibitively expensive," she asked.

"I'm afraid the price matches its beauty, but I don't believe it's prohibitive, not considering it's a once in a lifetime gift."

"I'll take it," said Frances.

The timepiece was beautiful, and Mr. Sack agreed to match it with a suitable gold chain for the same price.

"Now to who should it be inscribed?" he asked discreetly.

"Not to whom, just an inscription. I would like the date of September 23, 1881 and below it these words." She handed him a small scrap of paper. He nodded appreciatively, thinking of the many messages he had inscribed over the years.

"That is a beautiful thought," he said. "When would you like it?"

"I need it today. Is it possible to pick it up this afternoon?"

"It's a little tight, but since I do all the engraving here, we can make it. Can you come back about three?"

"Yes, thank you," said Frances, excitedly.

"And Miss?"

"Perry, Frances Perry."

"He's a very lucky man."
She was silent for a reflective moment. "Thank you."

* * *

The taxi came to a halt at Frances' door at exactly six in the evening. Rob instructed the driver to wait and stepped smartly up to the door. Frances answered the bell. She had a glow on her face.
"Hello," he said. Are you ready for a little dinner, miss?"
"I suppose I can work up an interest in that direction," she said lightly with a smile.
"The lady's carriage awaits."
They sat close on the ride to Rob's apartment, him with his arm around her and holding her hand. They were both in a light mood and excited to be together. It was only a short drive to Rob's and soon they were again in the privacy of his apartment.
"Could I interest madam in a glass of wine this evening?"
"That would be lovely, kind sir."
Rob went and opened a bottle of Chablis and filled two glasses. He began stirring around in the kitchen and she asked what she could do to help.
"Well, I'm not a great cook, but as a bachelor you do learn some things. I thought we could have a salad with pecans and mandarin orange wedges. Maybe you could start on that. The makings are in the icebox. For the main course, I've baked two Cornish hens and cooked wild rice. Also, I picked up some bread sticks at the bakery."
"Sounds scrumptious," she said.
Rob had prepared the small table in advance with a white tablecloth. From his sparse collection he was using his best plates and linen napkins, accompanied by a white candle within a hurricane globe as the center setting on the table.
"Rob, it's so elegant. Thanks for making it special."
When everything was in readiness, the couple seated themselves at the table in the kitchen. They made small talk about the food and how good it was to be together.

"I don't have a dessert for us," he said. "I'm not too good in that department."

"It was wonderful without it. I don't believe I could eat any more.

Rob rose from the table. "I have something I would like to give you. He walked over and opened a drawer in the side cabinet. From it, he took a small package back to the table and placed it beside her plate. Underneath was an envelope with a handwritten note inside.

"Let me make some room for you," he said as he cleared the plates. She opened the envelope and began reading.

My Dearest Frances,

In only a short time, you have become the most important person in my life. Although we have no idea where this relationship is headed, please know of its importance to me. I wanted to give you something that would show how much I love you and something that, with each time you wore it, would remind you of us. Its simple elegance seemed to express oneness. I hope you like it.

All my love,
Rob

Slowly she removed the wrapping and examined the box.

She turned it so the Great Southern Jewelers imprint on the top faced her. Still looking at him, she lifted the top. As the necklace gleamed in the box, she delicately removed it and held it up for examination. Rob hoped it seemed as beautiful to her as it had to him earlier in the day.

"Oh my god! Rob, it's gorgeous. You shouldn't have. It's much too expensive."

"Do you like it? It just looked like you. I wanted to get something that would symbolize the oneness of us. It's called the Tahitian Tiara."

"It's the most exquisite thing I've ever seen. But Rob, you shouldn't be spending all your money on me."

"I'd buy you the store if I could." He rose from his chair and went behind her. "Here, let me put it on you to see how it looks."

He unclasped the necklace and gently put it over her head and snapped the clasp. He placed a small kiss on her neck.

"I love you, you know."

"I know you do darling, and I love you, too. I must look at it in the mirror. She went to the hall and looked from different angles.

"It's almost haunting the way the color seems to change in the light. Now sit down. I have a small gift for you."

Rob sat as instructed and Frances went to her handbag and extracted a small package, also gift-wrapped. She placed it in front of him. "Now it's your turn," she said.

"Darling, I didn't expect you to get anything for me."

"I think it's probably more for me than for you. I don't want you forgetting me."

"There's very little chance of that."

Rob tore the paper from the box and removed the top. Frances sat across from him. Gently he raised the watch while holding the chain in his other hand.

"What a handsome timepiece. A Hampden, no less. I've never had anything so fine." He noticed the triple hinged case with the scroll enhanced shield on the front, bearing the initials R.L.T. "There's an inscription inside," she said.

He pressed the latch on the side and the watch sprung open. "Beautiful." he said, "It's just ultimate craftsmanship." He read the engraved words.

September 23, 1881
"From this day forward - One"

"Do you mean it?" he asked.

"With all my heart." Frances suddenly put her face in her hands with resignation and rested on her elbows on the table. "Oh Rob, what are we going to do?"

"I don't know. But I know we've got to believe in us. Always. Something will happen. Something's got to."

"Make love to me," she said. "I need you so much."

He nodded slowly. They rose from the table, and he led her to the bedroom.

* * *

Frances always struggled with good-byes and knew she wouldn't do very well if Rob went to the station to see her off. She wanted a more private parting than merely a final wave from the train.

"Rob, I don't want you to go the station tomorrow."

He answered slowly, knowing the answer but just mouthing the words. "Why?"

"I just don't want to share you with anyone at this time. Can't we be selfish in this one instance?" She paused a moment and then continued. "As much as you will be on my mind, I can't handle the finality of leaving you in a public place."

Rob looked directly at her. "I understand. I, too, feel very selfish about us at this moment. Let's say our goodbyes tonight. I can tell you, though, that tomorrow will be a long day."

Chapter 14

The train ride back to Florida was totally empty for Frances. She felt deserted and shocked, like a sacrificial lamb being led, dazed, to the altar. Life on her terms was over and that realization was setting in. All joy and happiness for her had been left behind in Savannah. Did Rob understand, or was he only being kind to her? Should she have told him she wasn't sure about her time of month and the possibility of conception? Questions, questions.

Now she must orient herself to the present. If she allowed herself to dwell on the past, and what-ifs for the future, it would only be maddening. What she needed was to get in a proper frame of mind. After all, she controlled her thoughts. They should not be allowed to control her. Should they?

Frances mentally took stock of where she was in life and where she was going. Again, she studied her father's dilemma and whether there were other options. As many ways as she turned the situation in her mind, the outcome was always the same -- Wales Watson was holding the stronger hand.

And what about her life and having to live in a small town like McIntosh? Could she resolve to make herself happy by jumping in and being a part of life in the tiny community? Again questions. Her mother often said there was no point in crossing the river before you got to it. Obviously, that was what she was trying to do. Better leave all those things in the hands of fate and deal with them as they come. The die was cast.

Reflective thoughts continued to pour out for most of the trip. Actually it made the ride shorter. She knew once she returned home she would have little time to sit around and reflect.

Hearing the conductor announce her stop broke her private thoughts. She looked out the window and as they rounded the bend, saw the McIntosh sign on the depot. Sam Perry was there to meet her.

Frances and her father exchanged small talk on the ride to the house, but he didn't probe about her trip to Savannah. She was relieved. Apparently, he was still overcome with guilt, and the last thing he would do was encourage a confrontation.

Frances knew she must again talk with Wales to plan the details of the wedding. She decided to assert herself. Since she was a reticent bride, she was determined to have the major say in the where, what, and when with the details. She decided it would be a family service in the Presbyterian Church. Only a few would be invited to attend. Her father, of course, would give her away. The reception following would be for the entire community. Announcements to that effect would be made in the churches, but no invitations would be sent. The wedding would be on Saturday, the 29th of October.

As she changed into her nightgown, she collapsed on the side of the bed and finally gave in to a choking cry. "Oh God, I can't believe this is happening to me."

* * *

"Let me get this straight," said Grant as he leaned back in his desk chair and lit a cigar. "This girl is in love with you, but she's gone off to marry someone else?"

Grant didn't want to be too hard on his friend. He could read the funk Rob was in. Silently he was thinking; something is wrong with both of these people if this is true.

"That's right. This Watson is practically extorting performance through a debt he's holding over her father's head."

They were sitting in Grant's second floor office on Bay Street. It was where most of Savannah's legal profession traditionally maintained offices. From there it was only a short walk to the courthouse and to city hall. It was about 5:30 in the afternoon. Grant had poured two glasses of single malt scotch that he kept in the office for special occasions.

"Rob, maybe the two of you were only ships in the night. It may be just one of those things that wasn't meant to be."

"Did I show you the watch she gave me?" Rob handed the timepiece and chain to Grant, who looked at the case studiously before snapping it open. For a moment he reflected on the inscription.

"Look, I don't doubt her intent, or yours. It could be just one of those things you can't control."

All the time Grant was thinking that if the situation was reversed, he would not let go so easily.

"When is the wedding? What can you do?" he asked.

"According to Fanny, it's set for the 29th of October, and I don't know what to do. I could go to Florida and attempt to stop the ceremony. If I succeeded in that, Watson could still foreclose on Frances' father, so that would end up accomplishing nothing."

"I guess not."

"I'll tell you something though, Grant. One day I'll have my say. Actions like this don't go unpunished."

"Maybe not by you, but by someone," said Grant.

"Have you ever felt like something has just been stolen from you?"

"You know," said Grant, searching for something comforting to say. "There's an old Chinese proverb that says if you let the bird go and she comes back, you own her. If you let the bird go and she flies away, she was never yours. Maybe you should apply that philosophy in this case."

Rob looked at Grant. "The problem, my friend, is that she is flying to the cage rather than from it."

* * *

It was the winter of 1864. Grant looked around at the faces of the men in his unit. There were only a few he had known from early in the war. The unit, like many, had seen its ranks decimated from the many campaigns they waged since 1861.

Each battle had taken its toll. Men on both sides had been butchered and maimed. All in the name of a just cause. Each side had been convinced of their purpose and knew they were right in God's eyes. Now the men were only convinced of one thing; the necessity of survival.

He and Rob had enlisted with the Oglethorpe Light Infantry under Colonel Bartow and were thrown together in training. He was a few years older than Rob and had not been a classmate of his in school.

Initially, he didn't even like him. He felt there was something about the man that just got under his skin. He saw him do it to others, as well.

Rob was not a man that took orders well. Hell, neither was he. People usually either liked Grant a lot or didn't like him at all. From his viewpoint, it suited him. He was not a person that needed the company of others. If it was there, fine, he enjoyed it. If not, no bother. He was truly a person comfortable in his own skin.

It was not until one evening, when he and a few others were on the town and sharing a drink, that he was introduced to the fierce loyalty in the man that would become his dearest friend. As those things usually start, someone said something that someone else took offense to. What, who, or where didn't matter, just that everyone was spoiling for a fight. Until at least, they went outside and it started.

When Rob came along, there was Grant, outnumbered three to one and one of his adversaries suddenly brandished a knife. In a twinkling, it was three to two, with Rob fresh in the fray and with a soberness and willingness that caught the immediate attention of the others. In quick order the tide turned and the others, including the blade, decided to retreat to fight another day.

"It's a good thing for them you came along," said Grant, staggering, his face covered with blood. "A few minutes more and I would have killed them."

Rob smiled wryly. "I'm sure they'll forever thank their lucky stars then that I did."

After the incident, the two had a newfound respect for each other. They still got on each other's nerves at times, but like all friends, they liked each other in spite of their faults.

Finally, in the summer of 1862, the unit started north. They were all surprised at the heat and humidity that existed in the Pennsylvania farmlands. Most southern boys had a preconceived notion that the northern climate was cooler – period. It was obvious they were wrong. Days on end of trudging the roads north soon let them know that Pennsylvania could be as hot as any of their southern homes.

Finally, they reached Gettysburg. Rumors were rampant. Word had it that the entire Yankee army had been spotted in the area. The feeling of most of the men was one of relief and anticipation. Few

110

doubted they could lick the Union forces in an evenly matched fight. There was no logic behind it, only southern confidence.

It was during the battle of Gettysburg that Rob, in a small group, was overrun by Union forces. Grant searched for him afterward in the dead and wounded all over the field. He was nowhere to be found. Some said he and a few others may have been taken as prisoners. Like most battles, there was a great deal of smoke, noise, and confusion.

Grant reconciled himself to it and hoped for the best. He knew that even if Rob and the others were prisoners, there was no guarantee of safety. As bad as Confederate prisons were, the Union had their own that equaled them in inadequate shelter and food, combined with gross mistreatment. As much as he hated it, he had to get on with the business of living. After three years of war he knew a person must live in the present. If all your faculties weren't focused on survival, you were at risk to be counted among the number who would never answer roll call again.

Almost a year after Gettysburg, at Cold Harbor, a much-thinner Rob came straggling into camp. True enough, he had spent the missing months in a prison camp in Maryland. One day, during a deliberate diversion, Rob and about twenty others escaped. He separated from them immediately, knowing his safety lay in going it alone rather than being part of a larger, more visible group.

For close to a week, he traveled at night and scrounged meager food from the land and neighboring farms. By day, he caught what sleep he could while being ever alert for Yankee patrols.

When Grant realized who it was, he made no attempt to conceal his relief. He went directly to Rob and encircled him in a huge bear hug.

"You're alive," said Grant. "Thank God, you're alive."

Rob smiled. "Yes, and hungry as hell, too. I thought you would have had the war won by now." Grant nodded appreciatively and smiled while steering Rob to the stewpot. "I'm working on it. But honestly, I could use a little help."

Actually, the South was in a slow retreat. Ever since the battle of the Wilderness, Lee had been pulling back, with General Grant in steady pursuit. The Union general knew the North had the numbers weighted heavily in their favor. In some cases, he was giving up two casualties for every one of Lee's, but he had the resources to expend.

He had more men, more supplies, and more time on his side. He became a relentless pursuer -- pressure, steady pressure, day by day. The South was pushed from the Wilderness to Cold Harbor and finally tried to dig in for a last stand at Petersburg. General Grant was marking time, waiting for General Sherman's army coming up from Savannah to catch Lee between the jaws of the Union vise.

In the spring of 1865, Lee's army left Petersburg and slipped westward toward a little town called Appomattox Courthouse. There in April, General Gordon of Georgia led the remnants of the Savannah Volunteer Guards along with other rag-tags in what would be the last Confederate attack of the war.

With his army greatly outnumbered and his rations gone, Lee knew further resistance was futile. It came down to a matter of numbers and they were all on the Union side. It was time to put it all behind them, to try to negotiate an honorable peace for his men.

Grant and Rob, along with thousands of others, started home. Thousands more, on both sides, would not. Their future was not to be. The Southern cause was lost and the war was over. But for many, the bitter feelings were just beginning.

Chapter 15

McIntosh, Florida
The Weekly Gazette

*On October 29th at the three o'clock in the
afternoon, Miss Frances Perry and Mr. Wales
Watson exchanged holy vows of matrimony. A
reception in the park under the gazebo followed
the wedding.*

Most of the town was in attendance. No one asked about the sudden romance and neither Wales, Frances, nor others in the family ever responded to the surprise of the townfolks. Besides, Wales held the trump card in the form of liens on the many farms in the area; so most people were intentionally uninquisitive. The weather was fine, the food delicious, and the farmers more concerned with the upcoming citrus crop than two people committing their lives to each other. Godspeed. Frances and Wales spent their first night together in the nicest hotel in nearby Gainesville. He had reserved the bridal suite. Frances realized the sexual concessions that must be made in order to cover what she hoped would be her conception with Rob. She braced herself for the worst. She felt like a whore.

Wales couldn't have been more gallant. He acted the perfect gentleman. He was tender, considerate and probably somewhat surprised that she had so little reticence in consummating their vows.

"Darling, if you would prefer, we can put this off for a while until you're more comfortable with me," said Wales.

"No," she said, "only let me change into my nightclothes and I'll wait for you in bed."

Wales deferred and joined her later under the covers after he extinguished the gas lamps. After some awkward fumbling, where she seemed more the aggressor than he, the two united. Few articles of nightclothes were removed.

"That was nice," said Frances. "I appreciate your being a gentleman. I look forward to getting to know you better." She turned on her side away from him and inwardly, she wept.

The couple honeymooned for a week in New York City. It was the first visit for Frances and actually the second for Wales. They stayed at the Waldorf, ate in expensive restaurants, and went to several Broadway plays. Through it all, Frances missed Rob terribly.

She realized how little about Wales she knew, other than he had been in the community for about five years. It was rumored he was from the North. First hand, her only knowledge of him was being his employee for several short periods over the past five years.

Now they were seated in the large lobby of the Waldorf, enjoying an afternoon cocktail and passing the time until dinner. Later, they would take in a show.

"Wales, tell me something about yourself."

"What would you like to know?"

"Just start with where you're from, your family, and how you came to be in Florida and specifically, McIntosh."

"There's not a whole lot to go into. I would imagine my history is much like many others trying to put their lives together after the war," he said in a measured tone.

"Perhaps, but I think I should know something about the man I'm married to. You know my limited history, and I think it's only right that I know yours."

"Fair enough. There's really nothing to hide. But by the same token, there's really nothing to tell."

"Try."

"I was born and raised in Maryland in a town by the name of Laurel. My father ran a dry goods store, and when I was old enough, I began working with him. It was from my father that I learned most of what I know about business."

"Did you have any brothers or sisters?"

"A younger brother who was killed in the war. I also had a younger sister who died of scarlet fever when she was three."

"That's too bad," said Frances. "I also had two brothers who were killed in the war. They were much older than I. Did you serve with the Union during the war?"

"For about two years. I was educated at a military academy in Virginia before the war. Because of that background, I was pressured to join one of the local units in Maryland and commissioned a second lieutenant. My unit was sent west and was stationed close to Vicksburg. We were under General Sherman's command and fought in several campaigns in that area. Later in the war, Lincoln appointed General Grant as head of Union forces. Since Grant always respected Sherman's ability as a field commander, he reassigned him to campaign in the south near Chattanooga and Atlanta."

"You served under Sherman?"

"Yes, and am proud of it. I know he isn't well thought of by the people in the South, but he was very much of a gentleman and one hell of a soldier."

"Were you on the march from Atlanta to Savannah?"

"Yes, I was there. We spent several months literally living off the land after leaving Atlanta. There were two columns covering a width of sixty miles through the heart of Georgia. There was no way to get word back to Washington with all the telegraph lines being cut, and everyone was wondering what happened to us. Finally, we surfaced in Savannah on December 22nd and Sherman presented the town intact to President Lincoln as a Christmas gift."

"I've seen some of the damage done by Union troops in Savannah," said Frances, thinking about Colonial Cemetery. "You may have presented it intact, but you sure didn't leave it that way."

"There was some damage done, some looting, but it was on a small scale and those guilty were punished. When we arrived, the place was literally starving to death. The streets were virtually littered with the dead carcasses of animals the people couldn't afford to feed."

"I've heard."

"Actually, Savannah had been gradually starving since 1862. That's when Ft. Pulaski, at the mouth of the Savannah River, was forced to surrender to a Union assault by rifled cannon. With commerce blocked on the river both into and out of Savannah, the town had no access to food and other supplies. Boats couldn't get in, boats couldn't get out."

"My aunt has mentioned that many times. She also tells how Yankee troops desecrated Colonial Cemetery in search of gold and silver and other valuables. Apparently someone started a rumor that the wealthy people in town had hidden their treasures in the cemetery vaults."

"Unfortunately, that's true. Anytime you get a body of troops far from home they have a way of doing things they would never consider otherwise."

"I can't believe you rode with Sherman. He is probably the most detested man in the South, especially Georgia."

"*Rode with* is not a true expression. I was part of his army. At that time I was a captain, not really a very high-ranking officer. Many of the men with Sherman who occupied Savannah thought it was the most beautiful town they had ever seen. I was one of them."

"It is a lovely city."

"Yes, I've always thought I would like to go back there to work. Even during its occupation, the people were friendly and showed a lot of class."

"My cousins have always been proud of their town."

"After leaving Savannah in January, we moved north into the Carolinas. The plan was to join up with General Grant's army and catch Lee in Virginia between two forces. That was close to the end of the war."

"Were you ever wounded?"

"Twice. I was hit by a small piece of shrapnel in the Vicksburg campaign, then caught a bullet in the hip in the Carolinas. That was close to the end of the war in April and really the end of my active service. I was laid up in a hospital till right at the surrender."

"Did you ever kill southern boys?"

"It's hard to say; I hope not. When we got close to captured prisoners, it was easy to see that they weren't much different in most ways. Not many of us on either side even knew what we were fighting for. Someone declared war and the side you ended up on was mostly determined where you lived or where your family was."

116

"What did you do after the war?" asked Frances as she took a sip of wine.

"I went back to work with my father. He prospered during the war and was able to expand his business into areas other than a dry goods store."

"Like what?"

"Dad had gotten into the wholesale produce business and was buying large quantities of vegetables and watermelons. He bought directly from the agents that came up from Florida, Georgia, and South Carolina representing the packinghouses that dealt directly with the farmers. I was assigned to supervise that business. Through that operation, I made many contacts with out-of-state people in the trade."

"And that's how you came to live in Florida?"

"Indirectly. Dad asked me to go to Florida to look into a packing house operation in Ocala, right down the road from McIntosh."

"What happened?"

"The facility was old and the equipment outdated. Most of the key employees had already jumped ship and gone to work for other companies. In short, it was not an opportunity but a pitfall. We passed it up."

"So you went back north?"

"For a while, yes. Also, I married shortly after war's end and my wife had developed a terrible problem with her breathing and a chronic cough. Later it was diagnosed as tuberculosis. I tried to be home with her as much as I could, but eventually we were forced to admit her to a sanitarium. A few months later, she died."

"I'm so sorry."

"I felt as if I had lost my right arm and wished it could have been me instead. I tried to lose myself in work -- anything to have a focus on things other than what would never be."

"Were there any children?"

"No, we were never blessed with children in the five years of marriage. I guess that's fortunate because I could not have handled them by myself."

"So what brought you back to Florida?"

"Another opportunity came up through one of the agents we were in contact with. He mentioned a bustling town in Florida on the rail line and there was a packing house and dry goods store for sale. Someone had passed away without heirs and the executor was searching for someone to buy the two businesses in the central part of town next to the railroad."

"And that was you?"

"This time the business and accounts were still intact and purchase seemed merited. My father agreed to finance the acquisition and gave me the option to buy him out with the profits generated. I think he realized it would be a good thing for me to get away and start over."

"So you moved to McIntosh."

"So I moved to McIntosh."

"And business has been good?"

"Business is business. It's like farming. You have good years and bad."

"And this year was good because you were holding all the paper on the farmers."

"No, actually this year was bad because farming was bad. As goes farming, so goes business in the town. When farmers have a bad year, they can't pay their debts and don't produce income for their families. That means they don't have the money to buy new equipment, clothes, and a host of other things they need. They have to cut back. Except they do have to replant for the coming year and hope it will be better. The only way to do that is to get the seed and fertilizer on credit from merchants like me. If they have two bad years back to back, I never get repaid."

"So you take their farms."

"Sometimes I have to. I have creditors that are demanding their money from me. The last resort is to foreclose on a property and hope to resell it. That takes time, and the proceeds are seldom more than barely enough to pay the debts. Farming is a business where everyone is constantly living on the edge."

"I thought it was one where big money could be made."

"It can be, when everything goes right a few years in a row and prices are right."

"What do you plan to do now?"

"I'd like to stay in the area and do well. I'd also like to make you happy. Is that possible?"

Frances looked down only briefly, collecting her thoughts. "As you can imagine Wales, I still have a great deal of resentment about this whole thing. It will take some time."

Wales nodded slowly. "Let's just take it a day at a time and go slowly."

LITTLE GRACIE

Chapter 16

Frances again settled into the McIntosh way of life. The town was small and the people were friendly. There was a strong work ethic in the town and everyone pitched in to help their neighbors. The protocol of the town operated on a strict regimen. The church was the focal point of all social activities.

Since Frances was a home girl, people in town were happy to see her stay in the area, and even marry someone so well thought of as Wales Watson. He had the respect of the town. Of course, almost everyone had an open account at Watson's Dry Goods with an outstanding balance. Respect for Mr. Watson was in their best interest.

Like small towns everywhere, there was gossip, but it was contained and cautious. After all, no one wanted to make a careless comment to the wrong person and have it get back to Watson. Most of the farmers needed credit at the store and retribution by Wales could place them in a most precarious position.

During the citrus season, and on into January, Frances was attuned to the subtle changes occurring in her body. She seemed to crave certain foods while others were totally distasteful. When the morning nausea began, she knew it was time to pay a visit to old Dr. Strange.

His office was located in the center of town at the rear of his huge Victorian house. Of course, as soon as Frances described her symptoms, he formed an immediate opinion based on years of practice. Frances too, agreed with his diagnosis.

A few days later, he indeed confirmed what both had suspected.

"Frances, I don't believe I'm telling you anything you don't already know, but it seems a child is on the way."

Frances beamed.

"Now I've also examined you otherwise and find you to be in a healthy state. There should be no problem with either the pregnancy or the birth."

"When do you project a due date, Doctor?"

"Probably sometime in mid-July."

Frances busied herself with the mental calculation of subtracting nine months from July.

"Congratulations," said Dr. Strange. "I couldn't be happier for you and Wales."

Frances too was extremely happy inside. She had accomplished what she wanted. She had no doubt as to who the baby's father was, but felt no guilt about Wales. He's got what he demanded and I've got what is important to me. Now she had a piece of Rob. If she could only tell him. No, she would keep it to herself. In time, it would come out. Now was not that time.

Wales was predictably ecstatic when she told him at the dinner table that evening. He rose and came around to her chair and kissed her on the forehead.

"It's wonderful," he said. "I couldn't be happier. Are you okay? What did he say you could do? When is the baby due? Can I tell people now?"

Frances was not quite prepared for Wales' overreaction. She thought he would be happy for her and generally pleased, but she didn't anticipate the excitement this caused for him. It was a side of him she didn't know -- the expectant father. Everyone seeing Wales on the street or in the store would comment on the coming event. He was all too happy to respond.

"Do you think it will be a boy or a girl, Mr. Watson?"

"How is Frances doing Mr. Watson?"

"I'm glad to see everything is going well, Mr. Watson, what will you name the baby?"

It was getting into the summer months, rather hot for central Florida, even for July. About a week before her scheduled time, Frances began having labor pains in the evening. Wales sent for Dr. Strange. It was early the following morning, July 10, 1882, that a baby girl was delivered to the Watsons. There were no complications and both mother and daughter were fine. Wales could not have been prouder.

"What shall we call her?" he asked. At that moment, he would have called her Rumpelstiltskin if Frances wanted, he was so happy.

Without hesitation she said, "I would like to name her Grace Perry. Perry after my family and Grace because I've always liked that name for a girl."

"Little Gracie," said Wales, "I like it."

The spare bedroom was converted into a nursery with pink bows and blankets. When Frances finished with the redecoration, there was no doubt the occupant was female.

Wales was busy passing out cigars and telling everyone who would listen how smart his new baby daughter was. He was truly the doting father.

Frances wrote to her cousin Fanny in Savannah. She knew the word would get to her relatives eventually. She was not trying to hide the news, but she was uncertain how Rob would react when he heard it. Savannah was still a small enough town and she was sure the news would reach him at some point.

Dear Fanny,

Exciting news. I have just given birth to a seven pound, two ounce baby girl. She is a beautiful gift to her father and me. The baby and I are both well. Wales is ecstatic. We have named her Grace Perry Watson. We call her Gracie. Wish you could see her. Hope her "father" is well.

Love,

Frances

* * *

The Watsons lived in McIntosh for another three years. Gracie rapidly developed into a beautiful child and was a young charmer for the entire community. She was blessed with long golden hair that seemed kissed by the sun itself. Her face usually carried an impish smile that preceded laughter. She was very outspoken and never met a stranger. Everyone was amazed at this precocious child.

Wales' business prospered as the area farmers were greeted with ideal growing seasons to give them the ability to pay their creditors and basically start again. A time and season for everything. Wales' focus seemed to be more and more on the hotel business; there could be no doubt he had found his calling. One afternoon he came home to talk to Frances. She noted his excitement.

"You're certainly in good spirits today."

Wales came to her and held her by the shoulders as he spoke.

"What would you think about moving to Charleston?" he asked softly.

"Charleston? What would take us there?"

"I have an opportunity to purchase a small hotel in the city." He turned and began pacing. "It's something I've been working toward for a number of months. Also, I've found someone from out of state that is willing to purchase my businesses here. The hotel can be sold to Betty McKoone; she has been my right hand in the business for years. I'll need to finance it for her, but that's not a problem. The town is growing and she can make the payments from her bookings. The hotel stays full all the time."

Frances could tell he was very excited about the prospect. She didn't know what to say. She certainly was not opposed to moving. Her greatest fear all along was being confined to the area and not being able to explore the outside world. In addition, going where no one knew them and were not prone to be whispering behind her back appealed to her. She would live in a city where there were cultural events and diverse people and she could have friends.

"I don't know what to say. What a surprise. Maybe we can talk about it more over dinner. When would we go? There is so much to consider, but if you think it's right, yes."

* * *

Charleston proved to be a godsend for Frances. She was a totally different person. Wales noticed the change immediately. Even Gracie seemed to thrive on being in the city.

They decided to live in the owner's suite of rooms within the hotel. The Planters' House on Meeting Street had been part of the Charleston scene for years. It was near the old market section of the city. The hotel boasted sixty rooms with a restaurant and lounge housed on the first floor off the lobby. It wasn't long before all the staff knew Frances and Gracie, who became an instant favorite.

Charleston was prosperous during this period and the hotel was overflowing with merchants, cotton brokers, and traveling vendors.

Shortly before they arrived, the first of two catastrophes broke. In 1885, a cyclone demolished the battery seawall at lower end of the peninsular and flooded many parts of the city. As bad as it was, it was only a taste of what was to come.

It was the following year, on Sunday, August 31, 1886, at 9:45 p.m., that calamity struck again. The day had been exceedingly hot, followed by an unusually sultry evening. The air seemed to hang with such stillness that many in town remarked on it.

Gracie had been in bed for about an hour and was now asleep. Wales and Frances were reading in the parlor of their suite. Wales looked up from his newspaper. "Did you feel something?" he asked.

Suddenly, like a creeping sensation, the trembler came lightly with a gentle vibration, much like a cat as it trips over the floor.

"Is it the building?" asked Frances getting up from her chair.

The tremor grew suddenly to sharp jolts that increased in intensity, each more violent than the last until the building was shaking like a toy.

Frances looked at Wales. They were speechless. They continued to stare at each other. The hotel began to rumble again. "Gracie," screamed Frances. She raced into the bedroom, gathered the child in her arms, and headed out the door and downstairs for the street. Her primary concern was to get away from what appeared to be a building in danger of falling. She knew if it were to happen, they would be crushed by the weight of falling debris from above.

"Hurry," said Wales as he rushed behind her, not really knowing what to do or for certain what was happening. The hotel lobby was jammed with panicky guests and staff people all trying to exit to the street. He ushered Frances and Gracie out a rear door and into the lane.

Terror stricken, people from surrounding buildings and houses rushed into the streets. Wales and Frances, joined by hotel guests, could only watch as some lost their lives to falling chimneys and walls from collapsing buildings in the area.

Finally, after one mighty wrench, the shock passed. Then began a low rumbling noise, unlike anything ever heard before. It lasted for about a minute, and then, stillness.

Almost in unison, the people in the streets began jabbering and speculating on the cause of the tremors. The din of noise and apparent confusion was increasing.

These were the first shocks ever known in this part of the country. Many had just returned from church services and hardly anyone had retired for the evening. All around, was the smoking rubble from scores of buildings that had collapsed. Their occupants had fled to the streets to distance themselves from the danger of falling walls and debris.

"Good Lord," said Wales hearing the wails of the injured and dying. The evening became filled with terror amid the ruins of the proud Southern city. What began as a peaceful Sunday evening was turning into a long, dreadful, summer night. Lighter tremors continued throughout the city, keeping the nerves of many keyed to such high tension that several lost their ability to reason.

Frances was beside herself, not knowing exactly what was happening or when it would occur again. She felt totally defenseless and vulnerable. What future threat might come seeking out herself or Gracie? She too, was in a state of shock.

Wales walked the short distance to Washington Park near the hotel that was only illuminated by the dim gaslight of the street lamps. There, he joined with others and gave help to the injured and dying. Downed electrical wires ignited several large fires in the city, adding their horror to the tragedy. Additional havoc was wreaked before the blazes were under control.

Fortunately for the Planters' House, no one was injured. Many of the guests joined the crowd in the park to assist in administering to the injured. People from all over the city united in responding to the unannounced horror that had befallen them.

Frances asked Wales, "Have you heard? How bad is it?"

His clothes were still covered with the soot and grime he accumulated in trying to respond to everyone who needed him. He paused, tired. "It seems eighty-three people, so far, are dead from the quake and the toll seems to mount daily."

It was not until the next day that the town was able to assess the extent of the calamity. Not a building in the city had escaped damage. In fact, almost all the buildings downtown were rendered unfit for habitation. Hundreds were down and many were roofless or without walls or chimneys.

The Planter's House escaped with only minor damage. The hotel was missing shingles from the roof, several bricks from the side, and multiple windowpanes were out. But in comparison with its neighbors, it was lucky.

St. Michael's Episcopal Church, the city's pride since 1761, was in shambles, with its tall steeple lying in the street. Most public buildings along with blocks of businesses were ruined. The only option would be to take them down.

Down the street from the hotel, Washington Park became a tent city where people lived while their homes were being rebuilt. Many others erected tents and lean-tos in their yards. Wales, in the spirit of citizenship and charity, allowed some of the displaced townspeople to reside in the hotel in excess rooms at no charge. Hundreds were homeless, and looting was rampant.

To add to their bewilderment, the people of Charleston were cut off initially from the outside world. Wires were severed, roads to and from the city were impassable, and most of the rail lines had been destroyed.

The day following the quake, a courier rode to Summerville, nearly thirty miles away, to give the world the news of the disaster.

When he returned, he was able to announce to the town's relief, that the world had not been destroyed. Rumors from outside the area were that Charleston and the surrounding coast had been swept away by a mighty tidal wave.

In the weeks to follow, lighter and lesser vibrations were felt at varying intervals. Gradually, they became less frequent and finally ceased. Thousands out of a population of 49,000 fled the city as soon as they could.

Frances wasted no time in conveying to Wales her fright and uneasiness about remaining in the city. He was unable to reason with her; she was convinced the town was shrouded with a bad aura.

* * *

There was concern, there was grief, and there was relief. The city had never experienced anything so colossal in its history. In California, on the west coast, sure, it happened frequently. But not on the east coast, and certainly not in Charleston.

Of course, certain predictable elements in the city panicked. Obviously, they said, it was a demonstration of God's wrath; God was punishing them for their wickedness. The end was near. The world was being destroyed, starting with Charleston. Although cooler heads didn't buy into this argument, they were still baffled. Was Charleston on a fault line, like California? Could it happen again? Would it?

Frances was scared. It was a continuing fear that she was unable to shake. She had experienced a first-hand look at what nature, out of control, could do. She wanted no more of it.

"Wales, I'm frightened. What if it happens again?"

"Frances, the scientists who know about these things say it's a freak occurrence. It shouldn't happen again."

"It shouldn't, but it may. I'm not happy. What if something happens to Gracie? With the first time, we had no warning. If there's a second, I wouldn't forgive myself. I don't see how you could either, knowing it could have been avoided."

"I know," responded Wales softly.

"Something has to be done. Wales, you must move us out of harm's way."

Wales, too, was concerned. Fear was beside the point, but he was determined not to let anything happen to his family. The fact that Frances was concerned and worried was something he could control and alleviate. Charleston had been good to them, but his family was more important than the town.

During the following two years, Wales put out feelers with all his contacts to let him know of business opportunities in other towns.

Finally his quest bore fruit. One afternoon he said, "Frances, I have something I would like to discuss with you."

"Yes, Wales?"

"I know your concern about us being here in Charleston after the quake. I know you've tried to make the best of it, but you're not happy."

"In light of what's happened, is that unreasonable?"

"No, but here's what I want to tell you. I have a business associate in Savannah, Richard Powers. He's someone I've known and respected for quite some time. Richard has made me aware of a prospective situation in Savannah.

It seems the Pulaski Hotel, one of the city's finest, can be purchased. He, too, has experience in the hospitality field but can't swing the necessary investment alone. He has asked me to come in with him as a partner. What do you think?"

She sat as the blur of memory of Savannah raced through her mind and wondered what would be changed if she returned. She knew through Fanny that Rob was still not married, but she didn't know if he was involved with someone. How would he feel with her back in the city? Did he still feel anything, or was she now alone with old emotions?

"Frances?"

It was an opportunity. It would be a bigger challenge for Wales, and Gracie would be safe. Actually, it was all she could hope for. She secretly felt the strong compulsion to closing the geographical distance between Rob and herself. She felt they were like two magnets drawing each other. Slowly, she came back to the present.

"I like it," she said finally. "I'll be afraid as long as we stay here, waiting for the other shoe to drop. It's probably an empty fear, but I'd rather go. Thank you, Wales. Please, let's go."

129

LITTLE GRACIE

Chapter 17

The Pulaski Hotel, on the corner of Bull and Bryan Streets was the finest hostelry in Savannah. It now boasted seventy-five rooms, each for two dollars per night, a restaurant, and a cocktail lounge. The Pulaski was the primary meeting spot in the city.

It had operated for many years and even hosted some of General Sherman's staff during Savannah's occupation. The army rested and regrouped for a month in the town after their long "March to the Sea". In January 1865, they headed north into the Carolinas to join General Grant's main force.

The Watsons took up residence in the owner's suite, just as they had done in Charleston. They were on the second floor with a view of Johnson Square. Frances and Gracie loved it. The hotel was the center of business life in Savannah, and by being there long enough, one could see almost all of Savannah's business community as it passed through.

Gracie liked to walk around the city with her father and especially go to Forsyth Park, the large municipal park, to feed the pigeons and squirrels. They practically became a fixture, walking through the squares along Bull Street to the big park. Soon, most of the residents along the way knew them. This was primarily through Gracie because most adults were inclined to approach them just to talk to her.

Frances was re-acclimating herself to the city, this time with a different perspective. They were invited to several parties where they met many of the business and civic leaders of the city and were welcomed accordingly. Richard Powers had arranged a reception in the ballroom of the Pulaski. Everywhere, Frances was conscious of the pssibility of seeing Rob, but after a month in town she had neither seen nor heard from him.

One evening, at a gala affair, she was wearing the necklace given her by Rob. Because of its elegance, she only wore it for special occasions. Always, it elicited comments. Frances was approached by a man who introduced himself as Samuel Hamilton. He welcomed her to the city and complimented her on such an exquisite piece of jewelry.

"It's a gift from a friend," said Frances.

"It's also the Tahitian Tiara," said Hamilton "-- your friend could not have given a more beautiful piece to a more beautiful lady. It's truly one of a kind."

Not long after being in town, she invited her cousin Fanny to lunch. Frances suggested they meet at the hotel. One of the advantages of being in the hospitality business, as Frances discovered, was that you were in a position to entertain friends and acquaintances at very little expense, and in a very gracious style.

Fanny was now married with two children. Her husband was a young physician, William Elliot, who had an affiliation with her father. Fanny had put on a few pounds, but Frances figured, after two children, she was entitled.

Fanny met her in her suite, and the two of them went downstairs for lunch in the main dining room. Frances had the Maitre 'd reserve a table in the corner. It was really the first time she and Fanny had been together to talk at length and in private.

"How exciting it must be to be moving around and staying in the best hotels," said Fanny, laughing.

"Right," said Frances, acknowledging the jibe, "Charleston was certainly exciting, but it's the type of excitement I can do without. I tell you Fanny, I've never been so scared. Ground shaking, streets splitting, new electrical wires down -- all in a matter of moments."

"Did you have any warning?"

"No. There was a slight tremor that got everyone's attention in respect to 'what was that?' but nothing more. Then, a few moments later, everything started shaking. The intensity kept growing and in places the earth started opening up. It looked like the end of the world."

"Do you think it could happen again?"

"I don't know. I just didn't want to risk it, and I lived in fear until we moved to Savannah."

"Savannah had a few tremors, too, you know."

"I know, but from what I've read, it should be safe. The geologists, who are supposed to know, say Charleston is on a major fault line on the east coast -- the same one that Port Royal Island in the Caribbean was on. You know, the town that sunk into the sea in the late 1600's.

This one is sort of like the San Andreas Fault on the west coast, except it's here. Anyway, Savannah isn't directly on the fault line, so it should be safe. At least, that's the theory."

"Well I for one hope they're right. Of course it doesn't say a whole lot for the town of Charleston. They seem to have had their share of it. Major fires, starting the Civil War, cyclones, and now an earthquake. About the only thing they have missed is a major hurricane."

"I liked Charleston, as a city. It's very much like Savannah. I loved the cobblestones, gardens, and winding streets; and I found the people charming. We made friends I hated to leave, but that's life."

For a brief moment there was a lapse in the conversation and silence between the two close cousins.

"Frances, you haven't said but I must ask you -- have you seen anything of Rob since you've been in town?"

This time it was Frances' turn to be reflectively silent. Finally, she responded.

"No, and I'm puzzled. You would think that Rob has heard by now that I'm in Savannah. You would also think I would have seen him on the street or at one of the functions we've attended. I know he would have been invited. Maybe he's avoiding me. Do you ever see him?"

"Sometimes. I'll see him at a party or rarely, on the street. He's always pleasant and always purposely avoids asking about you. I wonder if it's something that is too painful for him to bring up. He hasn't married, you know."

"I thought so. Do you know why?"

"Well he's certainly had many opportunities. He's one of the most eligible bachelors in town and I can think of at least half a dozen ladies who would love to snag him. But do I know why? -- yes, but so do you."

"What do you mean?"

"You know very well. Rob is one of those one-woman men. He found the girl he wanted to marry but it didn't work out. Since he couldn't have her, he's repulsed by any other commitment. I think Rob has become an emotional cripple; he can want, but he can't love."

Frances didn't respond and was quiet for a moment.

"Do you think you could arrange for me to see him?"

Fanny hesitated. "Do you think that's wise?"

"I don't know but it's something I want, and I think it's necessary."

"Frances, I don't blame you for what you did and I think in your place I would have done the same thing." Fanny diverted her gaze. "I'm speaking about your intimacy with Rob. Does he know anything about Gracie?"

"No."

Fanny sighed in resignation. "Where and when would you like to see him?"

"Tell him I will be in Emmet Park tomorrow during the lunch hour. I will be near the Harbor Light; he will know where."

* * *

"Mr. Truitt?"

"Yes, Mrs. Arnold?"

"There's a Mrs. Fanny Elliott here to see you. She said she didn't have an appointment."

Rob only hesitated a moment. The only Fanny he knew was Fanny Ellis, and he knew she had married a few years before. Even though he ran into her occasionally, he couldn't recall her married name.

"Please ask her to come in Mrs. Arnold."

Fanny swept into the room and gave Rob an affectionate hug. She was still filled with the same vivaciousness she had when he first met her.

"Fanny, how are you? You look wonderful."

"You big liar. After two children and some extra pounds, I don't look so wonderful. But aren't you wonderful for saying so." Rob indicated a chair across from his desk and Fanny perched on the edge of it.

Rob smiled. "What's going on with you these days?"

"Oh, the usual functions of life; children, schools, activities. But Rob, I'm not the reason I dropped in to see you unannounced," she said.

"That's perfectly okay," said Rob waiting.

"It's Frances."

"I see," he said with some hesitation.

"Obviously you know she and Wales have moved to Savannah. He's co-owner of the Pulaski with Richard Powers. He and Frances are living there in the owner's suite."

"Yes, I've heard."

"I'm only a messenger -- Frances would like to see you. She will be in Emmet Park tomorrow during the lunch hour. She said you would know where. And Rob?"

"Yes?"

"Be careful. Both of you."

Fanny rose to leave. Rob came around the desk and took both her hands in his.

"Thank you, Fanny."

* * *

The clock on the wall of the bank chimed the noon hour. Rob pulled his pocket watch and checked the time -- not because he doubted any variation, but because he was nervous. He glanced at the facing inscription and it seemed to stare back at him. ***"From this day forward – One."*** Every time he looked at his watch, he silently read it. It had become a ritual.

The watch kept perfect time and only once had he taken it for repair. Actually, it only needed cleaning. Mr. Sack, the jeweler, examined the watch and its inscription and then looked back at Rob. "This is a fine timepiece, Mr. Truitt, one you should be proud to own."

"Yes, thank you. It was a gift from a friend." Mr. Sack nodded in silence.

Rob put the watch back in his vest and announced to Mrs. Arnold he was going to lunch. He had been committed to a prior appointment, but was able to re-schedule on short notice. Rob left the bank by the Drayton Street entrance and headed toward the river. If he took the walkway along the iron fence on the bluff rather than the sidewalk on Bay Street, he would be able to see her before she saw him.

It would be about a ten minute walk to the park and Rob intently observed the activity on the waterfront as he gazed between the buildings on Factors' Walk. The rhythm always fascinated him with the cries of cadence from the stevedores as they tugged at the bales of cotton with their handheld iron hooks. The port was active and that meant business in Savannah would be good. Today however, his mind was focused on other things.

As he neared the Harbor Light, he saw a lady sitting on the bench where he and Frances had sat seven years earlier. He also noticed a small girl playing nearby with the squirrels. The lady turned as he approached and upon recognition, rose to greet him. Rob remained at a respectful distance and extended his hand. As she reached for it she came to him for a quick and friendly hug.

"Rob," she said sincerely, "how are you?"

"I'm fine." He looked toward Gracie. "It seems you've had an addition since I've seen you."

"Yes, this is my daughter." She looked at Rob. "Her name is Gracie. Grace Perry."

Rob looked at Gracie, then back to Frances inquisitively.

"How old is she?"

"Gracie is six. She was born July 10, 1882."

Rob looked at Frances again -- for clarification.

"Yes," said Frances, "Gracie is your daughter, Rob. Our daughter."

Rob sat down on the bench. Frances joined him. It was too much for him to assimilate at the moment.

"Why didn't you get word to me? Fanny could have told me."

"I thought it best you not know. "There was little that could be done by either of us to change things. It would have only made you worry about things you couldn't control."

"Were you alarmed when you became pregnant so soon after leaving Savannah and going into your marriage?"

"Rob, I lied to you. I was so much in love with you that I couldn't let you go. I felt if I had to sacrifice for someone else, I wouldn't feel guilty in doing something for me. You were who I wanted. If I couldn't have you, I would at least try to take a piece of you with me. I don't feel guilty for that and I'll never apologize for it. I was in love with you. I still am."

Rob stared away from her. There was too much happening he was unprepared for.

"I read the inscription in the watch every day. I've practically rubbed it off by repeatedly touching it. I love you, too, Frances, and I've missed you very much."

"Who are you, mister?" asked a small voice. "Do you know my papa?"

Rob turned to see a small girl with an expression of inquisitiveness on her face. She was somewhat flushed from chasing squirrels. She was dressed in a sailor suit with dark stockings and wore a tam-o'-shanter cap.

"Honey, this is Mr. Rob. He's a friend of Aunt Fanny's."

"Do you know my Aunt Fanny, Mr. Rob?"

"Yes Gracie, I do. She's an old friend."

"How do you know my name?"

"Your aunt told me a pretty little six-year-old would be moving to Savannah and to watch out for her. When I saw you, I knew you must be her because you were the prettiest girl in the park."

"Can you give Mr. Rob a hug, Gracie?"

Gracie came without hesitation to Rob and looked up expectantly. He knelt down and she threw her arms around his neck, squeezed him tight and then released him.

"Thank you, Gracie. That was nice," Rob said.

She ran off without further word to where a group of pigeons were feeding. Rob stood and Frances stepped closer.

"I would like to be able to see you but I just don't know how," she said.

Rob looked out at the river as if there he could find an answer. Abruptly, he turned back to Frances. "Do you have any secretarial or business skills?" he asked.

Frances looked mildly surprised. "I've posted the books for the store and many times I've assisted the night auditor in the hotel with balancing his daily sheet. I've also done my share of business correspondence. Why?"

"My personal assistant, Mrs. Arnold, is retiring from the bank after fifteen years of service. We are looking for a replacement. Is it something you believe you would like to do?"

"Does it mean I'll be working with you each day?"

"Yes -- setting appointments, handling correspondence, checking financial projections, and that sort of thing. Do you think it's something Wales would permit you to do?"

"Oh yes. That's not a problem. He knows I get bored if I have little to do other than amuse myself with lunch and afternoon tea with the ladies. I'm not a career girl, but I would like to feel involved and productive. Is there anyone you need to check with to approve me for the position?"

Rob laughed. "No. Executive level positions are expected to recruit and hire their personal assistants."

"Do you think we can work together given our history and feelings?"

Rob didn't answer immediately. He seemed to weigh his words. He knew Frances was too important for a flip answer. "Do you think we can live in the same town apart, given our history and feelings?" he asked.

"I know I can't. When would I start?"

"Mrs. Arnold's last day is Friday of next week. Can you begin the following Monday?

"Yes, Gracie is in school for most of the day and we have a sitter who can be with her for a few hours in the afternoon. Oh Rob, I hope this works out. I hope we're doing the right thing.

He looked at her direct. "Without a doubt."

Chapter 18

Rob needed to talk to Grant. He felt sure hiring Frances was the right idea, but he still wanted another opinion. Or, did he just want to ventilate and tell someone who knew the situation, someone he could talk to, someone with whom he share his excitement.

He stopped by Grant's office on his way back to the bank. Grant was out but his secretary checked his appointment book and saw no reason he couldn't meet Rob after work.

"Good," said Rob. "Tell him to meet me at Houlihan's at half past five."

* * *

That evening at dinner, Wales seemed to be in a jovial mood, and Frances thought it would be a good time to discuss her going to work.

"Wales," Frances began, "Fanny said there is a position as an executive assistant opening up at one of the local banks. If I'm interested, she knows the person hiring and thinks there would be no problem in my securing the job."

Wales put his fork down and took a small drink of water. He blotted his mouth with his napkin. "Frances, we went through this in Charleston. Why do you want to work? We have more than enough income from the hotel. We don't need the money you would earn."

"The money's not the point. That's just it, Wales. You don't need the money because you have plenty. The only money I have is what I get from you. It would be nice to know that some of my money is what I've earned and can spend as I wish without an accounting."

"I'm sorry, I know."

"Also, with Gracie now going to school, I have most of the day that I can do something else for a change. I want to feel like I'm doing something other than going through the motions of life."

"You must know you're valuable to me and Gracie. Which bank is it? Maybe we bank with them."

"It's the Southern Bank, here on Johnson Square. The executive's name is Truitt, Rob Truitt."

"Well, our primary account is at the Savannah Bank & Trust Company. I don't know Truitt. He sighed, "Do what makes you happy, Frances. Just keep me posted."

* * *

Houlihan's was in full swing with the afternoon watering crowd when Rob entered at 5:25. He didn't know if Grant would be there but knew, at any rate, he wouldn't have long to wait. One of Grant's positive traits was that he was always punctual. You could set your watch by him. If he was late, something was wrong. He had once explained his view on being late to Rob.

"When I was a kid in Sunday school," he said, "we were taught that the most valuable commodity a person has is his time. No one knows how much of it he has left. When you're late for an appointment, you're stealing that person's time. You're also saying that your time is worth more than his. It's the rudest and most presumptuous thing a person can do."

Rob knew also from serving in the war with Grant that he was a person you could count on. So many times it was of utmost importance to know someone would be where they said they would be at the time they said. He knew from experience that Grant would be there. He had not known him to fail.

Many people, friends and acquaintances, suffered from good intentions. Rob often thought he would hate to be sinking in quicksand and know his rescuer was that type of person. They were coming, they had good intentions, but something else diverted their attention on the way.

It was like the old story of who killed Cock Robin. No one had a direct hand in it but then again, no one lifted a finger to stop it. And when it was all said and done, Cock Robin was dead.

Grant was at the bar and had just started on a draft beer. There was an empty stool next to him. He seemed to be deep in thought on an insurmountable problem. On a pad at the bar, he was scribbling some thoughts.

"What are you working on?" asked Rob in a chipper fashion.

Grant glanced up. "It's a new story I'm developing for <u>Detective Magazine</u>. Every time I'm at a loss for a character, all I have to do is come in a place like this. Then, I'm covered up with actual people who will work perfectly with a few name changes."

"It is amazing, isn't it?" said Rob. "Savannah seems to have more colorful characters per block than any other town its size. It never lacks for interest." Rob signaled the bartender to bring him a draft by pointing to Grant's.

"You know," said Grant, "I've got you as a character in one of my stories."

"Great. What am I, a serial killer?"

"No, actually you're the alter-ego of the protagonist of the story, who is, of course, me. You see, I'm the sleuth on the trail of a missing art treasure and you're there to provide some comic relief."

"And you, of course, will save the day and recover the treasure and win the beautiful lady in the end. There is a beautiful lady, isn't there?"

"What story would be complete without beauty and romance?"

"And at the end, she's enamored with your macho persona. Ultimately, you win her?"

"It seems to bring the story full circle."

"And they pay you to produce that pulp for people to read?"

"Actually they pay me after the pulp is produced. And quite well, I might add. Also, while it may not be literature, it's not pulp."

"Good lord."

"What's going on with you? You seem to be more into friendly banter than usual."

Rob hesitated and smiled. He looked down to his beer. "I saw Frances today."

Grant looked at him while he reached in his pocket and extracted two cigars. He offered one to Rob, who declined.

"It's still there, isn't it?" Grant struck a match and cupped the tip with his hands while lighting the cigar.

"It never left," said Rob.

"I heard through the grapevine she was back in town with her husband. He bought the Pulaski Hotel with Richard Powers.

Apparently he's been successful in hotels as well as other businesses in Florida.

"Grant, I've asked Frances to come to work with me. She's to replace Mrs. Arnold, who is retiring."

Grant drew on his cigar and exhaled slowly. "Can she do the work?"

"She's trained in bookkeeping and has handled the correspondence for her husband's businesses. She can be trained on the specifics of the job."

"Can she be trained to work with you in a business-like manner so as not to arouse suspicion in any corner? With you two lovebirds working together every day, how are you going to avoid temptation?"

"We can make it work. She wants it to and I want it to, very much. It's the only way we can see each other."

"Kind of the reverse of husband and wife being apart all day and then spending time together in the evening. You too have your togetherness during the day and your separation in the evening."

"I know, I know. It's a damn poor excuse for a relationship, but I don't know what else to do."

"There's little I can tell you that you haven't told yourself, but let me tell you this with all gravity. You are playing with fire. You both are. Be careful, be damn careful. You're in a war again, but a different type. Don't let your guard down, and impress on her that she can't either. Be sure you're always in controllable situations."

"There's something else."

Grant looked at his friend directly. "I'm waiting."

"She has a daughter, Grant. Six years old, and I've never seen a more beautiful and precocious child. Her name is Gracie, named after my mother."

Grant held his cigar and looked at Rob expectantly. He waited with the certainty of what was coming.

"She's my daughter."

Grant drew again on his cigar and exhaled slowly. The smoke gently wafting in and mixing with other smoke in the room. "Good grief, Rob, when you dive, you plunge deep, don't you. Maybe *you* should be passing out the cigars."

"It should've been us together."

"Should've, would've, could've -- it's not! You can't should've done anything. It's already happened. All you can do is deal with what you can control today."

"I know, that's all I'm trying to do."

"How about another beer?" Grant offered.

"No, thanks," said Rob rising from his seat. "I've got a lot to think about and I need a clear head to do it."

* * *

Two months into the job, and everything was going along extremely well. Frances had proven to be a quick study, and while Rob always wondered how anyone would be equal to Mrs. Arnold's skills, he knew that, in time, Frances could surpass her. She was people-oriented and enjoyed dealing with the host of developers, contractors, and architects that were always in and out of the bank. Although her learning curve was steep, each day she was increasing her knowledge about construction costs and project requirements.

Most of the staff and bank officers thought her to be a warm and personable addition and wished that she worked for them, instead of Rob.

She and Rob were always careful to keep everything on a business-like basis, and many days personal talk was nonexistent. There were times of course, usually late in the afternoon when appointments were over, they were able to relax and converse freely.

Frances was ecstatic; it was like a dream come true. She was able to spend the working day in the company of the man she adored. Rob, too, was on an upper most of the time. It was like he had come out of a dark cave into the bright sunlight.

He would always ask about Gracie. How was she doing in school? What subjects did she like? What was her sitter like? Did Gracie like her? Frances went out of her way to keep him informed about the goings-on in her house, especially as they applied to Gracie. She said little about her relationship with Wales; it was an area Rob seldom

143

asked about. It was like he acknowledged his existence but he really did not want to know.

"Wales said he would like to meet you," said Frances one afternoon. "He plans to take me to lunch tomorrow and he said he could come for me here at the bank. Would that be okay with you?"

Rob barely hesitated. "Of course, I would like to meet him, too. Then I will have a better idea of the man you are talking about."

"He's not very outgoing on a natural basis. He can be personable when the occasion demands, but it's very deliberate, almost rehearsed. But I'm sure you'll find him very cordial on your first meeting."

Rob had to admit he was curious. When Wales showed up the following day, Rob went out of his way to be clever and sincerely complimentary of Frances and her work. He was also glad he had worn one of his better suits. Wales looked as though he had just stepped out of the pages of a gentlemen's fashion magazine.

"Rob, it's indeed a pleasure to meet you." He extended his hand. "Frances told me how she enjoys working with you and how patient you are in teaching her the fine points of real estate and finance."

Rob shook hands warmly and both men looked in each other's eye. Rob noticed Watson had a firm handshake and exuded confidence, but in his eyes there a slight blink that revealed a calculating mind behind a facade of bravado.

"Thank you, Wales. Frances has become a real asset to the bank and is a joy to work with. We're glad to have both of you in Savannah. I understand you're planning to do some major renovation at the Pulaski?"

"Yes. You know there's a group in town planning to build a deluxe hotel on the site of the old Savannah Barracks at the corner of Bull and Liberty Streets. They've chartered under the name of the DeSoto Hotel. People like new things, and in order for us to remain competitive, we need to have a face lift."

"The Pulaski is an institution in Savannah. It's hard to imagine another hotel replacing it as number one." "We hope you're right." He turned to Frances. "Dear, are you ready for a little lunch?"

Frances had been hovering nearby while the two squared off and sized each other up. Rob was probably an inch taller, whereas Wales was a little stockier. Rob was clean-shaven while Wales sported a full mustache. She was glad the meeting was finished.

"Yes," she answered; "let me get my hat and I'll be ready."

As they left the office and were out of earshot, Wales commented, "Well, he seemed to be a friendly sort and I hear he's very capable as well."

"Yes," said Frances, "he's very good at his job."

* * *

Rob reflected on this first meeting and the man who dashed both his and Frances' dreams for a life together. So that's my rival, he thought. Probably the best approach to the situation would be to act as though he didn't exist for the most part -- out of sight, out of mind. Rob believed in a philosophy of not reacting to others. This meant acting first, then letting them react to you.

He thought how in many occasions people would say, "because he said this or did that, I'm not going to . . . Or, he snubbed me and just wait until he tries to do it again and I'll--." Rob knew if you constantly reacted, you were you were letting people control you. He refused to do that.

LITTLE GRACIE

Chapter 19

The months slipped by and the Christmas season had come again. With it came a host of parties, for Savannah was a very sociable town. It was a time Frances and Rob wanted to spend together, but obviously couldn't. The most they could hope for would be to attend the same party and be together if only for a moment.

Traditionally, the bank had a party for all employees. Normally it was held at one of the hotel ballrooms, and this year it would be at the Screven House on Johnson Square. It was a time for the staff and their spouses to dine, mingle, and dance and generally enjoy the goodwill of the season.

In prior years, for Rob it had only been just one more party of the season. He knew the staff would be in attendance, dressed in their festive finery, with their spouses, and looking forward to having the party night of their year. The food was generally good, and everyone would be in a holiday mood. They would be eager to mix with the others they worked with and to observe what they would be wearing and who they were married to.

Rob had asked one of his more regular companions to the party so as not to come alone. Actually, he was active on the social circuit and there were a circle of ladies he normally escorted to functions when it was expected that couples would be the rule. This was such an occasion.

His date was an attractive widow in her mid-thirties. She and Rob had been together many times before and while there were no pretenses of serious affection other than good company, she was someone that most men would be proud to escort.

The evening had progressed in good order. Rob had spoken to almost everyone in the bank along with their spouses. Small talk of the holidays had been exchanged and everyone was enjoying the party. The band was beginning to play some of the favorites of the time and season.

Suddenly, someone appeared at his elbow and he could not deny her presence.

"Excuse me, Mr. Truitt, I know it's bold for a lady to ask a gentleman to dance, but I was hoping my boss would grace me with his presence on the floor for one dance of the season."

Rob turned. "Mrs. Watson. Aren't you the lovely one tonight? May I present Mrs. Kathleen Balfour, Kathleen, Frances and I work together."

The two ladies exchanged greetings and Frances turned back to Rob.

"Well," she said, "are you going to dance with me or not?"

"I would be honored. Will you excuse me, Kathleen?"

Frances and Rob made their way to the dance floor. The band was beginning to play a slow waltz. The floor was crowded with other couples.

"Isn't it funny?" said Rob.

"What?" she replied.

"How we wait all season to attend the same party, and then the most we can hope for is to share one quick dance as an excuse to touch each other."

"Maybe, but right now it's all I want it to be. Have you been aware of my presence tonight?"

"I've thought of little else. I think I've known where you were since the moment you walked in the room."

"Someone watching you would never have known. You cover your feelings very well."

"I feel like they're totally on my sleeve."

"Your date, Miss Kathleen, is very attractive. Should I be jealous?"

Rob laughed. "You make all the other women here look like boys and you know it. If anyone is jealous, it's me."

"Christmas is a time when people who love each other should be together," Frances said. "When you aren't, it can be a very depressing time of year."

"I know. This is the season when the bachelor lifestyle certainly takes a back seat to home and hearth."

"Don't be so sure. When you aren't living with the one who owns your heart, a house full of people is only that. Rob?"

"What?" he answered softly.

"Promise me that in the new year, we'll find a way to share some time together."

He pushed her away to look directly at her. "We will. We'll work on it."

"Promise me. I know if you promise, then we will."

"Then I promise," he said sincerely.

Frances squeezed his hand. "Merry Christmas, darling. I love you."

"I love you too."

From the side of the ballroom, Wales watched the two with feigned disinterest. Slowly, he stroked his mustache.

* * *

A few months later on a Monday afternoon Frances said, "Rob, my mother isn't doing very well."

"I'm sorry to hear that."

"Thank you. I received a letter from my father saying she had developed a cancer and it would only be a matter of time. I would like to take the Friday afternoon train and go down to see her for the weekend. Would that be a problem? I would be back on Monday so I would only lose the one day of work. I feel it may be the last time I'll have the opportunity to see her."

"No, of course not. Why don't you take Friday off, the entire day? That will give you some time to pack and arrange your things. Do you have someone to keep Gracie?"

"Partially, I've spoken to her sitter and she's agreed to extend her hours for the weekend. She said it would not be a problem. Gracie really almost keeps herself; she practically has the run of the hotel and the guests seem to love her." Frances faded within herself for a moment. "You know Rob, I wish you could go with me."

He answered thoughtfully. "Yes that would be nice. We've never had a trip together."

"Why couldn't you?" she said suddenly. "No one pays that much attention to what goes on at the station with all the people coming and going. We would never be noticed. What do you think?" She paused a moment and said tauntingly, "Remember, you promised me."

"It's too risky, too coincidental."

Frances bit her lower lip. "Damn," she said. "There should be a way we can be together for a little while."

Rob seemed to be lost in thought for a few moments. Suddenly, he turned his attention directly on Frances. There was an intensity on his face. "I know what could work," he said with assurance. There was a lilt to his voice.

"You do? What?"

"I'll board the train in Augusta, the last major stop before Savannah. In advance, I'll reserve a private compartment with a berth."

"So when the train pulls into Savannah, you will already be on it."

"Exactly. And since I will stay on the train, I won't be seen at the station in Savannah."

"But Rob, it means you will have to go to Augusta so much ahead of time in order to come back to Savannah."

"Not really. All I need to do is catch the morning train to Augusta, kill an hour there and board the train from New York that runs into Savannah and on down to Florida. I can book a compartment out of Augusta to Ocala and just stay on the train for one stop after you get off."

"Would you mind? Frances held both his arms with her hands. "It would just give us some time. That would be so nice."

"Then I'll make the arrangements."

"How will I know which compartment you're in?"

"After you're seated on the day coach with your bags, I'll come through and pass you a note giving you my number," he said. "After a few minutes, just get up and come to my car. I'll be waiting."

"Then what?"

"When we leave Gainesville, you'll go back to the day coach and I'll stay on to Ocala."

"Can you come back with me as well?"

He thought for a moment. "All I would need to do is spend two nights in Ocala and reserve a compartment again for the return trip."

"What would you find to do there? Have you ever been?"

"No, but it's a nice town and it will give me somewhere to explore for a while. Don't worry, I'll be fine."

"So, will you make the arrangements?"

"I'll take care of everything."

"What if something goes wrong?"

"Don't be such an alarmist. Nothing will, You'll see." Nonetheless, Rob had a feeling of dread growing inside him.

At lunch Rob went to the station to book his fare. He also reserved his return trip from Ocala. The only change he made in the plan was to get off at Brunswick, about an hour before the train would arrive in Savannah. This way there would be no suspicion at the station in Savannah when Wales met Frances.

He played it back in his mind. I go to Augusta on the 9:00 a.m. train Friday morning. I return on the New York- Florida Special, departing Augusta at 1:00 in the afternoon, arriving in Savannah at 4:00. I'll be in a compartment with no reason to be in plain view. Frances will board the day coach in Savannah. As soon as the train is comfortably outside Savannah and the conductor has called for tickets, I'll locate her on the train and give her my compartment number.

She will ride with me to Jacksonville and then go back to her seat. When we leave the station she will come back to the compartment until Gainesville. At that point she will return to her seat and get off in McIntosh. I'll go on to Ocala and spend Friday and Saturday nights. Sunday I'll board the train at 1:45 in the afternoon. We'll pick up Frances about 2:10 in McIntosh. We'll follow the same routine as before. I'll pass her the information on the compartment number and we'll ride together until Jacksonville. She will go back to her seat but return when the train leaves the station. Then, right before Brunswick, she'll again go back to her seat. I'll get off there and she will continue on to Savannah. I'll catch the local about an hour later and there won't be any problem with getting into the station. Rob could find no flaws in the plan.

He confided the strategy to Grant, who said, "I've warned you about this. You're going to get away with it once and then you'll get careless."

"Would you do it if you were me?"

151

"I'm not you and, yes, I would."

Chapter 20

"Everything is set," Rob told Frances.

"For real?"

"All you have to do is board the train in Savannah and get off in McIntosh. I've taken care of the rest."

Both were beside themselves with anticipation. The week dragged on. Each one knew the other would come up with a conflict at the final moment, but neither did.

On Thursday evening, they bade each other good night as they left work. Now, they each had something to look forward to. Frances could barely think about her mother, who was the reason for taking the trip in the first place. Even an indentured servant should be entitled to a day off, she thought.

Rob packed that night, and Friday morning at 8:30, he was at the station. The train was on time. His eyes scanned the terminal for familiar faces and he was relieved not to see any. What he did feel was the old tingle that he learned to live with during the war. It was the anticipation of what he would be involved in, the danger of it, and knowing he'd better stay on his toes.

It's strange, he thought. Here we are doing something against the laws of God and man and yet we're still willing to risk almost everything. Why? Rob could only answer for himself. She was the woman he loved, and it was like someone came in and whisked her away against his and her will. It was like she was one of the spoils of war, there for the taking.

In Rob's mind, he knew that was exactly what happened. Not so much that she was stolen but more that she was sacrificed by her parents.

The ride to Augusta was uneventful. Rob read the morning paper and browsed through several magazines he purchased at the newsstand in the station. One was True Crime Journal featuring one of Grant's more recent stories. True indeed, thought Rob. I wonder if the rest of the stories printed here are as made up as Grant's.

The train was thirty minutes late getting in to Augusta and Rob was beginning to feel concerned about making his return connection to Savannah. Finally, they lurched into the station. He was glad he only had one bag to bother with.

Briskly, he walked into the station and confirmed with the ticket agent the track number and departure time of the New York Special.

"Track seven and it's scheduled to depart on time," said the ticket agent. Rob was assigned compartment 18 in the forward sleeper.

He again purchased a few magazines along with sandwiches and juice to have in the room. The conductor punched his ticket and he boarded only one car away from his own. This made him feel more secure since it reduced the chance of his being recognized by someone from Savannah on a return trip from Augusta.

Finding his compartment was no problem and he immediately proceeded to acquaint himself with the few security precautions he would be in control of. He lowered the window shade and checked the door lock from the corridor after he had set the internal lock. It seemed to be in proper order. Nothing to do now but settle down and wait.

The return trip to Savannah was made without incident, just as the morning trip had been. About 4:15, the station call for Savannah was made by the porter. Rob looked out the small opening in the window shade for any recognizable landmarks. Almost immediately he had his bearings. He knew in a few minutes they would be in the station. He fully closed the shade so those on the station platform would be unable to see in. It gave him just enough of a peephole that he could see most of the activity.

As the train backed in, he spied Frances and Wales. Since he was in the next to the last car, he knew she would be boarding one of the day coaches toward the front. They would only be in the station about fifteen minutes, but he knew Wales would stay with her until the train departed.

He checked the time on his watch -- 4:20. In an unconscious movement, he rubbed his thumb over the inscription. Still "One" he thought, soon to be reunited. Shortly, the cars gave a slight jolt as the engineer took out the slack. It was always worse for the rear cars due to the cumulative effect. Another jerk and the cars started slowly forward. As he peered out, he saw Wales looking down the track where the train was heading. This confirmed that Frances was on the train; now he just needed to locate her.

Taking one of the magazines he had purchased at the newsstand, he proceeded forward. The car ahead of his was a day coach with most of the passengers facing toward the front except for those in a four way grouping, tête-à-tête. It was about two-thirds full. The seats were usually turned when the car was coupled. The railroads discovered early on that it was easier to reverse the seats than to attempt to connect the car heading in the right direction. He stood for a moment in the rear of the car to scan the backs of the passengers' heads. Frances' telltale auburn hair was not among them.

He proceeded forward through the car holding the luggage racks on either side for stability. Once under way, the cars had a side-to-side careening movement and it was on the side of caution to have a firm grip as one moved about. At the end of the car, he opened the connecting door and noticed again the immediate increase in the noise factor. The wheels on the steel rails screeched as they traversed the myriad of other tracks on the outskirts of Savannah. This combined with the rhythmic click-clack as they crossed the joining of one rail with another.

Rob opened the door to the car ahead. As he entered and the door closed behind him, the noise reduction was pronounced. This car, too, was a day coach and he noticed sitting near the rear on the right hand side, a pretty auburn hairdo under a smart pillbox hat. Frances was sitting next to window on a seat by herself. If one didn't know differently, they would think she was absorbed in the passing scenery. The car was about half full. He passed by her seat without acknowledgment and went to the front by the water cooler. He felt her eyes turn to him as he passed.

At the cooler he pulled a paper cup from a stack and drew a small amount from the tank. While drinking, he scanned the car for familiar faces. Seeing none, he walked back to the rear. As he neared Frances' seat he leaned over and said, "Miss, I have an extra magazine. You may wish to read it *after* the conductor has checked your ticket." He wanted to emphasize that she needed to stay until then.

"Thank you, sir, I appreciate it." Frances accepted the magazine and Rob left by the rear of the car. Again he scanned the car and to his knowledge no one had an interest in their exchange.

Frances looked at the magazine after Rob left. There was a small scrap of paper protruding from the pages at the top. She removed it and read, "Two cars back - No. 18."

* * *

There was a light tapping at the door. Rob had been waiting expectantly. He turned the latch and pulled the door inward. There she stood. All the anticipation and frustration was temporarily over; this was now and she was here.

"Come in," he said with a smile, reaching for her hand and drawing her inside. He firmly closed the door and slid the latch into place. Rob turned to her. "Come here," he said, extending his hand. She took it, her eyes intent on his, and he drew her to him. He tenderly held her face in his hands as he kissed her oh so gently.

"Oh Rob, I've missed you so much," she said as she hugged him tightly.

"I know, it's been like forever. I thought the week would never end."

"I'm nervous," she said. "I'm probably a few pounds heavier than the last time we were together. You may decide you don't won't to be with me at all."

"That's just pure nonsense and you know it. You're more beautiful than ever, and I'm more in love with you than ever. You're the girl I want."

"You promise?"

"I promise."

Rob kissed her again, this time with passion. He heard an audible sigh escape her throat.

"It's been so long," she said.

Frances was conscious of a million thoughts racing through her mind -- all unimportant. She was determined to concentrate on the present and the few hours they would have together. She knew it was a small window of opportunity and she wanted to make the most of it. Frances felt Rob's hands begin to caress her body, they were moving from the public to the more intimate. She pressed tighter against him.

Rob scarcely knew where to begin. Her body presented a feast and he was starved for her. By her response, he could tell she was just as hungry.

"Turn around," he told her, and began unbuttoning her dress. She complied as he began gently kissing the nape of her neck. His hands cupped her breasts and she covered them with her own.

The two lovers began assisting each other out of their clothes. When they were down to bare undergarments, Frances sat on the small berth in the compartment.

"Now *you* come here," she said.

Rob joined her on the bed and again they kissed eagerly. Suddenly, there was a loud knock at the door. Both hearts stopped. He placed a finger over her mouth and motioned her to keep silent.

"Yes?" said Rob.

Frances' face possessed a look of sheer alarm.

"I've got sandwiches and drinks. Are you hungry?" It was the newsbutch.

"Thank you, but no," said Rob. "We're well taken care of for now." Frances looked at him and stifled a giggle. He turned back to her. "Well aren't we?" he said.

"My hunger goes a little beyond food at the moment," she answered.

Rob felt the need to tell her all the things he had been thinking for so long: what she meant to him and how hollow his life had been in her absence. She, in turn, wanted him to know that he had been constantly in her thoughts since their parting.

They were caught in an emotional torrent of expression where neither was able to voice his feelings adequately. Rather, they let their bodies do their talking to express feelings their voices were unable to convey.

They tossed in a frenzy and were like animals in a death struggle. Their passion was high and all too soon it was over. Both were totally spent and collapsed into each other's arms. Only then were they conscious of the swaying of the coach and the clickity-clack singing of the wheels on the rail.

"I love you," she said, her lips pressed against his neck.

"I love you, too."

"What do you think has kept us together though apart for so long?" asked Frances.

Rob thought. He wanted to give her a truthful answer but was wondering himself at the same time. "I don't know. We probably knew the best thing for both of us would be to walk away. Unfortunately, I never could. I always felt you were stolen from me."

"I know. Do you think if we had married we would have lived happily?"

"Absolutely."

They redressed, knowing they would be coming into Jacksonville soon. Rob produced the sandwiches he bought earlier in Augusta. "These might be a little stale by now," he said, smiling, "but filling."

Frances left the compartment as the train began pulling into Jacksonville and returned to her seat. She knew the conductor would be by again checking tickets after a major stop. It wasn't a problem in between cities since passengers were frequently moving about the train to visit and going to the dining car.

A few miles out of Jacksonville, Frances again found her way to Rob's compartment. "Miss me?" she asked.

"Yes, I thought we would never get out of there. How much time do we have before your stop in McIntosh?"

"About an hour and a half." She looked at him and raised an eyebrow. "Perhaps we should use it well."

* * *

Sam Perry was waiting at the depot. Rob cracked his shade and watched as Frances left the train. She and her father walked down to the wagon. As the train began to move, she turned and looked for his car. Recognizing the drawn shade, she gave a small wave of acknowledgment as he slowly disappeared into the night.

"How have you been, daughter?"

"Fine. We're all fine. Gracie is now six years old and seems to be everywhere. Very little escapes her notice. How is Mother?"

"She has good days and bad. Recently, though, it seems the bad ones outnumber the good."

"What does the doctor say?"

"Dr. Strange gives your mother about one to three months. It just depends on how rapidly the cancer continues to spread."

"Has she seen other doctors to see if there is anything more that can be done?"

"No. We haven't had the money. Dr. Strange said we were welcome to go elsewhere, but that there were no breakthroughs in the treatment of cancer and there was very little to be done except to make your mother comfortable."

"How is she reacting?"

"She's accepted it. Now she's resigned herself to living out her days with dignity. She's okay."

"And you?"

"We've had a good life together, a lot of grief but also some happy times. There were days when we both were ready to pitch it all and surrender, but we didn't. Now it comes to this. We all have a time to go. Mine probably won't be far behind her's."

Her father let her off at the front porch and the twins came out to greet her.

"Hi, big sister." They both hugged her hello.

"Well hello to you. What's happened to my baby sisters? You're almost grown."

"Well, most of the boys in the area think we are," said Martha. "Grady Casey hangs around Mary so much you would think he lives here."

"You both have plenty of time," said Frances. "Is Mother still awake?"

"I'm not sure," said Martha. "She was trying to wait up for you. You might peek in on her."

Frances ascended the stairs quietly and walked down the hall to her mother's room. She stood in the open door and heard the regular breathing from her mother's bed. She tiptoed over and looked down on her as she slept. Other than her face, which was extremely drawn, she barely looked like the woman Frances knew as her mother.

Turning, she walked softly out the room and down the hall to her own. "We'll talk in the morning," she said to herself.

Chapter 21

Frances was up early and joined the twins who were fixing breakfast in the kitchen. Her father had eaten a generous serving of scrambled eggs, grits, sausage and toast and was having a second cup of coffee.

"What is Mother able to eat?" asked Frances.

"Almost anything," said Mary, "but her appetite is very small. Why don't you take her a tray of eggs, grits, toast, and coffee with cream and heavy sugar? I doubt she will eat very much, but it can be her choice."

Frances fixed a tray and after it was carefully balanced, she started off. Carefully and slowly, she climbed the stairs in the central hallway. The house seemed to talk as memories of her childhood were brought into focus by different objects in the house. It was another time, she thought. She stopped at the open door to her mother's room and noticed she was awake in bed and brushing her hair. She turned as Frances strode in with the tray.

"You must think me terrible for falling asleep before you came in last night. I tried but just couldn't make it."

Frances sat the tray on the bed and leaned down to give her mother a hug.

"I brought you some breakfast," she said.

"I'd like some coffee. I'm not really hungry, but I'll try to eat some eggs and grits."

Frances arranged her mother's pillow and put the extra one behind her and helped her to sit up against the headboard. The legs of the tray straddled her.

"I'm glad you came, Frances. I've missed you. With the twins growing up and being involved in their own circle of friends, the house has become very empty for your father and me."

"Yes, it's a big place. When the twins leave, there will only be the two of you."

Her mother arched an eyebrow. "You're kind, but we all know I'll be gone long before the twins are. Time now is on an allotment, and

I wanted to see you rather than have to say things to you in a letter. Sit here on the bed with me."

"I wanted to see you, too, Mother."

"Since your marriage to Wales, a cloud has been hanging over the family and a wall existing between you and your father and me. We never talk about it with you, but we all know it's there."

"Oh, mother!"

"Just listen." Her mother reached for Frances' hand. "I know what we asked you to do was wrong. It was extremely unfair to put you in such a position. You probably always know these things when you look back on them rather than when you rationalize them at the time. We were too much in the survival mode. We were more concerned with our lives and what the neighbors would think if we failed on the farm."

"Mother, we don't need to talk about this."

"A person needs to be true to himself. Your father and I found this out too late. We would do anything if we could undo the harm we caused you and return your life to you as it was.

"It all worked out. Maybe it was a part of growing up."

"Can you forgive us?"

Finally she will be able to have it all, Frances thought. The farm had survived and with it their continued position in the community, and now on her deathbed, she would receive the absolution from her daughter for her wrongdoing. They ran up the bill and she picked up the check. They had no idea the extent of the harm they had done to her.

"Mother you can't imagine -- ." Her thought went unexpressed.

"What, dear?"

Frances looked at her mother but only saw an old woman that was pitifully reaching out to those around her, trying to square accounts. She saw no gain in destroying her mother and rejecting her plea for redemption. She could not judge her because she hadn't been there.

"It's okay, mother. It all worked out for the best. I have a beautiful daughter and a good life in Savannah. You did what you had to, but it worked out. I'm glad we had this talk, too. Just know that if a wall existed, it's gone."

Her mother reached out to her and Frances obligingly leaned down and embraced her. She kissed her on the cheek.

"I love you, Mother. It's okay."

Frances quietly backed out of the room.

* * *

Rob watched Frances and her father walk to the wagon as the New York Special pulled out of the depot on its way to Miami. His thoughts retreated back to the morning when the day was ahead and the feeling was one of anticipation. It seemed like there were so many hours to fill and then suddenly, they were gone.

He reflected on the events of the day and replayed them all in his mind. Would Frances do the same? He knew she loved him, but he also knew all they had ahead were stolen moments. He thought back to Grant's admonition. "It's dangerous. Once you get away with something you're tempted to try it again. You get careless and then, you get caught."

Wales didn't concern him, but Wales could make Frances' life a living hell. Rob knew his heart was ruling his head. For the moment, he didn't care. They had been together for a little while and they would be careful again on the return trip. He heard the porter begin to call the stop for Ocala. It had only been a thirty-minute ride from McIntosh.

Rob got off the train with only a few passengers. They seemed to be businessmen and others who were probably returning home. The first order of business would be to find a room for the next two nights. He had no plans other than to kill Saturday and most of Sunday morning waiting for the return trip to Savannah.

Ocala was new to him, and he thought he might be able to learn something of interest. If not, it was not a problem. Having lived single all his life, he didn't need to be constantly entertained.

* * *

Frances knew this was probably the last time she would see her mother. Her thoughts were in conflict. As much as she resented the situation she had been thrust in by her parents, she still loved them. It was difficult to get out of her shoes and into theirs and what she would have done under their circumstances. Could she ever force Gracie into such a dilemma?

She made her way from room to room in the old house, touching and feeling. Many of the pieces of furniture were items passed down to her mother from her parents. Others were acquired in years when crops were good and money was available. Each seemed to have its own story.

She wondered about her brothers. What had they been like? If they had lived, would they be farming in the area like others that returned from the war? Now it would be just her, the twins, and her father. She knew his health, too, was failing and it wouldn't be long before he followed her mother. With her death, his reason for living would be gone. Already he was a beaten man, and had been since her marriage to Wales. All his pride and dignity as a man had been sapped.

And what about Rob? Would he be walking the streets of Ocala looking for something to fill the time? The question of "why" kept returning to her. Why her, and what if it had been different? She felt as if Rob was her lifeline. In the short time they had been reunited, she realized the degree to which she depended on him. Not so much in doing things, but for his opinion on decisions she needed to make. He was always there, only asking that she include him in what was going on in her life. She knew it was wrong, but also that she would never give him up. He was too important to her.

If things were different, if anything ever happened to Wales, she and Rob could be married and live out the dream that had been dashed before their love even bloomed. In that event, should she tell Gracie who her real father was?

And what if something should happen to Rob? Frances couldn't continue the process. It was not even possible to let her mind go there. She was unable to imagine going through the daily routine of life with no hope and no feeling. Only to awaken to grief and go to sleep with the ache of absence. She couldn't imagine being without him even though she didn't have him now. She only hoped when their time came, she would be the first to go.

The grandfather clock in the hall struck four and she mentally counted the hours before she and Rob would again have some quality time together. Less than a day to go, she thought.

Chapter 22

The New York Special was scheduled to leave Ocala at 1:45 in the afternoon. Rob was more than ready. He spent the better part of the last two days reading everything available at the hotel. He had walked the town and viewed the downtown area several times. Sunday morning had been quiet.

Rob strolled over to the station with his one bag at 1:00 p.m. As much as anything, he wanted a change of scenery, but he was also restless. In the back of his mind, he felt he needed the extra time to confirm his berth and be sure everything was in order. Again, he bought a magazine and planned to use the same ruse as before, if necessary.

Only a few people boarded the afternoon train. Rob recognized no one and assumed most passengers were on their way to Jacksonville or perhaps other large towns north of Savannah. He found his way to his compartment -- number six, in the car behind the dining car. Hopefully Frances would be riding a day coach not too far in front or behind.

As the train slowed into McIntosh, Rob looked out his window and around the curve into the covered waiting platform in front of the depot. Frances was there with her father. Good, he thought, everything is on schedule. As the train straightened, he lost sight of them. He mentally traded places with Frances, knowing she was aware of his presence on the train. This meant he just needed to wait for a few minutes after the train was comfortably away from the station. Then her ticket would be confirmed.

He could feel the slack being tightened in the cars as they slowly began to roll forward. After about ten minutes, he emerged from his compartment and made his way to the front. The dining car was only filled with strangers and he was relieved. Proceeding on, he entered the day coach. He recognized her hair immediately in a seat on the right toward the rear.

Since there were few others on the coach and no one seated behind her, he joined her in the seat. She turned and smiled and he handed her the magazine. A stub was protruding as before.

"Hi," she said. As she extracted the stub, she read silently, "one behind the dining car, No. 6."

"I hope your weekend was more exciting than mine," he said.

Frances laughed. "Friday was good."

"I can't argue," he said. "I love you," he mouthed silently.

"I love you, too," she silently replied.

Rob returned to his compartment anticipating her arrival. He removed his coat and began loosening his tie. Soon, there was a light feminine tap on the door. He cracked the door, and recognizing Frances, admitted her and closed and locked it behind them.

"Oh darling, I missed you. Were you okay in Ocala? I thought of you every minute. What did you find to do?"

"First things first," he said. He took her in his arms and kissed her passionately and deeply.

"That made my heart jump," she said.

"I missed you, too. Ocala was fine, but even fine can get stale quickly when your mind is somewhere else. How was your mother?"

"Failing. Trying to make amends and seeking redemption in the short time she has left. Her prognosis is a few more months."

"I'm sorry."

Frances paused. "Thank you. I suppose we must look at the options she has open to her. The preference we all have with a loved one is for them to remain in life and be healthy. In her case, she can't. I don't want her to linger this way. It's best she doesn't. She's had a good life, being married to the man she loves. She's had her share of tragedy, but it's from a family perspective and not her own heart." Frances paused. "Rob, have you thought about our situation?"

"Yes. It's practically consumed my thoughts this weekend."

"And?"

"I wish I had easy solutions. Do you think Wales would give you a divorce?"

"No. We've never discussed it, but I know his view on that type of thing. He would feel it to be a personal affront to his dignity. He would not permit it. He's not the type of man who would place himself in a position of ridicule by others. He would have no one talking behind his back."

Rob stood in front of Frances and his eyes locked with hers. He began unbuttoning her dress.

"I think better naked," he said.

She smiled, holding his eyes with hers. "Then obviously it's in our best interest for you to be in the state you're most astute in. She began unbuttoning his shirt.

* * *

They lay in the berth, entwined with each other. The sex had been good and they were still enthralled with each other's physical presence.

"What are you thinking?" she asked dreamily.

"I'm really not, I'm just consuming the moment."

"You know, when Wales and I have sex, he never talks. Why is it that we seem to have no problem communicating with each other, regardless of the setting we're in. I'm totally relaxed lying here with you without a stitch on and talking about anything that comes up. Do you feel that way, too?"

"Yes. Being with you has been better than thinking of being with you. I know that sounds obtuse, but it's something I believe many people go through. They anticipate a situation like this and what will be said and done but when they get to the actual event, they're disappointed."

"You mean their fantasy is better than the real thing?"

Rob's eyes were fixed on the ceiling. "Yes and no. The real thing is wonderful, it's just that when their mind is in the present, they're thinking about something else."

"What about you?" she asked.

"What about me? I guess that's what I'm trying to tell you, although I'm not doing a very good job of it. When I'm with you my thoughts are with you -- in the present, not drifting somewhere else."

"Rob, it's been a wonderful weekend, at least partially. When I leave this compartment, it'll be over for me. It's like going back to a prison cell. Do you think there will ever be an escape for me?"

"Something good has got to break for us. At least, thank God, I'll be able to see you tomorrow."

"Yes, and seeing but not touching will be torture. It's like checking a book out of the library and then having to return it to the shelf after a short period."

"If we continue to play this 'what-if' game it will drive us crazy. Just know I love you and want to be with you when we can. Until then, we'll do what we have to."

"I know. I guess knowing you want to see me, as much as I do you, helps some."

"In a way. I guess you better get ready to go back to your seat. Jacksonville is coming up."

Frances dressed and returned to the day coach -- the same routine as on the way down, only in reverse. The train stayed in station for about thirty minutes and then was again on its way north. She made her way back to Rob's compartment. Again she tapped lightly at the door.

Almost without hesitation, it swung inward. She knew he would be overly conscious of not making her wait in the corridor any longer than necessary.

"Hi," he said.

Frances brushed passed him with little acknowledgement. She sat on the day seat and removed her hat.

"You know," she said, "this is like having to sneak around to use things that belong to you. It's like having a sentry posted when you're using your silver and best china for a meal. Those are things that belong to you and are natural, and this is too. I hate this. It reduces us to the position of culprits, when we are actually the victims."

Suddenly the compartment became drab and confining. Although, she loved it for the privacy it offered, she hated it for not being what they were entitled to.

"I don't know what to say," said Rob, his voice raised an octave, "but I know how you feel. Even if things were different, I know I don't have the means to give you the things Wales has been able to."

Frances rose and came to stand in front of Rob.

"Happiness can never be measured in material things. They are only objects, don't you know that. Nice, it's true, but they aren't you and they aren't us. Do you have any idea how many nights I've cried myself to sleep and lain awake thinking about you? Thinking about us and what could have been. Against that, material things are just inanimate junk."

Rob only stared, not prepared to answer.

"Wales can give me things, but he can't be you."

Rob was silent.

"Why do you think I so deviously preyed upon you to have your child? Rob, don't denigrate what we have by thinking emotions and love can be replaced with wealth and comfort. I wanted you. I wanted your child. I settled for less. If we were together and had nothing, I would be the happiest girl in the world."

Rob opened his arms and Frances melted into them. They stood for a moment, holding each other as contentment rushed over them.

"Rob?"

Yes?"

Promise me that at this moment you don't want to be anywhere else or with anyone else.

"I promise."

"How far are we from your stop?" asked Frances.

"We're about 45 minutes from the Brunswick station.

"The time is running out of the hourglass, at least for now," said Frances. "Can we slow it down?" She looked intently at Rob and he nodded.

"At least for now," he said.

He took both her hands in his and kissed each one. With no other talk, he led her to the berth.

"Let me see your watch," she said.

Rob pulled his most treasured possession from his vest and handed it to her. She pressed the catch on the side and they watched as it sprung open. Both silently read the inscription.

She looked at him. "Do you still feel that way?"

"It's never left."

"I know, and it never will."

It was as if the two of them merged into one being. The intensity of their gaze seemed to go beyond the mere exchange of glances and into a reading of each other's soul. The lovemaking that followed was more an attesting to their feeling of oneness, than any sexual encounter.

They lay side by side, both afraid to speak, knowing it would break the cohesion of the moment. Finally Rob kissed her on the forehead and said, "It's probably time for you to go back to the coach."

"I know. Do you have long to wait for another train?"

"Only about an hour. It won't be bad."

"Do you think it was necessary to go to that extreme? I would think you could just wait to get off in Savannah after the platform has cleared. That shouldn't take long."

"Possibly, but we just don't know. This way we can be sure."

Frances finished dressing and turned to go.

"I miss you already. Please be careful."

He kissed her tenderly and lovingly as to leave no doubt that she carried his heart.

"Love you," he said.

"You too." She opened the door and stepped into the corridor. As the door closed behind her, he realized how empty a place can be when the one who filled it has gone.

Chapter 23

The casual observer of the meeting could tell immediately who was in charge and who was reporting to a superior. The little man sat in front of the large oak desk in the office of Wales Watson. He had a furtive look about him and only occasionally would meet Wales' eye. He held a derby on his lap with both hands.

"Now tell me exactly the way it happened," said Watson.

"Yes, sir."

The wood oil smell of furniture polish permeated the air in the office. It was definitely a man's room with hunting prints, leather furniture, and Oriental rugs covering the floor.

"I boarded in Savannah with Mrs. Watson and took care to sit unnoticed in the same car. When we got about five miles out of the city, a man came through and made the pretense of giving her a magazine to read. A few minutes later, she left her seat and went toward the rear of the train. I followed. She went back to the car with the private berths and was admitted. Other than coming back to her seat briefly in Jacksonville, she stayed in the compartment until right before her stop."

"Who occupied the compartment?"

"After she got off at McIntosh, I stayed on the train until the man in the compartment left at Ocala, one stop away. He checked into a hotel about a block from the station and I also booked a room."

"What name did he use?"

"According to the register, he signed in as Rob Truitt from Savannah."

Wales lit a cigar. The action interrupted the conversation for a moment. The little man hesitated accordingly.

"Go on," said Wales.

"The gentleman stayed around the hotel on Saturday, only going out for short walks and taking his meals in the restaurant in the hotel. It was like he was filling up spare time and just waiting. This same behavior also continued on into Sunday until about 1:00 in the afternoon. That's when he went back to the station."

"Did he see you? Was he suspicious?"

"No sir, I'm sure of that.

"Then he was unaware he was being followed?"

"Mr. Watson, I've been doing this type of work too long to be detected at it. He was not suspicious. He boarded the New York Special and I got on after him. I purchased a ticket from the conductor."

"Did Mrs. Watson catch the same train?"

"Yes sir, but not until it reached McIntosh. She again boarded the day coach and a few minutes later, the same man came and this time sat next to her and handed her a magazine."

Wales motioned with his cigar for him to continue.

"They laughed at some private joke and then he left. After a few minutes, she got up and went in his same direction. I followed, and again she went to the private compartments, one car behind the dining car. She tapped on one of the doors and was admitted."

"He must have stayed on the train in Savannah until we were gone."

"No sir, he actually got off at Brunswick and caught a later train. Obviously, he was being very careful."

Wales noted the man said "he" and not "they". It was a diplomatic way of phrasing it. "Mr. Joseph, I appreciate your service. As I mentioned when I retained you, I didn't want someone from Savannah because of the possible gossip. You have a reputation in Charleston as being someone who is discreet. It's also said that extends to not discussing your client's affairs with others."

"Thank you sir. I was glad to be of service."

"What are your charges?"

Joseph opened his inside coat pocket and presented a tri-folded paper to Wales who took it, looked at it briefly, and nodded.

"Very fair, quite reasonable," he commented. Wales rose and went to the small safe in his office. After a few practiced spins of the dial, the door opened. He came back to his desk, counted out some bills, and then looked at Joseph.

"There's some extra here for your continuing discretion." He made sure he looked Joseph in the eye as his said it so there would be not doubt as to the veiled threat.

"Yes sir, I understand."

The little man rose, thanked Watson again, and exited the room.

As the door closed, Wales sat again in his chair to mull over what he had learned. He wasn't surprised, just disappointed. His fears confirmed. Soon after moving to Savannah, he began to suspect something amiss in his relationship with Frances. First of all, she had been too eager to move. That was unlike her. Although he was aware she had relatives in the town, she usually liked to stay in one place after she was settled. Even with the earthquake, she seemed somewhat out of character in demanding the move.

Another thing that had bothered him for sometime was that just before their marriage, she made a hurried trip back to Savannah. That had been surprising since she had only returned from Savannah a short time before. He had been unable to guess the purpose previously but thinking about it again with his new information, he approached the question differently. Sometimes it's best to make assumptions and see if the events fit. Assuming she was involved with someone in Savannah, she would have felt the need for a formal good-bye.

When she returned to Florida, it was with a necklace that was much too expensive to have been handed down by her parents. It had "special" written all over it. Plus, the idea of going to work was something that had never driven her before. She was too happy now that she was working and that wasn't quite right, either. It occurred to him that she seldom talked about her job and the little irritations one encounters during a normal day.

Now, with all his suspicions confirmed, he was beginning to wonder about Gracie. She had been born a few weeks early according to Dr. Strange, but had she? A few weeks early from the time of their marriage, but perhaps right on schedule for an earlier interlude. Which was it, and did it really matter? Wales sighed. He had wanted a wife and child and he had them. Maybe his method was not a traditional one either, but now they were his and no one would know any different. "That's why this entire affair must be severed immediately," he said to himself. Frances would have to be confronted.

* * *

"Good morning," said Frances as Rob came into the office Monday.

"Good morning, Mrs. Watson." There was a lilt to his voice. I trust you had a good weekend?"

"Very nice, Mr. Truitt. I visited my mother in Florida and had a most fulfilling trip. Rob?"

"Yes?"

"We've got to do something."

"Well, it seems we have some private time. Why don't you come into my office."

Rob walked into his office. There were no others in this section of the bank this early in the day. Frances followed. He turned and embraced her tightly.

"Darling, it's good to see you. How could one evening without you be so long?"

"I know," she said, squeezing his hand. "I'm going to speak with Wales. Maybe I was wrong about his reaction. I wouldn't think he would want to go on living in a loveless marriage either. And after all, I feel like I've paid my dues. I've been with him almost seven years."

Rob sat behind his desk and nodded. "It's something I can't help you with."

"I know, but I'll feel like you're there."

* * *

Wales had been out to a business function on Monday and was not back until later. Frances didn't feel the time was right to bring up a matter that was certain to lead to bitter words. It was now Tuesday evening. Dinner was over and Wales had put Gracie to bed. Frances was busying herself with little nothings and turning over in her mind how she would broach the subject. No time was a good time but this might be the best. Should she try it logically or from an emotional standpoint, which would work best?

"Wales?"

"Yes?"

"Could we talk about something?"

Wales had just settled in his favorite chair and was sorting the newspaper he had just begun to read. He looked up and glanced at Frances.

"Of course."

Frances settled in a chair across the room. "Wales, I'm not happy and I think you know it," she began.

He only looked at her.

"There is more that I want out of life than just comfort," she said.

Wales folded his paper and put it aside. "What more do you think there is, Frances?"

She hesitated, trying to choose her words with care. "I want to feel alive. I want to feel emotion. I want to feel -- that I am my own person and not just Mrs. Wales Watson."

"What person do you see yourself being?"

"It's hard to explain." She arose from her chair and began to pace. Suddenly she blurted, "Wales, I want a divorce."

The statement hung in the air like a shroud.

After a few moments, he responded. "Is there someone else you're interested in?"

"No. It's just that I want to explore a life of my own and see if I can find self-esteem outside of being your wife."

Frances thought the conversation was going well and that Wales was accepting her stance on why she needed freedom.

"What about Gracie," he asked. "Where would she be left by all of this?"

Fortunately, she had anticipated the question. She played the card she thought would be the obvious. "Gracie is my daughter. At her age she needs her mother. She would go with me."

"Gracie is also my daughter. She needs a father as well as a mother. Maybe you've not considered my feelings in all this."

"I would expect you to see Gracie as much as possible. I realize the strong bond between the two of you."

"Maybe you have in mind that Gracie could also be adopted by someone else you could meet?"

Frances turned away from him as she answered. "Wales, I told you, there is no one else."

He got up from his chair, and walked over to the fire. He stoked it a few times with the poker leaning against the hearth.

"Not even your Mr. Truitt, with whom you work on a daily basis?"

She strode to him. "What are you saying? Rob Truitt and I only have a business relationship with each other. I have the utmost respect for him."

"What I'm saying is that your feelings and your relationship with Rob Truitt seem to go far beyond respect. I believe you and Rob are 'involved' and have been for a good while. If you are thinking of divorce, and taking Gracie, think about this." Wales raised his voice. "I won't agree to a divorce, and if you want to fight it I will prove in court that you're an unfit mother."

Frances was stunned. "I've never done a thing to harm Gracie. She has always come first and you know it. You know what she means to me."

"Then consider this. Consider how it will sound to a jury that Gracie's mother, and one Rob Truitt, vice president of a local bank, consorted together on a train from Savannah to Florida and back again."

The room was silent. There was no response. Frances went numb. She was speechless. He had me followed and watched, she thought, dumbfounded. By whom?

"You are concocting a wild story that just doesn't exist, Wales."

"Give it up. I have someone who will testify in court that you and Rob spent several hours in his compartment, each way, on your recent trip to Florida. The man is a professional investigator and very believable."

"You had us followed?" She was livid.

Wales was aware of the use of "us" by Frances although she herself was not.

"I began to have my suspicions and knew the two of you may be looking for an opportunity. So you used your mother's poor condition as the cover to go on a lark with Truitt."

"You bastard!" she screamed.

178

"In your opinion, maybe, but let me add this. If you are so determined to pursue a divorce--fine. But based on your actions, attested to by my investigator, I will be awarded custody of Gracie. Then, you will be the one who needs my permission for visitation privileges."

Frances suddenly saw red as the futility of it all came thundering in. This man who had stolen her life was now threatening to take her child. She lunged at him with arms flailing. Wales blocked her blows and in turn struck her with his open hand on the side of her face.

"Damn you," she screamed and slumped to the floor, sobbing. He stood over her with his hands clasped.

"Perhaps you and your Mr. Truitt, for whom you profess so much respect, had better talk again about your future. There *is* a trade-off, you know."

Wales left the room for the bedroom, retiring for the night. Frances remained on the floor, unmoving, for a long while. She felt like a cornered animal. She had run out of options. How could this have happened? With resignation, she pushed herself from the floor and moved to the sofa. There, she took stock of her situation. She now knew he was aware of her feelings for Rob. He also knew she was unhappy. Even if she was successful in leaving, he would keep Gracie. She would have to stay with him in a marriage where the only feelings were mistrust and resentment on her part, combined with possession and control on his. She lay on the sofa, pulled a comforter over her, and quietly wept.

Chapter 24

The following morning, Frances sent word to the bank, by one of the hotel porters, that she was ill and would not be coming in. When Rob received the news, his mind began racing with what-ifs. Although, it was only a short walk across Johnson Square to the hotel, to him it seemed like a chasm.

Frances never missed a day of work. She was never sick. Was it something with Gracie he wondered? Or, more likely, was it the aftermath of her talk with Wales? Did it go wrong? Was there a bad scene? Not knowing was killing him.

The only immediate outlet was to ventilate and that only meant one person - - Grant. Rob stopped by his office during lunch to see if they could meet for a beer after work. Grant was out but Rob left word. Grant should meet him at Houlihan's at 5:30, if possible.

For the remainder of the day, Rob accomplished little in the manner of business. He met with an architect, reviewing a cost estimate for a building to be erected on Gwinnett Street near Forsyth Park. The city was bursting forth with new construction and a feeling of prosperity was in the air. Today, Rob was no longer concerned with prosperity. He couldn't concentrate and watched the clock until the city exchange bell chimed the hour at 5:00.

He arrived at Houlihan's at 5:15 and took a seat at the end of the rectangular bar facing the door. He ordered two beers, one for himself and another for Grant to hold the seat. If he didn't show up he could always drink it himself. The afternoon crowd was beginning to drift in.

Rob continued to turn the "what-ifs" over in his mind. Was Frances actually sick and nothing more? Did she and Wales argue and because of it, she was emotionally distraught? He felt totally on the outside, attempting to peer in.

Grant's face appeared outside the window approaching the door. It was like taking an elixir, knowing the malady was already better because someone with a sympathetic ear was there to listen. He motioned to Grant as he saw him enter the room.

"Hey old man," said Grant smiling as he approached. "Is that for me?" He pointed to the beer beside Rob.

"It's yours; I ordered an extra, hoping you could come. Sit down."

"Well, tell me about your weekend rendezvous," said Grant.

"The weekend was perfect. Everything we hoped it would be -- just too short."

"No problems or close calls with being detected?"

"No, but I'm concerned. Frances didn't come in today and I can't figure out what's wrong. We talked yesterday about what we could do and she was planning to talk with Wales last night. She was going to ask him for a divorce."

"Oh god," said Grant looking into his beer, "I can see where this is heading."

"Well, she's been with him for seven years. By now you would think she's paid whatever debt her father owed."

"Look. It's like I told you before, you are playing with fire. I understand how you feel and I think what he did was unconscionable, but right now he's holding all the cards."

"Grant, the whole situation is just eating me up," said Rob. "What would you do?"

Grant took a sip of beer and thought. "I would leave it alone. I would go and try to build a life around someone else, if you feel you've got to have somebody. Look, women are everywhere. If one doesn't work out, another will be along soon."

"Oh thank you for that wonderful piece of advice," said Rob sarcastically. "Why didn't I think of that? It was so simple and right in front of me all along."

Grant paused and said more seriously. "What works for one doesn't always work for another. You will probably find out it's nothing with Frances. Maybe she's out of kilter today. It's probably only a coincidence that it's the day after she was going to talk to Wales."

Rob sighed. He looked at his friend. "I hope so. We'll know tomorrow."

* * *

Rob arrived at the bank Thursday morning about fifteen minutes ahead of his normal time, hoping to be there when Frances came in.

He was sitting at his desk when he heard the door to the department open. He got up and looked outside his office. She was busy putting away her purse and jacket, avoiding his gaze and not acknowledging him.

"Good morning," said Rob. "Are you okay?"

"Good morning." She still didn't meet his eyes.

Finally, she turned to speak and when she did she broke down.

"What's wrong?"

She continued to sob.

"Come into my office," he said.

Frances followed and sat in the chair by his desk. Rob hesitated for a moment so he would be fully focused in going forward in this conversation.

"It didn't go well," she blurted out. "He suspects us and said he wouldn't give me a divorce. If I still pursue it, and am successful, he will demand custody of Gracie based on my being an unfit mother."

"He's bluffing. He has no grounds for that argument."

Frances composed herself. "He had us followed the entire weekend. Down to Florida and back. He hired a professional investigator who is willing to testify we were together for several hours each way on separate days in your compartment. He would use that testimony against me to keep Gracie if necessary."

"Damn him!"

"It got violent. When he told me that, all the pent up resentment and anger I've held came surging forth. I lunged at him, trying to hit him. He grabbed me and struck me in the head in return."

"He hit you? The son-of-a-bitch. I ought to kill him." Rob could feel his blood beginning to boil. He realized he had underestimated Wales. He was dealing with a formidable foe that would do anything necessary to win. After all, hadn't he proved the lengths he would go in the situation with Frances and her father?

"He says he has proof and a witness?" repeated Rob.

"Yes."

Rob only stared and clenched his fists.

"There's something else," said Frances.

"Yes?"

"He's brought up the subject of Gracie and the whole pregnancy."

"Oh god."

"Yes. He accosted me with it Tuesday evening. He claims he's always suspected because of her coming before her time. He also said he knew there was something between us by the way we acted in each other's presence while he's around."

"I'll speak to Wales," said Rob grimly, "Now."

"I don't think that's a good idea."

"It's probably something I should have done early on. If I had followed my heart at the outset, none of the last seven years of hell we've been through would have occurred.

"Oh Rob, let it go."

"Not this time. At the least we'll have an understanding. We may as well head this thing off rather than have it fester."

"Do you think that wise?"

"I think it's necessary."

* * *

With determination, Rob walked across Johnson Square to the Pulaski Hotel. It was with single-minded purpose, and he was barely aware of those he passed in the park. He knew he had to control his temper but at the same time he wanted to wreak havoc on this person who would strike a woman, especially the one so dear to him. He was not sure what he would say to Watson. That would come when he saw him. Dammit, the time had come for a reckoning.

He strode into the lobby and surveyed the guests and staff. Not seeing Wales, he quickly mounted the stairs to the second floor where the business offices were located. As he entered the anteroom, Watson's secretary confronted him.

"May I help you?" she said with a challenging tone.

"I'd like to see Mr. Watson," said Rob.

"Mr. Watson is busy in a conference at the moment. Do you have an appointment?" she asked almost accusingly.

"No, but please inform Mr. Watson that Rob Truitt would like a minute of his time." He presented the truculent woman with his card.

She took it, eyed the card with disdain, and proceeded to the office door. She tapped lightly and entered. He overheard the exchange.

"Mr. Watson, excuse me, but this man is wanting to see you. He's quite insistent."

She presented the card to Wales. He looked at it briefly. Sitting across the desk was his friend and business associate, Richard Powers. Powers was the man who had encouraged Watson to come from Charleston to purchase the Pulaski with him. He now looked inquisitively as Watson studied the card.

"Would you like me to excuse myself?" asked Powers. "I can come back later."

Watson gestured toward him with the card. "No, why don't you stay. I may want you present as a witness." He then said to his secretary, "Ask the gentleman to come in."

The secretary returned to Rob in the outer office and said "you may go in." She was obviously in a huff that her authority over Mr. Watson's schedule had been overridden, especially by one she had developed such an aversion to.

Rob entered the room and was met with the inquiring stares of both Watson and his partner. Neither offered their hand nor asked Rob to sit down. Powers was known in the sporting circles in town. He owned a few racehorses that competed successfully at the Thunderbolt harness track. One was the local champion. He and Rob knew each other as business acquaintances, but Powers felt the tension in the room and kept his position in his chair as a silent observer.

"What can I do for you, Truitt?" asked Watson coldly. He had a condescending tone and a contemptuous expression on his face."

"I would like to speak with you in private about your wife, Watson."

"Powers is my partner. I have no secrets from him. Anything you would like to say to me you can say in front of him."

"Very well. Frances has informed me that you are of the opinion that there is something between her and myself that is more than a working relationship. She said you have accused her of things unbecoming a wife and a lady. Is that true?"

185

Wales replied with a steely even voice. "What is between my wife and myself is something that is our affair and none of your damn business, sir. In fact, there were no problems in our relationship or marriage until she began to work for you only a short time ago."

Powers shifted uncomfortably. He saw the conversation was escalating and becoming quickly out of control.

"Gentlemen, I don't think this is the place or type forum for a discussion of this nature," he said in a placating manner. Neither Rob nor Wales paid the slightest attention to him. They were locked on each other.

"Frances working with me has nothing to do with the problems she has with you. Those began long ago when you took advantage of a situation that had thrown a family into desperate straits."

"Interesting you know so much about my personal business. You could only know from one source, and how would you know if there was not more to the two of you than you pretend? What I ought to do is take you outside and swat you with my cane, you scoundrel."

"I don't think so," said Rob regaining his composure. "I think what's more in your style is abusing those you have no problem dominating physically -- like women."

Watson stood up behind his desk and walked around in front of Rob. Powers rose from his chair.

"Gentlemen please," Powers pleaded.

"And let me tell you this, you sniveling coward," said Rob. "If you ever lay a hand on her again I will personally emasculate you."

"You bastard," screamed Watson, lunging forward with a roundhouse right. Rob easily parried the punch and buried a right fist in Watson's solar plexus. He doubled forward from the blow, the wind knocked out of him. Rob automatically followed the punch with a chop to the back of Watson's neck. This sprawled him completely on the floor. Rob's adrenaline was now flowing feverishly. "Get up dammit, get up."

Watson didn't move. At that point, Rob exchanged looks with Powers, who stood silently and in shock. The bossy secretary had also re-entered the room, and now looked at him with terror. She acted like she had seen the devil incarnate. Rob turned and stormed out of the office.

He didn't want to go back to the bank, he was in too black a mood, but he had to let Frances know what was happening. He entered his office, still riled. Immediately, Frances knew something was wrong.

"What happened?" she asked testily.

"We fought. We actually came to blows, or at least I did."

"What do you mean?"

"He swung at me and I hit him. It was ugly. His partner Powers was there, as well as his secretary."

"Is he hurt?"

"Only his pride. The way I feel, he's lucky he's not."

Frances started pacing back and forth in the office. Her own adrenaline was beginning to flow. "What started it?"

"He accused us of having a relationship and I called him a coward. Then I told him he better never lay a hand on you again. At that point he lunged at me with a wild swing."

"You've embarrassed him in front of others. That's not good. That means he's lost face. That's even worse. I've seen it happen before. He will stop at nothing to even the score. It bothers me. It bothers me greatly."

"I don't think he'll come after me and I don't think he will hit you again either. Rather, I believe he will go lick his wounds and get his mind on something else."

"I hope you're right, Rob. I just have a bad feeling about this."

Chapter 25

Powers tried to help Watson get up from the floor. Apparently, he was not injured, except for his pride and a splitting headache from the blow to his neck. Watson shook off his assistance and pulled himself up by the edge of his desk.

"Give us a minute," he said to his secretary.

She backed quickly out of the office and Wales retook his seat behind his desk. Slowly, he massaged his neck.

"Since Frances went to work with that rascal at the bank, there's been nothing but friction. I've had a bad feeling about this all along. But I'll tell you one thing, he's not getting away with it. That's the reason I wanted you to be present."

Powers seemed to be deep in thought for a moment. He began pacing back and forth in the office. "Wales, I think the best thing to do is to let this go. Ask Frances to give up her job at the bank. Your request would certainly be justified after this incident."

"No! I'm not going to let that intruder come into my office without an appointment and humiliate me. I won't stand for it. He's not heard the last of it."

"What do you plan to do?"

Watson thought for a long moment then looked at Powers.

"I'm going to challenge him."

Powers was stunned. He came and stood in front of the desk across from Wales. "Have you gone crazy? This incident is nowhere near grave enough to elicit that magnitude of response. Besides, the Code Duello hasn't been sanctioned in polite society in Savannah in fifteen years."

"In my opinion, it's warranted. I'm not having word get out to the community that someone can push Wales Watson without consequences. And I'm not going to have him think there will be no reprisals for his actions."

Powers stood erect. "Wales, there's something you need to know."

"What?"

189

"That man, Rob Truitt, has a well earned reputation as someone you don't want opposite you when it comes to almost any type of physical violence. You've just had a first hand look at how he handles himself with his fists."

"That's not what I had in mind."

"I know, but what you don't, is that he is just as skilled, if not more so, with a pistol. In fact, he's one of the most naturally gifted marksmen I've ever seen."

"You've seen him shoot?"

"Once, at the gun club. It was simply astonishing. The man never practices and has no interest in joining the gun club. But I'll tell you one thing Wales -- he's deadly."

"Just the same, I will get satisfaction. You may be surprised; possibly there are some tricks I know that he doesn't."

"Wales, there hasn't been anyone killed in a duel in Savannah since 1870. The anti-dueling society has successfully squelched that endeavor in the last nineteen years."

"As I see it, it's the only avenue open. I want you to be my second."

"Wales -- . Powers began to pace again.

"Will you be my second?" he insisted.

"Yes, dammit, but you need to know this isn't a game. Either or both of you can be seriously wounded or even be killed."

"I'm aware of that. Now wait while I write something."

Wales took out his personal notepaper and began hastily scribbling.

Mr. Truitt:

In the events that transpired today in my office, you humiliated me before my associate and staff. In response to your loutish behavior and insult to my person, I demand satisfaction.

I request you meet me on the field of honor at a place and time mutually agreed to by our seconds.

Your formal apology will not be accepted.

Sincerely,
Wales Watson

Wales handed the paper to Powers. Now here, deliver this.

"I hope you're aware of the gravity of what you're doing," Powers warned.

"Just deliver it, Richard."

* * *

The knock at the door was not heavy but it was insistent. It was about 6:30 in the evening. There was a light fog in the air. Rob was reading the afternoon paper. As he opened the door he immediately recognized a nervous Richard Powers.

"Hello Richard, how are you?" said Rob.

"I'm fine Rob, fine, thank you." Powers looked down. "I'm afraid I'm here on some unpleasant business having to do with today's incident. I wish I could head it off."

"Won't you come in?"

"No, thank you, but no." Powers fidgeted with his hat that he held by both hands in front of him. I'm really here only to deliver this from my partner, Wales." He offered the note to Rob.

Rob unfolded the paper and quickly absorbed its contents. He looked back at Powers.

"The fool. What an utter fool. Very well, let me appoint a second and he will be in touch with you."

"I'm sorry, Rob."

"Yes, me too."

* * *

Grant opened the door with an inquisitive look on his face.

"What's up?" he asked.

"I need to talk with you. Are you alone?"

"Yes, come on in."

Rob entered Grant's apartment and noticed the periodicals and books that were strewn about the room. Obviously, he was in the middle of another story. He handed Grant the note and gave him a few moments to review the message.

"What's happened? Which 'events' would he be referring to?"

"You remember how concerned I was with Frances being out yesterday? Well, this morning she came in and told me she and Wales had a hard discussion when she approached him for a divorce. Quickly it grew to a bitter argument and finally ended with him striking her to the floor. That's why she missed work yesterday."

"Damn him."

"When she told me, I just saw red. I went over to talk to him, not really knowing what I would say. I just wanted to tell him to lay off. His partner, Richard Powers, was in his office with him."

"Powers is okay, just a lightweight."

"I know. Anyway, the exchange became heated. I told Watson if he struck Frances again it would be at his own peril.

"And?"

"He said he should take me out and teach me a lesson."

"Uh oh, big mistake."

I told him his style was more in striking women and that he was a cowardly bastard."

"I'll bet that got his attention."

"Right. Enough so that he tried to catch me with a roundhouse right."

"Did he?"

"No. You could see it coming all the way from River Street. I stepped aside and buckled him in the stomach and then chopped him to the floor."

"Good lord -- and now this?"

"Apparently. Powers delivered that a few minutes ago. I've got to respond, Grant. I want you with me as my second."

"Jesus, this is getting out of control. Let's defuse this thing now."

"There's no way. I'm damn sure not giving an apology-- and at this point I'm not accepting one, either."

Grant nodded. "Okay, you know where my loyalty lies. But let's be ready, I don't trust this man. If we're going to abide by the code, let's go on strict adherence to it. I'll write the response."

Grant went to his desk and extracted a clean sheet of his personal stationery and began composing.

Mr. Richard Powers
Acting Second for Mr. Wales Watson

Dear Mr. Powers,

Mr. Truitt, having been duly challenged by Mr. Wales Watson, has asked me to act in the capacity of his second, as you are doing for Mr. Watson.

Mr. Watson has stated that no apologies will be accepted. Mr. Truitt advises that none will be forthcoming and neither accepted by him at this point.

Our choice of location is the bluff at Bonaventure Cemetery near the Mongin-Stoddard vault. The time will be at sunrise on this coming Saturday morning. Choice of weapons will be yours. The first choice of place or count will be decided by coin toss at the meeting.

Your obedient servant,

Grant Dawson
Acting Second for Mr. Rob Truitt

"I'll deliver this tonight to his suite," said Grant.

"How familiar are you with the precepts of the "Code"?" asked Rob.

"Somewhat rusty, although I have a copy of the Code of Honor here in my library somewhere. I'll have to brush up on it."

"I seem to remember you were challenged yourself right after the war."

"Yes, it seems I wrote a short parody about life in Savannah for the Morning News. I thought the characters were well disguised, but one I apparently didn't disguise as well as the others."

"Didn't the event take place by old Fort Wayne, the dueling ground?"

"Right. "The man was true to character and such a fool that he made himself a greater laughing stock by such ridiculous behavior. But you know Rob, today I have a lot more respect for that man. Not in terms of his demeanor because he's still a fool, but because of his courage."

"Challenging someone to a duel is a gutsy call, no doubt about it," said Rob.

"He proved to be a formidable adversary. He missed on the first shot and I hit him in the thigh. I asked if he would like to try another and he said yes, if he could get to his feet."

"What happened?"

At that point the seconds intervened and decided the dispute was finished and the encounter was over."

"Well, since you've had first-hand experience, you should be comfortable being a second."

Grant nodded seriously. "I'll take care of it. Just remember though, according to the Code, from this point forward, you and Watson are out of it. All decisions and arrangements will be made by Powers and myself."

"What do you think he will choose as weapons?"

"I would imagine rifles. That will give him a better chance against you rather than with a pistol. Powers has no doubt told him of your prowess with firearms. A rifle will give him more distance and more time to aim for a surer shot."

"I would tend to agree. At any rate, he can choose and supply the weapons."

"Who do you want as an attending surgeon?"

Rob thought for only a moment. "Ask Dr. Elliott. You know, the one who married Fanny, Frances' cousin. He seems like a decent sort and probably is still young enough that he won't mind getting up early for a little sport."

Grant folded the note and inserted it into an envelope. As he turned to the door he came to face Rob and grasped his upper arms. He knew this would be one of the few moments presented for gravity. "Are you okay with this Rob?"

"Yes, I feel we have crossed the Rubicon. Let's proceed."

LITTLE GRACIE

Chapter 26

Like his partner Watson, Powers resided at the hotel in a small suite of rooms. It worked out well for him as a bachelor, since he could avail himself of both room service and laundry facilities at the hotel. Another advantage was that he could take his meals whenever he wished.

He was settling in for a late dinner when he heard the light rap at the door. Not expecting anyone at this late hour, he slid back the peephole and looked through as a precaution.

Standing on the other side was Grant Dawson. Powers knew immediately the nature of the call and it filled him with dread. He knew of the closeness between Grant and Rob, and knew they had been friends since the war. The whole idea of being on the other side of any violence involving the two of them caused him to shake.

Grant had the feline quickness of a cat and would have no scruples about defending himself or his friends in any manner he deemed necessary. Powers knew he would be loyal to Truitt regardless of the circumstances of what precipitated the encounter. "Damn, damn, damn," he muttered under his breath. Slowly he opened the door.

"Richard?" Grant said with inquisitive inflection and a hint of a smile behind his vacuous gray eyes.

"Hello, Grant. Are you here why I think?"

"I'm here in the capacity of second to Mr. Rob Truitt, representing him in what looks to be an unavoidable appointment."

"Please come in, Grant."

Powers opened the door to his suite and Grant entered as invited.

"Could I offer you a cordial. Maybe some port or sherry?"

"Thank you, but no. I think it best we conduct the business of our principals and leave civilities to another time. In fact, I'm sure you're aware as seconds we have the responsibility of guaranteeing proper conduct of our principals and if something goes awry, we're charged by the Code to seek retribution for our principal. I would regret drinking your wine then be forced to dispatch you a few days later. It would be bad manners."

Powers caught the veiled threat, but knew Grant was absolutely right. As seconds they would both be standing with loaded pistols, as would their principals. If someone violated the Code of Honor, it was incumbent upon his second to extract retribution in his behalf. If the other second opposed him when he was in his right, he was expected to post the other second as co-conspirator and coward.

"Let's hope it won't come to that," said Powers.

"Let's, but who would have thought it would come to this? I'll tell you Richard, I don't have a good feeling about this. It's only a gut feeling, but I feel this is setting off a chain of events that only begins with this. What we have is a continuing agitation in the cauldron that Watson has been stirring. I hope he stands ready to pick up the bill for the consequences."

"I only hope you are wrong, Grant. What have you got for me?"

Grant put his note in Powers' outstretched hand. It only took a moment for Richard to digest the message.

"Very well. Let me confer with Wales on weapons and you can expect a response without undue delay."

"We'll be waiting." Grant turned and left the suite without further conversation.

* * *

The following morning was Friday and Wales found a message on his desk from Powers.

Wales –

Please meet me for coffee in my office at 9:00 a.m. There are certain arrangements we need to discuss.

Richard

It was currently about eight o'clock, and Wales decided he would use the time to catch up on pending invoices and other hotel correspondence. He had neglected to mention anything to Frances about the quarrel or upcoming clash with Truitt. She will find out soon enough, he thought.

At five minutes to 9:00 he walked over to Richard's office, across the hall from his own. Powers was seated behind his desk drinking coffee from a cup and saucer with the Pulaski House colors and logo.

"Good morning, Wales. The pot of coffee was just delivered up from the kitchen. Help yourself."

Wales poured a cup of coffee and settled in a chair across from Richard. "Where do we stand?"

"I delivered your challenge to Truitt right after work yesterday afternoon. He didn't have much reaction to it other than to say we would hear from him."

"Is that all?"

"No. Later in the evening I was called on by Grant Dawson, who will serve as his second. They've set the time as Saturday at sunrise, on the bluff at Bonaventure. The choice of weapons is ours. That's what we need to discuss."

Wales took a sip of his coffee. He crossed his legs to make himself more comfortable. "You say this Truitt is a crack shot?"

"Yes."

"Well, for what I have in mind, I choose pistols, at close range."

Richard registered surprise. "Why? I would think to level the playing field you would be more inclined to go with rifles. Then you would have more time to ready yourself and line up your shot."

"Do you still have those French dueling pistols in your collection?"

"Yes, they're Henry Lapage models. They're also in mint condition and have only been fired a few times."

"What is the caliber?"

"Forty-fours. Why?"

"And the barrel length?"

"Ten and a half."

"Perfect."

"What do you have in mind, Wales?"

"Just working on a plan. Inform Dawson we agree to the time and place and we choose pistols which we will furnish."

"Isn't there anyway to settle this otherwise?"

"No. At this point it's gone too far. Somehow word has leaked out to the town. It's best to go ahead and get it over."

Powers shook his head. "I'll inform Mr. Dawson."

* * *

Frances arrived at work the usual time on Friday, still concerned about the infraction between Wales and Rob. Wales had purposely worked late last evening to avoid her and when he arrived home, he did little to encourage conversation. This was fine with Frances, since she had little she wished to say to him. She just didn't know what to do.

Rob came in a few minutes after her and she could tell by his expression there were things that happened of which she was unaware.

"I guess Wales told you what is going on," he said. As he looked at her he noticed she was wearing the black pearl pendant. Was she trying to make a statement?

"Wales and I have not spoken two words since our 'discussion' the other night. What has happened?"

"He's challenged me to a duel, the fool. He feels I've shamed him in front of his partner and staff and he demands satisfaction."

Frances just looked at him incredulously. The ramifications of what he said were too much for her to absorb.

"What?" she said incredulously. "When?"

"Tomorrow morning at sunrise. On the bluff at Bonaventure. His partner, Powers, is acting as his second and I've asked Grant to act as mine."

"Rob, this is insanity. You could be killed. You could both be killed. If anything happens to Wales, Gracie has no father. If anything happens to you, I have no life. Don't do this."

Rob replied with level voice. "I have no choice in the matter. By rule of honor, I can't back out now and be deemed a coward. I won't do it."

"And what about me and how I feel? Doesn't that matter to you?"

He rose from his chair and went over and closed the door to his office. He came back to Frances and for once he didn't care about the consequences. They seemed to melt toward each other and were soon entwined in each other's arms. He kissed her deeply and tenderly.

"Darling, you're all that matters to me, but you must realize, this is something I can't back away from. The option isn't mine."

"Then I'm going back to the hotel and speak to Wales. I'll call this insanity off. These are no longer primitive times. No one settles personal disputes with guns any longer. This is crazy."

* * *

Grant was just finishing with a client when his secretary came in to announce Mr. Richard Powers had requested to see him. Grant replied without hesitation, "Please show him in." She returned with Powers trailing.

"Good morning, Richard. You have come to tell me this nonsense has been called off, I trust?"

"I wish it were so, Grant. Actually, I've come to respond on the choice of weapons."

"Very well."

"We choose pistols, at five paces."

"Five paces, you can't be serious."

"Unfortunately, we are. I have a French dueling set in my collection. Smooth bore, 44 caliber, cap and ball. Are you familiar with the loading of those?"

"Yes, we learned in the war. Actually, I may leave the loading to you and just observe since we'll have first choice."

"Of course. Well, it seems that completes our business. Oh, I haven't mentioned our selection of a surgeon -- Dr. Read, from Brampton Plantation has agreed to serve. He's become the family doctor and friend to the Watsons since they've been in town."

"Then we'll see you at sunrise, about 6:30 I believe."

"Yes."

"We'll meet on the bluff. If there is any change, you can find me here the remainder of the day."

"Likewise, I can be reached at the hotel. Good day sir." Powers turned and left the office.

201

* * *

Frances went directly to Wales' office. His secretary, Mrs. Holder, said he in was in a meeting but should not be long. Frances asked that she inform Mr. Watson she would be in their suite and would like to see him. All the while she had the feeling the secretary was somewhat condescending. She went to their apartment.

After about ten minutes, Wales entered and announced brusquely, "Mrs. Holder said you wished to see me."

"Yes. Rob told me at work this morning what you've been up to. Why couldn't you at least tell me so I wouldn't have to walk into that situation unawares?"

"I felt you've already made a good enough mess of affairs and would find things out eventually anyway."

"Listen Wales, I'm your wife. I think you at least owe me the courtesy of telling me what everyone else in town seems to know."

Wales seemed to acknowledge the omission of his actions. "You're right; I apologize."

"You've got to call this ridiculous duel off. Do you think it's romantic and you're avenging your precious honor? Don't you know this isn't play. You can get killed doing this?"

Wales pulled a handkerchief from his coat pocket and wiped his forehead. Replacing the handkerchief, he took a deep breath.

"That man shamed me in front of my partner and secretary. I'm not letting anyone do that. It has nothing to do with what's between the two of you. For him to parade into my office and tell me about my personal business -- I won't have it."

"And what if something happens to you and Gracie is without a father?"

"I would think you would be overjoyed. It would remove your primary obstacle, wouldn't it?"

"You fool. Don't you know this isn't a game any longer? It's in your power to stop it. If anyone is hurt because of this, I'll never forgive you."

"By hurt, you mean Truitt, don't you?"

"I mean what I said. Don't do damage you can't reverse, damn you. If anything happens to him you'll live to regret it."

"This conversation is over, Frances."

LITTLE GRACIE

Chapter 27

"Everything's set," said Grant. He and Rob sat in Houlihan's having a beer.

"What did he select?" asked Rob.

"Pistols at five paces."

"You're kidding?"

"Ridiculous, isn't it. Powers will furnish the firearms. We'll meet them on the bluff at 6:30. A coin toss will determine choice for position and the count will go to the loser."

"Pistols at five paces is murder," Rob pointed out again. "That's much too close for a duel. What is he trying to do?"

"I don't know. But I do know this. Get all those chivalrous thoughts out of your mind. That man is out there to kill you, and don't get it into your head about shooting his hip to give a warning. You shoot to kill, too."

"I know. What's the caliber?

"They're forty-four's with ten-and-a-half-inch barrels."

"Jesus."

"Yeah. Listen, I know it's a morbid thought but is there anything I can do for you that you would rather not talk about?"

Rob was silent for a moment. He looked at Grant and saw the concern on his friend's face. The tie between them was still strong and he knew Grant would walk as far by his side as circumstances would permit.

"You're named the executor of my small estate. Dispose of any effects as you wish. If it comes to it, I would like Frances to have my watch. As you know, it's very special between us. Otherwise no."

"You want to hang out for a while tonight?" asked Grant.

"No, I think I'll go home and catch up on the newspapers and get a little rest."

"Okay partner. I have a carriage rented so Dr. Elliott and I will pick you up at 6:00 in the morning. Don't oversleep."

* * *

After spending a fitful night, primarily filled with thoughts of Frances, Rob awoke at 4:30. May as well get up and wake up, he thought. The kitchen stove still had some embers from the prior evening, so he added some paper and coal. He filled the coffeepot about half full and added some grounds.

As the coffee was brewing, he went about washing his face and shaving. The brew was hot and strong and he carried his cup with him to his closet, trying to decide what he would wear. After debating between casual for freedom of movement and dress for appearance, he chose dress. He figured Watson would be dressed in full business attire and he was determined not to be outdone. By the time he was dressed and into his second cup of coffee, he heard Grant's knock at the door. He checked his watch. It was ten minutes before six.

"Good morning," said Grant. "How are you?"

"Oh, I'm ready."

"Dr. Elliott is in the carriage."

"Let me get my hat and I'll be right out."

Rob walked back in the house and took a final look. Everything seemed to be in order. He picked up his hat and closed the door, locking it behind him.

"Good morning, doctor," said Rob as he swung onto the front seat beside Grant.

Dr. Elliott looked at Rob solemnly. "Good morning, Rob. This is bad business, I wish there were some other way of resolving it."

"Yes, but at this point, Doctor, I'm afraid there's too much water under the bridge."

The drive to Bonaventure was brisk on the early spring morning. At 6:20, they arrived at the gates. The cemetery was still private and operating as the Evergreen Cemetery of Bonaventure. The gates were already open so they knew they weren't the first on the premises. Grant guided the horse to the right, past the Gaston Tomb and down the road toward the bluff.

Rob's mind ran back to the first time he and Frances came to Bonaventure on that Sunday in an autumn afternoon. As they passed the ruins of the old plantation house where the Tatnalls lived, he remembered her comment on the eerie ambiance of the area. Ahead, he could see another carriage on the bluff near the Mongin vault.

Grant drove near the other carriage and halted. The three got out and Grant walked over to where Powers, Watson, and Dr. Read were standing. Dr. Elliott, recognizing Dr. Read, also began walking in their direction to speak with his colleague.

"Good morning, gentlemen," said Grant. "The dawn seems to be developing on schedule."

"Quite," said Powers.

Grant motioned Powers aside and asked him again, as a worthy second would, "Is there any possibility of reconciling these two and avoiding needless bloodshed?"

"Grant," Powers began, "I wish to God there was, but Mr. Watson reaffirmed on the way out that this is the only course of action acceptable."

"I'm sorry to hear that," said Grant. "Do you have the weapons?"

"Yes, they're in the carriage. Before we match for position though, I would like to confer with my principal one last time."

"Very well."

Powers went back to the carriage where Watson was waiting.

"We're ready to match for position," said Powers.

Wales was dressed in a light-colored suit with a black border around the lapels. A white shirt with a lace front, string tie and a black vest accompanied this. "Here is what you do, Powers. If he wins position and you get the count, I want you to speed up the cadence. Normally we will fire on three. Do you understand?"

"You want me to cheat on the count so you can fire first?"

"You better my friend, or you'll find yourself without a financial partner."

"And what if we win position?"

"Then that's my problem."

Powers retrieved the walnut case with the pistols from the carriage and went back to where Grant stood. He opened the case to show the pistols to Grant and suggested they mark position before they were loaded. As he spoke, Grant detected a slight nervousness in Powers that wasn't there before.

They decided to mark the places in the road. The bluff road ran in a northeasterly direction so the rising sun would be over the left shoulder of the principal facing southwest.

"I don't think it makes a whole hell of a lot of difference at five paces," Grant pointed out. They drew a box about four feet square in the road and both counted off five paces, or about 12 feet. Agreeing on the distance, they again marked off a designated box in the road.

"Are you ready to load?" asked Powers.

"I'll observe you," said Grant.

Powers went back and opened the case and extracted one of the pistols. It was a fine looking weapon indeed.

"These are cap and ball, so loading isn't that complicated," said Powers, as he completed one. With practiced dexterity he hurriedly loaded the other. "Are you ready to toss a coin for position?"

"You toss, I'll call," said Grant.

Powers nervously dug in his pocket for a coin. He tossed it in the air, catching it with his right hand and placing it on the back of his left. He looked inquisitively at Grant.

"Tails," called Grant.

Powers lifted his hand to reveal the coin.

"Tails it is," he said. "What's your pleasure?"

Grant went to confer with Rob for only a moment and returned. "We choose the northeast position."

"Very well," said Powers nervously. "I'll call the count. The choice of pistols is yours."

Grant chose the first loaded. He returned to Rob and asked him to take his position. Powers did the same for Watson. It was customary, according to the Code, that once the principals were on their positions, the seconds would cock the pistols and offer them to the combatants. They in turn, would take them with their left hand and not transfer them to their right until they were ready for the count.

Accordingly, Powers and Grant handed over the loaded weapons to their principals, who then waited.

Powers and Grant also took loaded pistols, two 38-caliber double-action revolvers, and positioned themselves at right angles to the two men. Essentially, the four men were stationed at the four corners of a square. This was for the purpose of ensuring fair play. If a second's principal was unfairly wounded or killed, it was expected that he would use his weapon to bring retribution on the adversary at fault. The second too, was knowingly in harm's way.

Rob and Watson eyed each other. "Close enough for you, Watson?" said Rob.

"I'll see you rot in hell, Truitt."

"Gentlemen," said Powers. "I will count to three. On three you can fire. Agreed?"

Both men nodded in ready assentation.

"Please follow my directions. Transfer your cocked weapons to your right hands and assume the ready position."

Both men did so, their pistols pointing toward the ground to give neither an advantage.

"On my call," said Powers, "one - - - - , two, three," he said hurriedly.

On the count of two Watson's pistol was already rising, anticipating the quick count. A single shot rang out.

Chapter 28

The two adversaries continued to face each other. Watson now with a smug look on his face. Slowly, Rob crumpled to the ground, his unfired pistol still at his side.

"You cheating bastard!" screamed Grant to Watson as he charged over to where Rob lay. He turned him from his side to his back. A gaping hole in his chest was surging with blood. Grant lifted Rob's head and held it in his hands. Rob looked at him with eyes that were wide but beginning to dilate.

"You warned me." Rob coughed. "I should have been ready for his trickery. Anyway, we've had a hell of a run, haven't we?" His voice began to fade.

"Yes," said Grant. "We really have."

"Remember to do what I told you," said Rob as the life ebbed from him and his eyes glassed over. Doctor Elliott knelt beside him to check his vital signs. He looked at Grant and shook his head.

"He's gone Grant, I'm sorry."

Grant felt the tears streaming down his face as he dashed to where Watson was conferring with Powers, still in his marked position. He rammed his pistol under Watson's chin.

"You son-of-a-bitch," he screamed. "You cheating son-of-a-bitch. I'm gonna kill you myself." He jammed the weapon harder into Watson's neck. Watson stood with his spent pistol, fear in his eyes, looking to Powers.

"It was a set-up deal," Grant said to both of them. "You both knew all along the count would be rushed."

"Now wait a minute, Grant--" said Powers.

Grant turned on him with his pistol. "Now I know why you were so nervous all of a sudden. "You knew what would happen." Powers said nothing, only standing in fear, alternating his eyes between Grant and the pistol, his own held limply by his side.

"I'm not going to kill you now, you two conniving cowards. I'm going to post you in the paper. I'm going to tell the city of Savannah the type of chicanery you two indulged in because Watson was not man enough to face Rob in a fair fight. You planned murder all along and both of these doctors are my witnesses."

Neither Powers nor Watson responded. They knew they were facing a man who could quickly dispatch them both and by the Code Duello was entitled to. Grant turned to go, but stopped and turned back to Watson.

"Frances will know what happened here. I will tell her personally." At that point, with a lightning motion, Grant pistol-whipped Watson across the nose, leaving a nasty gash. Then he turned to Powers and backhanded him across the face.

"If either of you have a problem with that, I'm at your service."

Grant walked back to Dr. Elliott who still stood where Rob lay. Dr. Elliott said, "I'll help you take him to the carriage."

"No," said Grant, his voice cracking. "I'll carry him myself. God knows he carried me long enough in my life."

With tears on his cheeks, Grant picked Rob up like a ragdoll and carried him to the back of the carriage. Once there, he gently laid him down, straightening his body. Delicately, he reached inside his vest pocket and extracted the watch while unfastening the chain. He popped the catch on the side with his thumb and read the inscription. "One," he muttered quietly to himself. Then, like someone tucking a child into bed, he covered his friend with the blanket in the rear of the carriage and finally pulled the blanket over his face. He and Dr. Elliott climbed in the front and started out.

"Where would you like to take him?" asked the doctor quietly.

Grant's mind was elsewhere, reviewing the many years and events of friendship. Finally he came back to the present. "I guess to John Fox's. Rob always spoke well of him.

As they drove off, Powers and Watson were attempting to regain their composure, a distance away from Dr. Read.

"Well, it went off as planned," said Watson, holding a handkerchief over his nose. "Now that's a piece of business I'll no longer have to worry over."

"I don't think so, Wales, said Powers, massaging the burning welt on his cheek. "When word gets out as to what went on here, I think we both will suffer a lot of character slippage in the town's eyes. And I'll tell you another thing."

"What?"

"The last thing I want is to get involved in an altercation with Grant Dawson. He would just as soon kill us both as look at us."

"What if he posts us?"

"That would be much the lesser of the two evils. I think we should leave it alone, especially you."

As they walked back to the carriage where Dr. Read awaited, they noticed the doctor was unusually quiet. Dr. Read had witnessed several duels in Savannah during his lifetime -- some on his own property at Brampton Plantation. Dr. Read's father had been a charter member of the anti-dueling society in Savannah formed in 1846 by a consortium of the town's leading citizens. With that in mind, he had accepted with great reluctance Watson's request that he serve as his personal surgeon today.

"Doctor," said Powers, "I'm glad we didn't need your services today other than this small cut."

Dr. Read didn't respond but set himself busily to attending to the laceration on Watson's nose. He also noticed the red puffiness on Power's cheek but knew medical attention wouldn't be required. After a few moments he said, "This wasn't right Wales, and you both know it. It was contrived and obvious and nothing more than murder. It's something you both will have to live with on your consciences. But I'll tell you something else; deeds like this have a way of coming back to haunt you. What goes around comes around. So be aware."

On the remainder of the drive back to the city, there was little conversation.

* * *

Grant went directly to the Pulaski while Dr. Elliott proceeded on to John Fox's funeral parlor. Once there he immediately went to Frances' apartment and let her know the events at the cemetery.

When she opened the door she only had to look at his face to know the outcome of the scheduled clash. What she didn't know and Grant was determined that she would, was how it transpired. He omitted none of the details and let her know of Power's role in abetting Wales. Frances listened quietly and when he was finished asked, "Where did they take him?"

"He's at John Fox's. I'm about to go there myself. He asked that I give you this." Grant placed the watch and chain in her hand and clasped her hand over it with both of his.

"Someday," she said softly. "We kept living for someday. It never came." Frances sat with a vacuous stare.

"Will you be okay?"

"Yes, I'm sure Wales will be here shortly. Thank you Grant."

Powers dropped Wales at the side entrance to the hotel and he went straight to his suite. As he entered the apartment, Frances was on him in an instance. "You bastard," she screamed. She flailed against Wales, attempting to strike him anywhere. He easily defended himself against her aggression and finally held her arms. He was just as angry.

"I made it very clear to you that no one is going to besmirch my reputation and get away with it. No one."

"What the hell do you think you've done to it and to us? You've gone out and murdered someone, a person much more the man than you, in what was never intended to be a fair fight."

"Grant was here?"

"Yes, and he told me everything. How can you expect me to even look at you anymore with anything but disgust? It's just more of your same behavior. Having a superior position and taking advantage of it. Get out of here, get out of my sight!"

"Frances, I think we just need some time."

"Time for what? For you to continue to use your wealth for destructive purposes? Have you noticed how people have started to look at us? With disdain, Wales, with total disdain. Just stay away from me!"

Grant left the hotel by the main entrance and walked toward the funeral parlor on Liberty Street. It was Saturday and he had no other pressing business for the day. Normally he spent several hours absorbed in writing.

As John Fox saw him enter, he went to offer condolences and let him know it would be several hours before Rob's body would be ready for viewing.

"It's okay," said Grant. "I still would like to spend a few minutes alone with him before you start."

"Of course," said Fox, "I understand. It's no problem." Fox led him to a rear room where he saw Rob on a white gurney. "I'll just leave you here for as long as you like. Take your time." Fox quietly closed the door behind him as he left the room.

Grant slowly walked over to the porcelain cart where Rob lay. He was still in his clothes from the morning. His blood-caked jacket was undisturbed. As he looked down on him, it was hard for Grant to believe the life had expired from his comrade's body. He covered the back of Rob's hand with his own.

"Well old friend, we never expected it to come to this, did we?" Grant paused, uncertain as to how to continue. "Why would you let yourself get so drawn in to such an impossible situation? It's almost like you were lockstep to destruction. You were smitten from the start. After her, no one else could measure up. You kept comparing all the ladies to her and what could have been. She became your benchmark."

Grant observed Rob's peaceful countenance and all the past moments of their companionship came rushing up; two boys who went to war and molded a friendship that continued for almost thirty years. He had never known a better man or friend.

And now it's all come to this, Grant thought. To survive four years of war and then be murdered in the end by a dirty Yankee coward. Grant looked again at Rob.

"God, what a waste. I talked to Frances and told her what happened. Knowing you, you would have said, 'let it alone,' but I couldn't. I couldn't let that son-of-a-bitch get away with one of his devious schemes again." Grant again placed his hand on Rob's.

"Frances was frantic. I don't know what she will do. I also gave her the watch, like you asked."

The feeling of aloneness began to sink in on Grant. He and Rob weren't constant companions but he knew he was always there if he needed him.

"Jesus Christ, what am I going to do without you?" His tears began to flow without shame.

Chapter 29

Frances' thoughts were swirling. How did it ever come to this? All she wanted in life was happiness. When she thought she found it, it was ripped away. In its place, she received a burden, unfairly bestowed, and unfairly asked by her parents that she carry it. By appeasing Watson, she was foolish enough to think she could bring it all to closure. Was she ever wrong. For seven years, all she could do was think about what could have been.

Thank God she had Gracie. She was the only piece of Rob she could claim. As she watched her grow, she continued to be amazed at her mannerisms and expressions. If Rob could have only known her, and she him. She reached in her pocket and lifted the watch Grant had left. She rubbed the case with her fingers lovingly.

"Oh Rob," she sobbed, "how could you leave me like this? Now I have nothing. Now I want nothing."

She threw herself on the bed and buried her face in her pillow. A darkness was consuming her and she gave in to her grief. She was unaware of how long she lay there.

Gradually Frances regained her composure and was aware of Rob's watch in her hand. She opened the case as she was sure he had many times and rubbed the inscription.

"From this day forward - - One." "One," she said. "Not two and not what remains of one."

Suddenly a calm descended over Frances like a comforting veil enshrouding her. With it her mind cleared. She knew exactly what to do. Her grief abated. She began thinking about her wardrobe. Wales would not win. She would be the victor in the ultimate battle. She realized she still had an option to play.

Frances opened her closet and looked over the dresses she kept for various occasions. Most were ones she wore to the office and others were for more festive times. Toward the back was one she hadn't worn for years and really only kept for sentimental reasons. She touched it. It was the burgundy dress she wore the first night she and Rob went to dinner at the Pink House. She pulled the hanger and held the dress to her as she stood facing the mirror. As she looked at her image, she knew this was the one.

Frances stepped into the dress and it fell into place around her as she buttoned up the front. Again, she looked in the mirror and was pleased to see very little change in the fit compared to seven years earlier.

From the jewelry box she took the necklace Rob had given her and clasped it around her neck. His watch, she put in her pocket. Satisfied, she rose and went to the small kitchen, opened one of the cabinet drawers and took out a small packet. It's contents were emptied into a glass of water and stirred thoroughly. Frances felt no emotion, just a calm deliberateness.

Trancelike, she carried the glass back to the bedroom and placed on it on the dressing table that was backed by a mirror. Carefully, she unbraided her hair and watched as it fell to her shoulders. In one of the drawers she found a sheet of paper and a pen.

Taking only a moment, she wrote a few lines, placed the note in an envelope addressed to Wales, and sealed it. With everything in readiness, she took the glass, looked at it hesitatingly, and then drained the liquid. Calmly, she replaced it on the dressing table and began to brush her hair, but in a preoccupied manner.

Suddenly, the door burst open and in rushed Gracie, excited from having been in the park with her sitter.

"Momma, momma, Mrs. Kinzie and I met two other girls in the park my age. We were playing tag."

Frances continued brushing her hair and gazing in the mirror. She could feel the first effects of the dosage coursing through her system.

"That's fine, Gracie. Come, give your mother a hug and go downstairs. I feel a slight headache coming on."

Gracie came over to the dressing table where her mother sat. She was looking in the mirror but when Gracie looked in the glass as well, she could see her mother's vision was distant and not at all on her hair she was brushing.

"Mother, I've not seen you in that dress before. And you're wearing your pretty necklace. Are you going to a party?"

"Mother's playing dress-up, Gracie. She's just wearing some pretty things she hasn't tried on in some time. Give me a hug."

Frances turned around on the stool and brought Gracie into her arms. She held her longer than normal.

"I love you, darling," she said.

"I love you too, Mother. Have you seen Papa?"

"No, he's probably downstairs in his office. Why don't you go look for him?"

Gradually, she could feel her limbs beginning to retract and her body growing cold. She knew the end would come soon. Gracie kissed her on the cheek and ran out of the room. Frances turned back to the mirror and the tears again began to flow. She held Rob's watch and looked at the inscription inside the case. She had meant it literally, from the day it was etched inside the watch. They would be separated no longer.

"Forgive me Gracie," she murmured as she brushed her hair a few additional strokes. Then, slowly, she slipped from the stool to the floor and united with Rob.

* * *

Wales sat pondering the events of the day. Already he was aware of the silent stares he was getting from the staff and guests in the hotel. He thought it would be better if he stayed out of sight and spent the remainder of the day in his office. His secretary, Mrs. Holder, made a point of bringing up the incident.

"Personally, I'm glad for what you did, Mr. Watson. He had it coming. To barge in here and attack you the way he did. Pure riff-raff, if you ask me. Can I get you anything?"

"Thank you, but no Mrs. Holder, I'll be in my office."

It wasn't long before Gracie showed up to check on her papa and to see what he was doing.

"Hello, Papa."

Wales looked up to see Gracie. Suddenly he realized why he had gone to the lengths he had -- nothing was more important than his family. Keeping it together justified everything. Gracie came around his desk and climbed on his lap.

"How's my girl?"

"Gracie's good." She kissed him on the cheek. "I've been playing in the park and then I went to visit with mother."

Wales sighed. "And how was your mother?"

"She's fine. She was acting strange, though, and she was all dressed up. She had on a new party dress and her special jewelry. Are you and mother going out?"

Wales began to tense. "What did the dress look like Gracie?"

"It's burgundy with lace. I've never seen it before. Mother looked pale and she had her hair down."

It didn't sound like Frances and it was not at all the response he expected. Wales didn't like the sound of it. He thought he better go check on her again. "Why don't you go downstairs in the lobby while I look in on your mother. Okay?"

Gracie slipped off his lap and trotted out the door. Watson rose and walked briskly down the hall in the direction of their suite of rooms.

Wales opened the door cautiously and entered the suite.

"Frances?" he called softly. Walking toward the bedroom he called again, "Frances?"

Lightly he tapped on the bedroom door and still getting no response he pushed it open. "Frances?"

Still on her side where she slipped from the stool, she lay crumpled. Her skin had already turned a bluish cast and she was cold. Splayed from her right hand was a man's open pocket watch with a gold chain encircling her wrist.

"Oh my god," said Wales. He picked her up and placed her on the bed. Running down the hall, he encountered Powers.

"Get the house doctor here, fast! It's Frances." He turned and ran back to the suite.

Frances was still on the bed, unmoved from where he laid her. Her eyes were still staring with the same wistful expression that had gazed into the mirror. Finally, she had found her release. Wales sat on the bed next to her and held onto her hand. The tears began to flow.

"You were so beautiful, I wanted to own you. I was certain in time that you would love me as much as I adored you. With anyone else, it would have been so. Why didn't you tell me your heart was already committed? What have I done? What in the world am I going to tell Gracie?"

The entire history of what he contrived and attempted to control ran before his mind. He had tried, like so many others, to buy happiness and discovered too late, he couldn't. To him, money had been no more than a tool. An effective tool to purchase goods, power, and people. Now he knew he could buy the people but he couldn't own them. Their souls and feelings stayed with them. Happiness couldn't thrive where there was no seed.

Wales dropped his head, a beaten man. He remembered an oft-repeated verse from scripture, "for what is a man profited, if he shall gain the whole world, and lose his own soul?" What indeed? he thought.

* * *

The doctor confirmed what Watson already knew. The poison was strychnine. They found the envelope, and the amount consumed was more than ample to do its dirty business. Frances left a short note having to do more with the disposition of her remains than the effects of her action.

Wales,

In trying to make everyone happy, I've only destroyed everyone involved. I don't forgive you for placing us in such a position. It was selfish and cruel. These things all come with a price. You gave me no way out, I had to find my own.

Please bury me in the hillside cemetery in McIntosh. That's where I remember life being clean and innocent and it's where I can overlook the lake.

Take care of Gracie. She needs her father.

Frances

It was mostly a family affair, a small graveside service. The group was shocked and silent -- Frances' parents, her mother in a wheelchair, and the twins, Mary and Martha. Her father only hung his head and continually repeated, "forgive me, please forgive me."

Wales stood erect to one side with Gracie and had little to say to the others. He knew the whole story had been told to them through Fanny and they would form their own opinions. Gracie placed a red rose on her mother's casket, as did Wales. Immediately after the service, Gracie was led away by her father, and he didn't look back.

He and Gracie caught the first train back to Savannah. As she watched the trees flashing by, Gracie asked her father. "Papa, why did mother leave us? Why did she do what she did? Didn't she love us?"

Wales reached over and took Gracie's hand, searching for an elixir of words to make the truth more palatable, but he knew Gracie wasn't ready for the truth. Maybe she never would be. At any rate it would only be the truth as he construed it.

"Darling, sometimes we love people so much we can't hear them when they tell us they need some time to themselves. It's like when you're in school and you have things you want to do but everyone is telling you to do what they want you to do. Finally, you need some quiet time for yourself."

"Did Mother love us?"

"Yes darling, she loved us very much. Your mother was a very special woman and you are going to be a lot like her. She was beautiful and she had spirit. She was passionate about life and tried to live it her way. She was not a person who would go along only to get along. In the end, she just broke."

Gracie was slumped down in the seat, staring at her little pocketbook. "I miss her, Papa. What will we do?"

"I don't know, darling. It's just the two of us now. Gracie, you are very precious to me. I want you to come to me with anything that bothers you. I can't replace your mother, but I want you to know your papa loves you very much."

LITTLE GRACIE

Chapter 30

For weeks following the deaths of Rob and Frances, the staff of the hotel was respectively cordial toward Watson and went out of their way for Gracie.

She responded and seemed to spring back. Her focus was always on what was in front of her at the time. It was Wales who continued in a deep funk. A few days following the duel with Rob, he and Powers were both posted in the newspaper by Grant Dawson. He was a man of his word.

Posting was a usual course of action for someone failing to gain satisfaction when challenging another to a duel. Being turned down or the victim of unfair play, as was the case with Rob, the perpetrator was "posted" in the local newspaper, or other prominent place, as a coward. In Grant's case he posted the following in the <u>Savannah Morning News</u>:

To All Citizens:

Be aware that on last Saturday Mr. Rob Truitt of
Savannah met Mr. Wales Watson on the field of honor
at Bonaventure Cemetery. Unknown to Mr. Truitt, Mr.
Watson, along with his second and co-conspirator, Mr.
Richard Powers, had pre-arranged the meeting to give
himself the advantage of knowing the starting count
would be speeded up. It resulted in the cold-blooded
murder of Mr. Truitt.
It was a cowardly act by both men, and I charge them
to answer for it. I am at the service of either, or
both, to answer this charge.

Grant Dawson

Watson was quite aware of the posting but had no intention of going up against Dawson. He knew Grant would be intent on one thing only -- avenging his friend's death. He would not leave the field until

Watson was dead. He could not risk it now, being solely responsible for Gracie.

Power's aversion was even greater. He knew Dawson was a killer and wanted no part of it. He was afraid to even leave the hotel after dark. He rued the day his partner had ever enlisted him to be a part of this dishonorable scheme.

Wales realized Gracie was all he had. His two marriages had ended with two wives buried and only one child to show for them. Based on his investigation and suspicions, he was not even certain Gracie was of his blood. No matter, he thought. I've raised her, I love her, and she's mine.

As the days passed, Gracie and her father spent more and more time together. She loved showing him her schoolwork from day school, and he was more than gratified in having her show it to him. There was a tighter bond growing between father and daughter than ever in the past. Each was looking to the other to fill the void left by Frances' passing.

Many of the hotel guests were businessmen who stayed at the Pulaski when they knew they would be in Savannah. They were regulars. Gracie made them all feel part of the family. She had an uncanny knack, even at her young age, to remember the names of regular guests, as well as the new ones.

Hardly anyone passing through the lobby escaped Gracie's field of vision. She loved people and loved being the center of attention. As one guest put it, "Gracie delights in mingling with the guests and they delight in her doing so."

No one new to Gracie escaped her question, "Where do you come from?" Many said Gracie was Savannah's good-will ambassador, a pint-sized chamber of commerce.

They all knew her situation with the recent death of her mother and most wanted to claim her as their own little girl. "Wouldn't you like to go home with me?" they would ask.

"Sure," Gracie would reply, "but I'd rather you stay here with us." Everyone loved for her to come talk with them. She never became a burden or nuisance and knew not to act spoiled or mean.

It was in the spring of that year and it was nearing the Easter season. Wales had promised Gracie he would take her shopping for a new dress and have her picture taken. Monday before Easter, he and Gracie strolled down Broughton Street, Savannah's shopping district, looking for just the proper attire.

They made quite a pair, this twosome, with the proud father holding the hand of the jabbering and inquisitive six-year-old.

She charmed all the clerks and knew quite well which were the fashionable stores. She and her mother had spent many hours together in Dryfus Brothers, B.H. Levy, and Appel & Schawl.

Finding the perfect dress, she twirled for Wales and asked, "Do you like it, papa?"

"It's beautiful Gracie. You're beautiful in it."

"She's quite a striking little girl, Mr. Watson. I know you're proud," commented the sales lady.

"Quite," he acknowledged. "Thank you."

Then it was on to the portrait studio. Mr. Charles Payne was always in demand due to the quality of his work. A visit to his studio was practically an annual ritual for many Savannah families.

"Mr. Payne, this is Gracie. Do you think you could possibly take a picture of her that would make her pretty," Wales joked. "I'm afraid she may break your camera even with this new Easter dress she has."

"Pshaw – don't listen to your father Gracie. He acts like he doesn't know he has the prettiest daughter in the city. Now you sit right up here on this chair and we'll show him how much the camera loves you." Payne saw he was playing to an appreciative audience.

"How do you want me to sit Mr. Payne? Which way should I face?"

"Just sit up like a proper little girl and rest your hands in your lap. Here, kind of like this." He positioned her hands.

"Now look this way and I'll tell you when to smile and get ready."

Payne took his position behind the camera and pulled the dark hood over his head. As he peered through the lens, he framed the countenance of a young lady with angelic expression. Her legs were crossed at the ankles with her right arm on the arm of the chair and her left facing down in her lap as he directed. Of prime importance, though, was the wistful and far-away look on her young face.

Payne snapped it. He had been in the business long enough to know you didn't waste the opportunities you were given. He shot a few more, but knew that first expression would be difficult to recapture or surpass.

"It will be toward the end of the week when you can pick them up, Mr. Watson."

"Very good." We thank you so much."

"Goodbye, Mr. Payne," said Gracie.

"Goodbye, darling," said Payne, feeling strangely sad.

* * *

Hotels are temporary lodging places and even those who reside in them are exposed to many people and forces in the course of a week. Such was the case with Gracie. Being a child, her immune system was not as resistant as an adult's to the many strains of viruses and flu that were brought to the Savannah hotel from many parts of the country.

It had only been thirteen years before, in 1876, that yellow fever had reared its ugly head again in the town. It was one of the worst epidemics on record. Over 1,000 people in the city had fallen victim to its black scourge. Most of the townspeople and doctors attributed the fever to the low-lying marshes around the city and the vapors that rose from them; no one suspected the mosquito. It would be the turn of the century before Dr. Walter Reed in Washington connected the two.

Gracie had to be called several times on Tuesday to wake up and dress for school. Finally, she informed her father that she felt ill and didn't wish to go.

"That's okay, honey," said Wales. "You stay home today and rest and you will feel much better tomorrow. There are plenty more days left in the week." He was able to arrange for her sitter to come earlier than usual. Gracie stayed in bed most of the day and in the evening began to run a fever. Her appetite had also vanished with the onset of her illness. Wales called for Dr. Read, who arrived at the hotel at 8:30 in the evening.

The doctor had not looked forward to visiting the Pulaski. It seemed his last two meetings involving the Watson family ended in tragedy. First, there was that bit of deception on the river that cost Rob Truitt his life. What a waste, and later the same day, to be called to the hotel to attend to Frances.

He hadn't actually attended her. What he did was confirm the cause of death with the physician on call with the hotel. Read knew it was nothing more than cause and effect tied in to the death of Truitt. Obviously, the two had been in love in earlier years and somehow the relationship had been thwarted by Watson. Read had been privy to the rumors. Hell, most folks in town had. Frances had taken her own life when the light had disappeared from it. When Truitt died, she died.

Someone once said, when your dreams die, you die. Perhaps that's what happened. No one really knew how close the two were. Separated in reality but not in spirit. When Watson came to the same conclusion, he orchestrated the duel as merely a means to murder Truitt. It was all bad business.

Dr. Read was ushered into the suite by Watson and led directly to Gracie's bedroom. As he entered, Gracie forced a tiny smile, still acting as the little hostess. She clutched a small teddy bear to her side.

"Hello, Gracie," said Dr. Read. "Your father tells me you aren't feeling too well today." He removed a thermometer from inside his jacket and asked her to open her mouth.

"No sir. You aren't going to hurt me, are you?"

"Of course not. I'm just going to take your temperature. Now put this under you tongue." He felt her brow as he placed the thermometer in her mouth. With his thumb he pulled the bottom of Gracie's eyes down so he could check their color. "Hummmmm," he said softly to himself. Then he took the thermometer from her mouth to read the gauge.

"Not too bad, only elevated a bit. Now Gracie, I want you to get some sleep tonight so you will be ready for Easter. Do you have a new dress to wear?"

4

"Yes sir -- Papa bought it for me yesterday. I had my picture made, too."

"I know you're going to be the prettiest girl in church Sunday."

"Do you think so?"

"Without question. Now you go to sleep while I talk to your father." Dr. Read led Wales out into the hallway and gently closed the door.

"What do you think, doctor?"

"I'm not sure at this point Wales. Probably nothing. Just a cold or mild case of the flu coming on. There are hundreds of viruses floating around in the air and you never know what could light at any one time. It's late in the season to be getting sick. I don't know of anything contagious going around.

"What do we do?"

"Why don't you just keep an eye on her tonight, and tomorrow and we'll continue to monitor her. Give her an aspirin every four hours for the fever and get her to drink a glass of water then as well. I'll check on her tomorrow."

"Goodnight, doctor."

"Goodnight, Mr. Watson."

Chapter 31

The night was restless for Gracie and for most of it, Wales sat in the chair by her bed. He followed Dr. Read's orders to the letter and even insisted on Gracie drinking large quantities of water she didn't want. She was able to sleep fitfully for some of the night. As he touched her head, he still detected a fever.

In the morning she was no better and refused her breakfast. Wales was partially successful in getting her to drink a small amount of orange juice.

"It tastes bad," said Gracie, who coughed a few times and seemed to be fighting congestion she didn't have the day before. Dr. Read came again about ten in the morning.

"How is Gracie feeling today?" he asked her.

"I hurt," said the little girl.

Dr. Read placed his stethoscope in his ears and asked her to breathe. As she did so, he would move to different locations on her chest and back.

"Take a deep breath and hold it." He paused. "Now let it out. Another."

"It hurts."

"I know, this won't take but a minute. We're almost done. Cough for me Gracie."

She emitted several congested efforts but was unsuccessful in clearing her lungs.

"Did she take the aspirin and water?" he asked Wales.

"Religiously, all night long, right on schedule." Wales paused. "What do you think it is, doctor?"

"I don't like the cough or the fever that is lingering. It could be something more than a chest cold. It could be the signs of early pneumonia."

"Pneumonia?"

"Possibly, but it's treatable at this point. We need to have her sit up as much as possible and make her cough every hour or so to keep her lungs clear."

"Pneumonia?" Wales repeated in disbelief.

"She's going to be okay, but it's probably going to be later than Easter before she gets to wear that new dress."

Dr. Read began making frequent trips in to see Gracie. He had seen many cases of bacterial pneumonia in his years of practice and knew it could be a silent killer. The cases were all different, and he never knew if some were preordained to live and others to die. He prayed for Gracie. Not this little girl, he thought.

Wales was getting more distraught with each hour. He was spending full time in his suite now and would not leave Gracie's bedside. He instructed Powers to make whatever decisions they normally made jointly, and he would trust his judgement.

He kept looking for a sign from Gracie, any indication she had reached the bottom and was bouncing back. It wasn't happening.

Thursday came and went and Wales didn't venture out of the suite. His meals were sent up from the kitchen. Gracie obviously had no appetite and it was increasingly difficult to get her to even take fluids. Dehydration was setting in.

By Friday evening, she was extremely weak. Dr. Read, too, was staying with her on a full-time basis. He told Wales he was doing all he could. "She's just got to fight it," he said.

Wales looked at him and mustered up all his courage. "Is she going to make it, doctor?"

"Dr. Read faced Watson and reached out and touched his shoulder. "It's in God's hands, Wales," he said quietly. "It's in God's hands."

Wales could only nod without meeting his eyes and then dropped his head to stare at the floor.

* * *

Gracie was now coughing up a great deal of phlegm but was still unable to clear her lungs. This congestion, combined with a high fever, had driven her to delirium.

"Momma? Momma? Is that you Momma?"

"She's out of her head," said Dr. Read. Even as he said the words to assuage Wales, he knew it was a dangerous indication. Dr. Read had been around the dying many years and knew as they began to pass to the other side, they sometimes talked to their loved ones who predeceased them.

"Momma, you're beautiful. Who's with you, Momma?" said Gracie.

It was now almost midnight on Friday. Gracie was coughing up a rust-colored sputum and was racked with chills and a high fever. Dr. Read had been unsuccessful in bringing it down.

Wales was sitting beside the bed where he had been most of the evening. He was now dabbing Gracie's forehead with an alcohol-soaked cloth, doing everything he knew to break the fever.

"Oh God, please don't take my little girl," He said with despair.

Even as he said this, Wales knew the chances of Gracie pulling out were getting slimmer. Her color was bad, she ached, her fever had not broken, and her lungs were more congested than at any time since she had been stricken.

Wales remembered the words Dr. Read had spoken as they were leaving Bonaventure after the duel -- "Deeds like this have a way of coming back to haunt you, so be aware."

As far as Wales was concerned, it was only a coincidence and a matter of personal misfortune. Besides, Gracie was going to be alright. She just had to be. He sat on the side of her bed and kissed her head. Gracie seemed to focus again on the present for the moment.

"Papa?"

"Yes darling, I'm right here. What is it?"

"I see Mama, Papa."

Gracie opened her eyes and for a moment looked clearly at Wales.

"I love you, Papa."

"I love you too, darling."

She reached toward Wales and he took her small hand in his. As she continued to look at him, her eyes dilated and she lapsed back into the dark void from where she came.

"Gracie! Darling?"

As he said the words, Wales looked at Gracie and realized his little girl had slipped away. She still maintained the same expression on her face, much the same as when she posed for her portrait, and much the same as her mother in her recent misfortune. Both were possessed with that wistful gaze focused so far away.

Wales took her little hand and pressed it to his lips. Dr. Read came over and placed a reassuring hand on his shoulder.

"I'm sorry, Wales. I'm so sorry."

"Oh no, not my little girl. Not Gracie, she's all I have left. Why not me? If anyone deserves to die, it's me."

"It's God's will," said Dr. Read.

Finally, the tears came and Wales begin to cry with great choking sobs -- a grieving man in unsuppressed release. The room was dimly lit and suddenly grew larger as the focus of all attention for the past few days had been lifted. It was over.

"I'm being punished by God, I know I am. He's taken my wife and now my precious little girl. I have no one. No one."

Dr. Read gently placed a hand on his shoulder and asked, "Would you like me to call John Fox to come over?" He knew Fox handled the arrangements for Frances and was certain Wales would want him to follow through with Gracie.

"In the morning. Now please, just leave me alone with my little girl."

Dr. Read nodded and quietly left the room. He stopped by Fox Funeral Home on his way back to Brampton Plantation and left word with the clerk on night duty what had happened. The clerk assured him they would call in the morning.

Now it was only Wales and Gracie together in the room. Wales knew he was alone but couldn't bring himself to believe Gracie was gone. He thought about all the plans he had for the three of them. The funds were available to send Gracie to the better schools and even boarding school and college. She would meet a nice boy and marry. He and Frances would travel. Everyone would be happy. That had been the plan.

Again, he remembered the passage. "For what is a man profited, if he shall gain the whole world, and lose his own soul?" He knew it was a Biblical verse but was unable to remember where it was located.

He let the back of his fingers pass gently over Gracie's face. Dr. Read had closed her eyes before he left and she seemed to be out of pain for the first time in days. Her life was gone and although Wales was unaware of it, his emotional life was gone, too. He sat, and waited, and cried. There was nothing else to do.

* * *

About eight the next morning, Saturday, John Fox and his attendants came for Gracie. By this time the staff and guests were informed of her passing. A totally subdued atmosphere pervaded the hotel. Richard Powers was now with Watson in his family suite.

John Fox quietly and diplomatically met with Wales. Death was his business, but times like these let him know there is no magic way of dealing with the bereaved -- especially in the case of Wales who had now lost both a wife and daughter in the course of a few months. Death of a loved one was always crushing but one never recovered from the loss of a child.

"Wales, I'm sorry, but we need to take care of a few details. Are you able to help me at this time?"

"I'll try," said Wales.

"Can you give me your preference of a minister? Would William Bowman at the Lutheran Church of the Ascension be your choice? I know he presided over the memorial service for Frances."

"Yes," said Wales, "he would."

Powers noted the composure of his friend and partner under these circumstances. He was responding but was unable to focus. He paced the room, staring at nothing. It occurred to Powers that regardless of a man's burden, he was always supposed to rise to the occasion. To be ready to stand and deliver. No matter his internal agony and heartache, he goes on. He carries on, but all the disappointments, tragedy, and heartache take their toll. He is still there and still functioning, but is no more than an empty shell.

"Would you like to have the service at the church or at my small chapel?"

Wales reflected for a moment. "Gracie loved going to Sunday school and church," he said not really to anyone. It was such a beautiful sanctuary. However, the chapel provided by the funeral home would probably be more than adequate. But wait. Gracie loved the hotel more than anywhere. It was her home and where she held court with all the guests. It might not be protocol but she would lie in state in the parlor and the service too would be conducted there.

"I would like Gracie brought here. I would like her to be available for the guests and staff she loved so much." He looked at Powers. "Do you object?"

"Absolutely not. This was her home. This is where she should be."

Chapter 32

It was the afternoon of Easter Sunday. The people came, and came, and such an outpouring of grief, the town had not seen for some time. Gracie was placed in the parlor of the hotel, laid out in the Easter dress she had planned to wear.

Flowers were everywhere. It was hard to imagine how one little girl had touched so many people. Maybe they could look at Gracie and see what could happen in their own lives.

Most were unaware of the full circumstances of the triangle that existed with the three recent deaths in the city. At this point, it wasn't important. A child had been taken, and their lives were the lesser because of it.

Grant Dawson came, not to express sympathy to Wales, but to pay his respects to the child of his friend. He was one of the few in the crowd who possessed all the pieces to the puzzle, but it didn't matter. They had all experienced loss, some directly, others indirectly. As Powers saw him enter and catch his eye, he slipped unobtrusively into a far corner and attempted to mingle with the others.

Reverend Bowman preached an eloquent funeral. He spoke of young life and innocence, of children being cut down before their time. He addressed the age-old question that always appeared at times like these -- why? Why must a young innocent child be taken when there are so many others who deserve to be? As always, you were only left with the age-old answer -- God's will. He spoke of Gracie, her sweetness and charm and how she had been such a favorite with the hotel staff and guests, how everyone she came in contact with went away a little richer.

Finally, the time came to close the casket. The time for one last goodbye from the family. At that point, there was only one left to bid her goodbye. Wales approached the small metal box and looked down on his only child. For the one thing he had wanted so much, he had forced the will of those around him to conform to his own. She was his because he could make her so. The cost had been staggering.

With his right hand, he tightly clutched the edge of the casket and with his other, he gently touched her face with the back of his fingers.

"Goodbye, darling. You were too good for this world. I wanted so much for you and for us. Now, I only have the price to pay." He felt his tears as they descended his cheeks. Turning, he slowly returned to his seat.

John Fox announced to the assembled body of friends that the burial would be private. Only the family and a few close friends would attend. He thanked them for their attendance.

The hearse and five carriages made a grim procession to Bonaventure. Behind the hearse was Wales, then Powers, then Fanny and her husband, followed by Dr. Read, and finally Grant Dawson. As the party assembled at the gravesite, Wales noticed Grant but shrugged it off. He knew he was entitled.

Wales had purchased the lot, especially for this occasion. It was only a short distance from the road where Rob and Frances had taken their Sunday drive seven years before. Gracie would be placed in the center. It was one of the saddest spectacles Bonaventure had witnessed; a small casket followed by a stoic but empty father.

Reverend Bowman read a few passages of scripture alluding to being in the arms of the Lord. John Fox quietly asked Wales if he would like to come back after the burial was complete.

"No, John, thank you. I can't leave now. I must see it through."

Slowly, Gracie's tiny casket was lowered into the earth of Bonaventure, and she became one with the ages.

"Now, it's over," Grant said silently, to no one.

* * *

The following month, John Walz, a young sculptor, opened a studio on the corner of Bull and Jones Street. Walz had studied in Europe – Paris, Florence and finally in Vienna with the great Victor Tilgner. Tilgner had been commissioned to do six statues for the new Telfair Academy of Arts and Sciences in Savannah. Walz served as his understudy on that project.

One of his first patrons in Savannah was Wales Watson, co-owner of the Pulaski Hotel. During his visit, he surrendered to his emotions and could barely speak. He could only hand Walz a photograph. It was recent, having been made the week of Easter.

Walz was immediately captivated by the projection of innocence combined with a knowing wistfulness. He only hoped he would be up to the challenge of capturing the little girl in the photograph.

Watson finally regained his composure and said, "I want the statue be life-sized and carved from no less than the finest marble. Gracie was pure and I want that to show through in the whiteness of the stone."

Walz devoted himself to the work.

LITTLE GRACIE

Epilogue

Now you know my story. Grant buried Mr. Rob in Laurel Grove, across town. No one was quite sure where. Mother, of course, is on the hillside in McIntosh. She was always happy down there. Isn't it strange how the three of us were apart in life and now even in death, we're separated? Apart in the flesh but one with the spirit.

You may wonder how I know the story of Mr. Rob and mother. The best way to explain is that although your presence is gone, you still have your consciousness. You know what you are meant to know. You know who you are.

Is there a lesson to be learned? Perhaps. Mr. Rob and mother were always hoping something would happen to change things. There would be a way out and a place for them - - someday. Something did happen, but not what they wanted. And someday never came.

Sometimes it's best to be selfish, especially when the prize is worth fighting for. So many try to govern their behavior by what they think is best for the greater good. Life is precious, and we are only allotted one. Be happy. When you find the person you are happy with, be selfish.

Papa stayed in Savannah for a number of years after the three of us left. Soon after my funeral, he was approached by Grant Dawson in the hotel. Mr. Dawson told papa he was the executor of Mr. Rob's estate and he was there for the watch that belonged to his friend. After a long silent exchange, Papa said, "Very well. I'll have it delivered to your office."

A few years later, Papa assumed the management of the new DeSoto Hotel. He never remarried. To his friends, he was functional but reserved. He was never again able to assume his warm personal demeanor. I loved Papa. He was a wonderful father. Eventually he left Savannah and headed north. At that point, he seemed to be absorbed by time and geography. I still miss him.

Mother's mother died a few weeks after she did. She, too, joined Mother in the family plot on the hill. After she left, Grandpa was only going through the motions of life. The following year he went to be with her.

Mary and Martha married and moved away. Mary with Grady to Jacksonville and Martha to Gainesville. Aunt Fanny and Dr. Elliott didn't seem to be as intended for each other as they thought when they married. In time, they were divorced -- a radical act in the polite society of the day. She remarried in about a year. Her new husband was none other than -- Grant Dawson. Their marriage lasted almost twenty-five years, until his death.

Time passes -- days, months, and years. Bonaventure is filling up. From my vantage point, looking toward the river, I see many of my generation as well as those of later ones, who have come to join me. I see the bluff where papa and Mr. Rob carried out that senseless ritual. It makes one wonder. Was it a preordained finish to the pledge of oneness between Mr. Rob and mother? It's obvious, looking back, that their love ran deeper than even they knew.

Was Papa being punished for his actions? I don't know. At any rate, he's gone. Mr. Rob's gone. Mother's gone. They're all gone, but I'm still here. I'm Little Gracie, and I'm all alone in Bonaventure.

The End